Thiago

Delaney Diamond

Garden Avenue Press

For the lupus warriors

Thiago by Delaney Diamond

Copyright © September 2025, Delaney Diamond

Garden Avenue Press

Atlanta, Georgia

978-1-946302-89-2 (Ebook edition)

978-1-946302-90-8 (Paperback edition)

www.delaneydiamond.com

Chapter One

Thiago Santana's bare feet struck the mat in a steady rhythm as he moved through the *ginga*—a fluid, swaying motion that was the foundation of *capoeira*. He dipped low, then rose into a spinning kick that sliced through the air, close to his trainer's face. Sweat dripped down his bare back, soaking into the waistband of the white, loose-fitting pants he wore.

In the background, the steady twang of a *berimbau* spilled through the speakers in the practice room. The single-string instrument didn't look like much, but it controlled everything— the rhythm, the energy, the pace of his movements. It dictated whether the moves remained playful or turned into a real fight.

"Nice," his trainer said, stepping aside as Thiago lunged forward and pivoted into a defensive crouch. Dexter was a tall man with coffee-colored skin, a capoeira master Thiago had been lucky to find. "You have the fire of *capoeira* in your gut."

Thiago let out a breathless, appreciative laugh.

Capoeira was Brazil's oldest martial art, created by enslaved Africans and indigenous Brazilians. It incorporated self-

1

defense techniques, acrobatics, and dance choreography and provided a good workout. He had learned *capoeira* during his time in Brazil. What started as a curiosity quickly became an addiction that gave his restless energy somewhere to go. Demanding focus, the art form left no room for distractions.

He needed to focus—especially now, with the pressure that came from taking over his father's company. Running a multi-million-dollar company was no easy task. He dreamed of expansion and had already moved the company away from some of the systems his father had implemented over the years. Thanks to all his hard work, Santana International was turning into the type of conglomerate he envisioned—a streamlined juggernaut upending the norms across various industries: consulting, tequila manufacturing, real estate, and more.

Thiago launched into another sequence—step, duck, spin, strike—enjoying the high from the fire in his limbs and the burn in his lungs. *Capoeira* didn't give him answers to the questions he faced each day, but it gave him space to think while keeping his body fit.

Their one-hour session ended minutes later, and Thiago thanked Dexter, grateful for the workout before he had to start the workday. Chest heaving, he rested his hands on his hips.

"I'll see you next week," he said.

Dexter nodded, using a remote to turn off the rhythmic music. "Same time?"

Thiago also nodded. "Same time."

As Dexter left the house through the front door, Thiago jogged upstairs and took a shower. When he exited the bathroom, his clothes were already laid out on the bed by his housekeeper. While he dressed, his brain ran through everything he had to do when he arrived at the office. Take phone calls, respond to messages, and conduct meetings, all required for building relationships, strategic planning, and networking.

Briefcase in hand, he walked down to the first floor.

"Good morning," his housekeeper greeted him as he entered the kitchen.

Thiago took the paper sack and the travel mug filled with coffee from her, balancing them in his free hand. "Good morning. I was thinking, although I won't be back for dinner, I would like you to make something light in case I get hungry later in the evening." On Friday nights he didn't eat dinner at home because he had plans.

"Yes, Mr. Santana."

He left the kitchen, exiting through the front door and into the frigid February air, where his chauffeur was leaning against the black limousine, waiting.

He straightened when he saw Thiago.

"Good morning, Mr. Santana."

"Good morning, Gonzalo. Looks like rain today," Thiago said, glancing at the gray clouds overhead.

"Fifty percent chance of thunderstorms," Gonzalo said, opening the door.

Thiago groaned while his chauffeur chuckled. Atlantans didn't know how to drive in heavy rain. There would be accidents galore, blocking traffic and causing delays.

They drove away from the house, and Thiago pulled out his phone to review a report. As he read the document, he ate the breakfast burrito filled with cheese, eggs, and chorizo that his housekeeper had prepared.

He worked hard all week, but later tonight, it would all be worth it when he had the opportunity to relax for a couple of hours.

* * *

With a soft chime, the elevator doors opened, and Thiago stepped onto the executive floor. Typically, he was one of the first to arrive, which gave him a period of quiet time before the buzz of activity began when employees came through the doors. He strode across the carpeted floor, numbers and strategy dominating his thoughts.

Halfway down the hall, his ruminations were interrupted when he heard low, tense voices around the corner. His steps slowed as he listened.

"I understand, but she—she's my daughter. She's still in the hospital, and I need another day to be with her. I'm only asking for one more day." He didn't recognize the voice, but the man's plaintive tone revealed his distress.

"You've already used all your leave. You can take off, but if you don't come in on Monday, we'll have to dock your pay." The other voice was clipped, irritated, and one he recognized. Sam, the VP of logistics.

Thiago rounded the corner, and both men straightened up.

"Good morning, sir," Sam said, shooting Thiago a friendly smile.

"Good morning," the other man said with less enthusiasm, his voice dull and defeated.

Thiago recognized him, though he didn't know his name. He'd obviously come in early, making his way up to the top floor to have this meeting with his supervisor.

Thiago nodded at the men and continued down the hall as if he hadn't heard their tense conversation. He pushed open one of the heavy double doors to his expansive office, which he'd created by merging two offices into one during a custom renovation.

The space was the epitome of sleek sophistication, perched high above the city with floor-to-ceiling windows wrapped around two walls and flooding the office with natural light. The design matched his office in Brazil, where he'd spent most of his professional career working in the consulting arm of Santana International.

The room was minimalist and masculine, with clean lines and polished concrete floors. The sitting area featured dark-brown leather chairs offset by colorful textured pillows, and a glass coffee table with a metal base in the middle of the grouping. Beyond that, a conference table made of smoked glass and brushed steel provided a dedicated space for high-level meetings.

Thiago placed his briefcase on his glass-topped executive desk, which was supported by a geometric chrome base. Using the remote control, he lowered the shades on the windows closest to him, effectively cutting off the sunlight pouring through and reflecting off the chrome accents in the room.

He sat in his leather chair and took time to skim messages for emergencies from other time zones overnight. When he didn't see anything that needed his immediate attention, he picked up the phone and dialed Sam's number.

"Yes, Mr. Santana," the VP answered.

"I need to see you in my office," Thiago said, hanging up without waiting for a reply.

Sam arrived right away, the same friendly smile on his face as he approached. Thiago didn't have guest chairs in front of his desk because they encouraged people to sit and stay, which he wanted to discourage. He had a lot of work to do and didn't like wasting time in pointless conversations.

He leaned back in his chair and steepled his fingers together. "Do you have children, Sam?"

Startled by the question, Sam's eyebrows shot higher. "Me? Uh, yeah. A boy and a girl."

"You love them?"

He laughed. "Yes, of course."

"So if one of them were seriously ill, you would be a mess, wouldn't you?"

He nodded vigorously. "Absolutely, I..." His voice trailed off as realization dawned.

Thiago deliberately let the seconds tick by without saying a word, observing the color in Sam's cheeks go from pale to pink. "If someone on your team needs time off because their child is in the hospital, you do not threaten to dock their pay," he said evenly.

Sam shifted on his feet. "H-he's completely out of leave, Mr. Santana. He has no sick leave, vacation, or PTO left. It would be unfair to the rest of the staff if I allowed him to take approved time off. Going against policy would set a bad precedent."

"Come to me if you are concerned about breaking the company policy. Explain the situation and advocate for your staff. I can override the manual, Sam," Thiago said in a derisive tone.

The director swallowed, the color in his cheeks deepening as he became aware his response had reflected badly on him.

"Give him all the time he needs and make sure his paycheck stays the same. Understood?"

Sam gave a stiff nod. "Understood, sir."

"Close the door on your way out."

Thiago watched him walk out of the room with a lot less bounce in his step than when he first came in. When the door clicked shut, he shook his head in disgust. "And people say I'm an asshole," he muttered before opening his laptop and diving into the day's agenda.

He spent the next few hours working uninterrupted. By ten-fifteen, he had finished reading the morning reports and responding to electronic correspondence that had come in overnight. Taking a break, he stood and rolled his shoulders.

Then he traversed the room, his footsteps muted by a plush charcoal rug grounding the central area.

He approached a double-door cabinet built into the wall, which blended into the surrounding paneling. Opening it revealed a stocked refreshment center with an array of premium bottled waters, protein bars, trail mix, and other snacks, along with a selection of the finest spirits, including the company's premium tequila—Don Bene—named after his father.

He lifted out a protein bar and a small bottle of sparkling water, consuming them as he mentally reviewed the rest of the morning. In a few minutes, members of the marketing team would arrive to present their new ideas for the company's tequila.

Anticipation hummed beneath his skin. Not only because he'd finally see the marketing proposal that could help him meet his second-quarter goals for the company, but also because he'd get his first glimpse of the woman who occupied way too much of his thoughts. His favorite distraction.

India Monroe.

Chapter Two

W hen a firm knock sounded on the door, Thiago was behind his desk. "Come in," he called.

India Monroe, vice president of marketing for the United States, marched into his office as if she owned it, and his body thrummed with awareness. Flanked by two members of her team, she moved with the confidence of a woman who knew her worth and had the results to back it up.

Her short hair was cut in a fade, the glossy tendrils brushed flat to frame her striking face, highlighting her high cheekbones. As usual, she was dressed to the nines in a monochromatic designer outfit. Today, she wore a tailored ivory blazer cinched at the waist, paired with an ivory button-down and ivory slacks that elongated her graceful figure.

Except for the small gold hoops in her ears, she was a no-frills woman. Sleek and well put together. Polished. Sophisticated. But not cold. No, she was smoking hot and had a friendly smile when she chose to use it. She didn't wear much makeup on her chocolate-brown skin, but her lips popped with a deep berry color, bold without being loud. On her feet were pointed heels, which added a couple of inches to her fit frame.

India hadn't said a word yet, and already the temperature in the room had shifted. The faintest flicker of something warm tightened Thiago's chest, and excitement made the pulse in his wrist pound faster.

He rose from his chair. "Is this everyone?" he asked.

"Yes," India replied.

She seemed to look through him, with a gaze as powerful as her presence. Direct. Discerning. Unbothered.

No one would ever guess the transformation that took place when she was beneath him, thighs shaking to let him know he was doing a good job. Heat surged low in his gut as an erotic image flashed in his mind—his fingers curled around her throat, lust filling her eyes, and her cool voice turning warm as she panted through an orgasmic release.

Thiago forced himself to keep his mind on business as he followed the marketing team to the conference table, which was not easy. India always smelled so damn good, no matter the time of day. A couple of months ago, he had learned that his favorite scent layered beneath her perfume came from honeycomb soap. The light fragrance was sweet and feminine and damn near made him salivate. Lucky for him, it was the only soap she seemed to use lately.

Thiago sat at the head of the conference table while India sat at the other end.

"What do you have for me?" he asked, keeping his voice crisp.

"We've completed our market research for Santiago Migos and prepared preliminary projections for capturing some of their market share," India replied.

Two weeks ago, a scandal rocked the tequila industry. Lab tests from a competitor—Santiago Migos—had shown a significant amount of the alcohol came from cane sugar instead of the agave plant, though they claimed it was crafted from 100 percent pure blue agave. That prompted a class-action lawsuit and presented an opportunity for Don Bene to grab market share.

India glanced at the younger woman to her left—Beth Ann, a redhead who had come to work for them from a prestigious firm up north.

Thiago listened as Beth Ann gave an update on the lawsuit and then launched into the demographics of their competitors' customers. While she talked, Thiago flipped through the packet in front of him, which provided additional details.

Then their male colleague, Stefano, discussed projections for taking over the Santiago Migos market share, as well as a preliminary marketing strategy. Thiago's eyes flicked over the illustrations Stefano handed him. When he finished talking, India gave a short wrap-up, stating a six- to eight-month time-line for seizing their competitor's territory.

Thiago tossed the presentation and marketing collateral on the table. Looking at each of them in turn, he said, "Not good enough. We cannot assume we have time to win over their customers simply because they are preoccupied with fighting the lawsuit."

India responded. "I don't disagree, but their problems give us an edge. We currently have the second-highest market share for premium tequila, and—"

"I want their market share now, not eight months down the line. I want results by the end of the next quarter."

Beth Ann quietly gasped, and Stefano's eyes widened. They both looked at India. The end of the next quarter would be June—four months away.

India folded her hands on the table. "That's extremely optimistic. We haven't finalized our marketing plans yet, and then we have to prepare collateral, work on commercials and social media. The rollout will take time."

"We do not need a rollout. For all we know, the lab results could be wrong, and they might be able to prove the discrepancy was all a big mistake."

"You don't really believe that," India said.

"What I believe is irrelevant. The point is, a slow rollout is a mistake. We need to hit hard and fast while they stumble around trying to deal with this mess."

"The tequila market is huge. If we move fast—"

"Are you saying you cannot meet my deadline?" Thiago cut in.

Silence filled the room, and he saw the subtle shift in her already excellent posture as her back straightened. One thing was for certain, India never backed down from a challenge.

"We can meet your deadline," she said, resorting to her frostiest tone.

"Good. Then I expect to see major progress in the coming weeks. We do not have much time." Thiago stood, indicating the meeting was over.

India and her staff stood as well.

"India, I would like you to stay behind, please," Thiago said.

The other members of the team avoided Thiago's eyes, but Beth Ann shot a furtive glance in India's direction before following Stefano out the door.

After the door closed behind them, tense silence reigned between Thiago and India.

One hand on her hip, she fixed her dark eyes on him.

"Do you have something to say to me?" Thiago asked, taking a seat on the edge of the table and folding his arms.

"You undermined me in front of my team."

"You brought me an unacceptable strategy."

Her jaw tightened. "We're marketers, not magicians. I brought you a strategic rollout after you asked for a proposal less than two weeks after the scandal hit the news. You want quick results, then expect half the quality. Unless you want me and my team to pull all-nighters every night."

His eyes flicked over her, the way she stood with one hand on her hip, her full lips pressed together in anger, challenging him with her voice and a deadly stare. She was acting as if she was the one in charge, looking at him as if she were ten feet tall.

So damn sexy. He fought the smile threatening to pull the corners of his mouth upward.

"Careful," he said, his tone low and dangerous, hiding his amusement.

He watched as she moved closer. "You don't scare me, Thiago."

"Hmm. That's a problem, don't you think?"

She held his gaze, her chest rising and falling with shallow breaths. Electricity crashed between them—anger laced with sexual awareness. He ached to reach for her but resisted the urge. They didn't cross the line at work. Too risky.

"Was there a reason you asked me to stay behind?"

"I wanted to make sure you can meet my... demands."

She flicked her tongue to the top left corner of her mouth, toying with him. "Don't I always?"

Thiago clenched his hand into a fist on the table. Damn, this woman. Insatiable desire for her consumed him with no end in sight.

India turned on her heel. "If I'm going to meet your deadline, I have to go."

She was halfway to the door when his voice stopped her. "India."

She stopped but didn't look back.

Thiago

Thiago pushed off the table and took a few steps in her direction. "Are we still on for tonight?"

She turned her head slowly, eyes narrowing into an expression hot enough to curdle milk. "Maybe," she said coolly.

Thiago exhaled through his nose, the corners of his mouth twitching upward. Then she walked out without waiting for a response. She was infuriating, but she was the best part of his week.

Knowing her, she'd remain pissed right up until he saw her later.

Which meant the sex tonight would be incredible.

Chapter Three

India silently cursed as she marched toward the front door of Beppe's Cucina Italiana. She was running behind because she had left the office later than planned. She was usually good about leaving on time on Fridays, but she'd gotten sidetracked pulling together more information for the Santiago Migos plan. She had plenty of other work to do running the marketing department of an international conglomerate's largest territory, but Thiago had given them a ridiculously short timeline, and she was going to damn well meet it.

She entered the bar of the crowded restaurant and told the man behind the counter that she was there to pick up an order. As soon as she paid, she rushed through the door with the paper sack in hand and climbed into her vehicle, a gray pearl Audi A7.

In less than thirty minutes, she was at her building, parking in the below-ground garage. She took the elevator to her floor, anxiously tapping her feet the entire time. When she entered her apartment, the tension drained from her body, and a smile touched her face.

This always happened when she arrived at home. She decompressed and relaxed. Her one-bedroom apartment was, in essence, her escape from the world. Much different from the dingy apartments she and her mother had lived in or the decades-old house she had moved to when her grandmother became her guardian. Not for the first time, she wished her mother had lived to see how well her life had turned out, but she took comfort in knowing her Grandma Selah had lived long enough to enjoy the fruits of her success.

She crossed the polished hardwood floors to the kitchen, which was hardly used since she didn't know how to cook. One day she hoped to use it more, but for now, the quartz countertops and stainless steel appliances were in pristine condition. A trio of pendant lights hung above the small island in the middle, where a bowl of fake lemons added a splash of color.

Several feet away, the layout opened to a dining area before stepping down into the sunken living room. Because of the size of the living room, India had set up a home office on one end, with framed charcoal drawings—the cityscape outside her window, a Jaguar hiding in tall grass, and an eagle soaring over mountains—hanging on the wall above her desk. Elsewhere, abstract pieces dominated with hints of gold, blue, and red. Her furnishings were all high-end, consisting of clean lines coupled with comfortable, plush chairs in cream and maroon. The high ceilings and tall windows allowed in plenty of light and gave the space an open, airy feeling.

India unpacked the food she had bought, removing the paper cover with the restaurant's name from the pan of lasagna and covering it with aluminum foil. Next, she placed the container in the oven to stay warm and stuffed the bag and other evidence of her food purchase into the trash.

She hurried into her bedroom, where soft lighting encouraged relaxation, but she couldn't relax at the moment since she was short on time. She hurriedly undressed and then slipped into the shower, letting the warm water beat down on her skin. After a long day, the soothing spray was a welcome relief for her achy joints, but she couldn't stay under the spray very long. It was almost seven o'clock. Thiago would arrive soon.

She hopped out of the glass stall and rubbed scented lotion on her skin. Then she donned a sheer black teddy with strategically placed rose petals that covered her nipples and a thong that slid between her butt cheeks. She examined her body from different angles in the mirror, adjusting the strap on her shoulder before smiling with satisfaction and smacking her own ass. Of course, it was always better when Thiago did it.

She was standing in front of the closet, searching for something to wear, when the doorbell rang.

Shoot! That had to be him.

India picked up her phone and checked the live feed to the hallway outside. Sure enough, he stood in front of the door. He looked up at the camera and stared right at her, as if he could see her, quietly demanding she open the door.

The camera feed always distorted the appearance of visitors, but not Thiago. A while back, he had told her that he'd done some modeling in the past but hated having his looks constantly picked over and, in general, found the work to be boring. He also hated the spotlight, which was better suited to his younger brother, Ignacio, who had followed in their parents' footsteps and become an actor. But if Thiago ever changed his mind, he'd have management companies beating down his door to represent him.

India retrieved her kimono from the closet and slipped her arms through the voluminous sleeves. Short and lavender, it hit midthigh and showed off her smooth legs. Since Thiago was early, she'd let him in, but then he'd have to wait while she finished getting dressed.

She padded barefoot down the hallway and opened the door. Without a word, Thiago entered slowly.

"You're early," she said, closing the door and heading to the kitchen to turn off the oven.

"I decided to knock off a little earlier than usual."

From the nearness of his voice, she could tell he had followed her to the kitchen. Though they'd been seeing each other for seven months, his deep, accented voice still sent a thrill through her.

India turned to face him, arching an eyebrow. "Why?"

He shrugged. "Long week. I needed to get out of there, I suppose."

Interesting. She always got the impression that he was exactly like her, getting a high from working hard and winning. He rarely took off—even on the weekends.

But she understood. More often, she looked forward to her weekends off. There was something to be said for downtime. Work-life balance, the modern gurus called it, though the term only seemed to apply to people in their positions. Did anyone care about work-life balance for people with two or three jobs trying to make ends meet?

"You can't continue at the pace you're going," she remarked, though she doubted he'd listen. He hadn't listened any other time she pointed out he needed to slow down.

"I have too much to do, and I will not be satisfied until the numbers for next quarter come in."

She should have known. He had a goal he was aiming for, and as she'd learned since getting to know him, failure was not an option.

Using oven mitts, India removed the food from the oven and set it on top of the ceramic stovetop.

"Smells amazing," Thiago said.

"It's lasagna tonight," she said, removing the gloves and placing them on the counter.

"When did you find time to make that?"

She smiled through the twinge of guilt nicking her chest. "I made it last night, and then all I had to do was warm it up in the oven when I came home."

"Smart," he said, sounding impressed.

Again, there was a niggle of guilt for lying.

The deception had started by accident. One night, she had bought dinner and served the meal on ceramic plates. When Thiago saw the plates, he assumed she had cooked the meal. He had been deeply appreciative and surprised she had gone to so much trouble for him.

She hadn't had the heart to tell him that she'd bought take-out, and so the deception continued every Friday night they had spent together since then.

India poured a glass of wine and handed it to Thiago.

"Thank you," he murmured, tugging on his tie.

"I have to finish getting dressed, so—"

"Finished getting dressed? Are you naked under there?" He tilted his head to one side, examining her intensely, as if he was trying to see through the lavender kimono.

India decided to tease him. "Not completely. I'm wearing this." She pulled aside the robe and exposed her thigh and a hint of black lace up to her waist.

"Is that new?"

Thiago put down his glass and reached for her, but she slapped away his hand and backed up. He arched an eyebrow.

"I don't know if we should have sex tonight," she said, though her body was already craving his touch. She had been angry earlier in the day, but in a way, arguing was like foreplay for them.

Thiago smirked. "You are not still upset about what happened at work, are you?"

"As a matter of fact, I am. So I'm going to get dressed and decide how the evening will proceed." She spoke with calculated coolness but didn't move an inch.

He slowly walked toward her, like the predator he was.

"Thiago," India warned, backing up.

He ignored her, moving closer until she hit the wall.

Locking eyes with her, Thiago loosened the knot at her waist and let the robe fall open.

The black teddy covered the important bits, but barely. Her nipples and the space between her thighs were hidden, but the sheer lace clung to her curves, leaving little to the imagination and putting her rich brown skin on full, tantalizing display.

India straightened her back so her full breasts sat up higher, holding her breath as she awaited his response.

Thiago's nostrils flared, his eyes trailing down her body in male appreciation. "This *is* new, isn't it?" he asked, his voice thick and husky as his fingers trailed along the edge of lace stretched over her breasts. "I like this design. I see you, but I don't see you." The tip of his finger smoothed over her nipple.

He bent his head and kissed the crest of her breast, his beard brushing her soft skin and making her breath catch.

India pressed a hand in the middle of his chest, pushing him back. "I didn't say you could kiss me."

"You did not say I couldn't." He caught both her wrists in one hand and stretched them above her head. "You don't have to bother getting dressed," he informed her in a low voice.

"Oh? And why not?" India whispered, her breathing shallow as sexual excitement coursed through her like liquid fire.

"We have more important things to take care of."

"Which are?" India whispered, unable to look away, captured by the intensity in his dark eyes.

"My need for you. Your need for me." He pressed his arousal against her stomach, and desire throbbed at her core.

Thiago kissed the tip of her nose and then teased her with a swipe of his tongue across her lips.

India lifted one leg to grind against his hardness. Her breathing labored as she savored this erotic dance with him, she panted, "Don't tear this like you did the last one."

Thiago wasn't exactly known for his patience, and he had torn her last piece of lingerie. Matter of fact, one of the first times they had made love, he had torn her panties off her hips. No man had ever behaved in such an animalistic way toward her, and his reaction had been both shocking and thrilling.

"I cannot promise that." He smoothed his hands down her stretched arms to her back, then let them glide lower beneath the kimono to squeeze her butt cheeks.

A whimpery moan escaped her throat. His touch already had her helpless, moisture seeping between her thighs. Her cold, indifferent act easily crumbled beneath his caress.

A slow smile crossed Thiago's lips. "I think you will agree that dinner can wait, yes?"

He lifted her from the floor, and she wrapped her legs around his waist.

Her fingers climbed into his soft hair as she eagerly pressed her lips to his, hungry for the pleasure only he could give.

With his hands cradling her bottom, Thiago marched toward the bedroom. Once inside, he kicked the door closed.

Chapter Four

T hiago dabbed his mouth and placed the napkin on the table. "Delicious."

"Thank you," India said.

Months ago, when a protein snack wrapper had fallen out of his pocket at her apartment, she learned during the ensuing conversation that he had come straight from the office. That was why she had started providing dinner at her place.

She watched him take the dishes to the kitchen, now wearing only a shirt and slacks, looking more relaxed than when he had arrived in his suit. His minimal attire didn't diminish his presence, however.

Two inches above six feet, he was the kind of man women fantasized about. He moved with the effortless confidence of someone accustomed to demanding attention, with his swarthy skin and appealing features. A neatly trimmed beard framed his strong jawline, the dark hairs lending a rugged edge to his facial structure—high cheekbones, a straight nose, and sinfully sculpted lips that had wreaked havoc on her skin earlier.

His dark-brown eyes were often unreadable, but when she

and he were alone, they carried a simmering heat when he looked at her, making the rest of the world fall away.

And damn, his body. India bit the corner of her lip as she relived the heated moments they had spent in her bedroom.

It was a sculpted work of art from years of sports and martial arts. As a boy, he had excelled at soccer, boxing, and martial arts before settling on martial arts in his late teens. He was proficient in kickboxing, having earned a second-degree black belt in the sport, a third-degree black belt in taekwondo, and held a white belt in capoeira.

His body was a machine made up of tight muscle, with six-pack abs beneath the dark hair on his torso, powerful, muscular thighs, and a firm bottom she enjoyed gripping as he thrust into her.

While Thiago placed the dishes in the dishwasher, she went to sit on the maroon sofa. Minutes later, he joined her, carrying two fresh glasses of wine.

He sat down with a heavy sigh, stretching an arm across the back of the sofa. Turning in his direction, she took in his striking profile as she curled her bare feet under her bottom and sipped her wine.

Since the start of their... relationship? Situationship? Affair, maybe? Whatever it was, much had changed since the first night he came to her apartment.

In the beginning, he used to show up, they had sex, and then he left. Once she started feeding him, they ate dinner, had sex, then he left. In their current stage, they ate dinner, had sex —or the reverse, like tonight—and he stayed for a while and they talked, often about business where he confided in her, and they brainstormed ideas. Sometimes they discussed other topics, sharing bits of information with each other but not too much, as if they couldn't risk getting too close. Conversation was fine. Intimacy was not.

India took another sip of the full-bodied wine. "Did you recognize that bottle?" she asked.

"Of course. I brought it for you a few weeks ago. I'm glad we're finally getting a chance to enjoy it."

"You have good taste. Stop frowning," she said in a teasing voice, gently smoothing her fingers across his forehead to remove the frown lines.

He grunted and then graced her with a faint smile.

"I have a question for you. Why the hard push for next quarter results? You want to see improvements, which I understand, but we have time."

Thiago didn't answer right away. "The truth?"

"Always."

"I have a specific goal in mind."

"I figured. Which is?"

"I want to hit a billion dollars in revenue."

"We're almost there, Thiago. We've seen astronomical growth since you took over. The expansion in Asia had a few hiccups but went mostly well. I'm sure by the end of the third quarter—"

He shook his head decisively. "Not by the end of the third quarter. By the end of next quarter, I want to see that number reflected, and the Santiago Migos fiasco practically fell in our lap and will allow us to achieve it. I ran the numbers. If we can take twenty percent of their market share and keep all our other businesses running as smoothly as they have been, we will reach the goal I've set, which will look very good when we... go public."

India drew in a silent breath at the bombshell he dropped.

Now everything made sense. The big push. The fact that he was seldom satisfied with their initial proposals. The reason why he worked so hard every single day. She thought his dedication was because he needed to prove to everyone his father had made the right decision in turning over the company to him, but he had his own agenda, which made her respect him more. This was self-inflicted pressure, which she understood.

Thiago was self-motivated, and she wanted him to achieve his goal. Not only for him, but for herself as well, to prove she was capable of hitting the milestones set before her. It would be another accomplishment she could add to a long list of achievements.

"How long have you been working on this?"

"I've had the idea since I was based in Brazil, but when my father stepped down as CEO, I saw the opportunity to make a stock launch a reality. I brought in a consultant to help with the prep work, but my father is not yet convinced going public is a good idea."

"You're the one in charge now. You can move forward if you want."

"I can, but I respect his opinion. He spent decades building this company, and though I am now the one in charge, I do not want to ignore his concerns. Only my father and the COO know about my plans—and now you. I will make a formal announcement to the rest of the executive team at next week's meeting."

India felt honored he had trusted her with such confidential information. "I won't say a word before you're ready to announce."

"Do you think you can help me meet my goal by the end of next quarter?" Thiago asked.

"Have I ever let you down?"

"No, which is why I know I can count on you." He drained his glass and rested it on the table in front of them. "By the way, I won't be coming by next week. My sister is getting married, and the family is having an engagement party for her and her fiancé."

"Oh. Monica, right?"

He nodded, running his fingers through his hair. "The reminder popped up on my phone today, and I haven't bought a gift yet."

"You need an assistant to handle those details for you. I've told you so a thousand times," India chided.

"I have an assistant."

"A *personal* assistant who knows you and your needs. Not that concierge service."

"I will be fine. I will ask my sister Audra to buy the gift. She has great taste and knows what Monica would like." Thiago stood, obviously not planning to stay long tonight.

India placed her glass on the table beside his. "I'll get your jacket and tie," she said.

She padded to the bedroom and picked up his clothes from the chair in the corner. On her way to the door, she paused, lifting the collar of his jacket to her nose. Her eyes drifted closed. His scent clung to the material. Notes of bergamot, leather, and something dark and smoky made her chest tighten in an inconvenient way.

Embarrassed, she quickly lowered the clothing.

She found him waiting by the door and handed over his clothes.

"Thank you," he said, folding both items over his arm.

"You're not planning to go back to work tonight, are you?" she asked.

He checked the Rolex Land-Dweller on his wrist. The timepiece was sleek, with a platinum band and an ice-blue honeycomb motif on its face. Cool and elegant, like its owner.

"I will be working but not at the office. I have a few calls to make."

Thiago cradled the back of her neck with a possessive hand and pulled her into his firm body. He kissed her, his lips lingering and making heat coil low in her belly. He seemed reluctant to leave, and deep down, she wished he'd stay.

"If I didn't have to go..." He whispered the words of regret against her lips.

India trailed her fingers through his soft hair. "You can make it up to me in two weeks," she said, hoping her voice and expression suggested playfulness, instead of the disappointment lying heavy in her chest.

"I will." He plucked her bottom lip between his teeth for a gentle tug before kissing her lips again. "Good night."

"Good night."

India closed the door and used the monitor in the entryway to watch him. He glanced up at the camera with a faint smile before striding down the hallway with his broad shoulders and purposeful gait. When he disappeared from view, she turned and faced the stillness of her apartment, in stark contrast to the energy he brought whenever he walked through the door.

Thiago always filled any space he entered, and though he was no longer there, his scent lingered in her nostrils. A scent she had no business missing.

A sharp, unwelcome thought flicked through her mind.

He didn't invite me.

He was going to his sister's engagement party and had mentioned the event so casually and, just as casually, let her know he wouldn't see her next week.

Did he at any point think to invite her?

Of course not, she thought with quiet disgust. They didn't have that kind of arrangement. What they had was no promises. No expectations. Only Friday nights, quiet dinners, and the invisible wall between them.

Still, disappointment curled hot and bitter in her throat. Which didn't make sense. She appreciated this arrangement. It was casual. Detached. Safe. She was just off tonight. Not only tonight, if she were being honest. Lately.

She had become soft. She used to be "that bitch" in her relationships, but now... now she only ordered the honeycomb-scented soap from Europe that he liked, bought sexy lingerie in the style and colors he preferred, and made sure he had a meal to eat whenever he came by.

"India, girl, what is wrong with you?" she muttered.

She collected the glasses from the living room and placed them in the dishwasher. Then she poured herself a glass of water, turned out the light, and padded down the hall to her bedroom, where she opened the drawer of her dresser to take out one of several prescription bottles. She tapped a pill into her palm and swallowed it down with the water.

She changed into her nightgown and went into the bathroom. She washed her face, moisturized, and then turned out the light. In the dark, the apartment seemed even more quiet.

Climbing under the covers, bergamot and leather once again teased her nose, filling her mind with images of her and Thiago in sexual poses, each one passionate and demanding. Up against the wall. Bent over the arm of the sofa. They most frequently made love in the bedroom but had christened every room in her apartment to satisfy their boundless desire for each other.

India restlessly shifted positions. She should get up and change the sheets but was too lazy at the moment. She'd leave a note for the housekeeper who came in on the weekends and ask her to do it.

She wouldn't be able to handle another night of Thiago's scent clinging to her bed, which was a sobering reminder of his absence.

Chapter Five

"**A**ll done." Mikah, India's barber, turned the chair around so she could see the finished product.

She turned her head to examine her profile as she smoothed a hand down the newly trimmed sides of her fade. "Perfect, as usual."

"You know I got you," Mikah said, passing her a hand mirror.

She checked the back, which looked as good as the front and sides.

"What would I do without you? Don't go anywhere," India said.

He laughed as he untied the cape from around her neck.

She was joking but serious. After her last barber closed up shop, it had taken her months to find Mikah. She had visited three separate barbers in the process, none of whom had done a good enough job and had left her so frustrated she had contemplated learning to cut her own hair.

"I'll see you next month," India said, handing over cash.

"Have a good one," Mikah called as she walked away.

As she strolled out of the shop, the eyes of several of the men followed her. Oddly enough, she seemed to get the most attention when she was dressed down like she was today, in burgundy joggers, tennis shoes, and a sweatshirt with *Not Adulting Today* on the front. The shirt had been a gift from her best friend, Kiara, as a reminder to slow down and do nothing sometimes. India had ended up purchasing two more in different colors.

Despite the shirt, she had a little adulting to do today. It was Saturday, so she was on her way to the grocery store. She climbed into her Audi A7 and drove to Whole Foods. After parking, she walked into the store, mentally going through the short list of items she needed.

She took her time in the produce section, examining apples, grapes, and strawberries before adding the chosen ones to her cart. Slowly, she browsed the other aisles, stopping to toss in a bag of chips before moving toward the refrigerated section with milks and creamers. She smiled briefly at a mother pushing a cart with her toddler seated in the basket, the little boy babbling away while his mother absentmindedly nodded and *mhmmed* as her eyes scanned the shelves.

In front of the refrigerated section, India gently gnawed the inside of her lip. There were so many choices for non-dairy milk nowadays. Not only almond, oat, or soy, but also organic, sweetened and unsweetened, vanilla flavored, and on and on.

She sighed. She just wanted something to splash in her morning coffee.

"First world problems," she muttered to herself, swinging open the door to the case.

She reached for a carton of unsweetened almond milk but stopped when pressure bloomed in her chest. Tight and suffo-cating, the sensation spread quickly, clamping like a vise around her ribs and stealing her breath. Her heart thudded against her sternum, erratic and heavy.

Her hand gripped the refrigerator door for balance as a wave of nausea rolled through her. Suddenly, the overhead lights seemed extra bright, and the distant hum of the conversations around her were rather loud. Downright harsh.

India pressed a palm against her chest, a panicked whisper of air slipping across her lips.

Oh no.

Was she having a heart attack? Like her mother had suffered when she passed in her late twenties?

Panic kicked in. She wasn't ready to die yet, and certainly not in front of the non-dairy milk products of her local Whole Foods.

"Ma'am, are you okay?" The mother with the toddler trained concerned eyes on her.

Unable to speak, India could only give a vigorous shake of her head. Then she shoved the milk back onto the shelf and power-walked away, switching to a jog as she neared the front of the store. When she slipped through the automatic doors, a man coming in gave her a strange look.

"I'm fine, I'm fine," she muttered to herself, as if saying the words out loud would make them true and force the pain in her chest to disappear.

She couldn't remember the last time she'd prayed, but she uttered a quick one now. "Please don't let me die," she whispered desperately.

As she approached her Audi, she removed the keys from her shoulder bag with a trembling hand and hit the power button. The doors unlocked, and she climbed into the driver's seat. After quickly buckling herself in, she peeled out of the parking lot with her hands gripping the steering wheel.

* * *

Where is the darn doctor?

Clutching her purse on her lap, India shifted restlessly, the paper on the exam table making a crinkling noise beneath her. She shouldn't be so grumpy. They'd led her back for tests right away when she told them she might be having a heart attack, but as far as she was concerned, that had been the easy part. The hard part was waiting.

She was terrible at waiting, and that's all that ever happened in an emergency room, it seemed, which was worsened by the smell—like some horrible combination of antiseptic and overused grease from a fast-food restaurant.

She sighed, looking around the white room. At least her chest had stopped hurting. A good sign, surely.

A soft knock sounded on the door, and she perked up. In walked the doctor, a good-looking man with tanned skin, wavy hair, and glasses. He wore an easy smile and held a clipboard in the crook of his arm.

"India Monroe?"

"That's me." She breathed quietly through her mouth, waiting for his assessment.

"I'm Dr. Stone."

They shook hands. His were large, enveloping hers in a warm grasp.

"I have great news," he said, looking down at a sheet of paper on the clipboard. "Your EKG was normal, and the labs look fine. I can say with confidence you were *not* having a heart attack."

India exhaled, her muscles relaxing. "Thank goodness. Then what the hell happened?"

"Classic case of heartburn. Dramatic heartburn, but heartburn nonetheless."

She stared at him. "You're kidding, right?"

"No, I'm not," he said with a laugh. "It happens. Stress and diet are among the biggest contributors. You'd be surprised how many high-powered execs come in thinking they're dying after eating a spicy meal."

"What makes you think I'm an executive?" she asked, considering how she was dressed.

He studied her for a moment in silence. "You have that look about you."

"I'm not sure that's a compliment, Doctor."

"It is," he assured her.

The direct, interested way he was looking at her made her cheeks flush with heat.

India cleared her throat and sat up straight. "Well, I'm glad to hear I wasn't having a heart attack. My mother died of heart failure at only twenty-eight years old. I assumed I was about to join her in front of the non-dairy milks and creamers." She grimaced.

A crooked smile touched his lips. "Not today." Then he sobered. "I'm sorry to hear about your mother."

She waved off the comment. "It happened a long time ago. I was only ten at the time, but the reason for her passing stayed with me. I'm very careful about my exercise and diet."

"As everyone should be, but you especially. I see here you have lupus?"

India nodded. "Complications from lupus killed my mother, and I was diagnosed in college."

The pain started in her hands, persistent and eventually spreading to her shoulders. The first doctor she went to suggested she might have arthritis but couldn't find any evidence of the disease. When the pains expanded to her legs, she went to see another doctor who gave her a blood test and noted the elevated markers for lupus. They referred her to a rheumatologist, who confirmed the diagnosis and started her treatments.

With subsequent research, she learned her mother hadn't died from simple heart failure. Her mother had complained of aches and fatigue for years, and by the time she died, rashes had broken out on her skin. When India searched through her mother's paperwork, she found the truth: her mother had suffered from lupus, which had inflamed her heart and ultimately caused her death.

Leaning a shoulder against the wall, Dr. Stone folded his arms. "How are you doing now?"

"I'm fine. I had a bad episode about five years ago where I was hospitalized for a while, but I'm better now, thank goodness. Occasionally I have a flare, but nothing extreme. It's mostly under control."

"You're taking care of yourself, taking your meds?"

"Always. Like clockwork," India said.

"Good, but I do need to scold you a little bit. You should not have driven yourself to the emergency room. That was very risky."

"I know, but I didn't want to waste time calling 911—"

"If you were really having a heart attack, you could have lost consciousness and caused an accident, injuring yourself and others." He interrupted her with a gentle but firm no-nonsense tone.

"You're right," India said.

He arched an eyebrow. "That was surprisingly easy."

"I'm a reasonable person," she said with a smile.

"So next time you'll call 911 or have someone bring you to the ER?"

"Hopefully there won't be a next time, but I will if it happens."

The truth was, there weren't many people India could

count on in such a situation. There was her best friend, Kiara, but she was visiting her mother out of state, and India didn't have any close family in town. She couldn't call the man she was sleeping with because of their no-strings relationship.

The doctor straightened. "Do you have any questions for me?"

India shook her head, distracted by her sobering thoughts. All she had going for her was work. How sad. She'd turned into her mother without realizing it. At least her mother had her, a child. India had no one.

"Since you narrowly escaped death, I suggest celebrating with a non-acidic meal."

"I will," she promised, thinking about her abandoned cart at Whole Foods. She needed to finish shopping. One of their frozen family meals typically fed her for a few days.

"I know some great places if you ever want a recommendation, or company while you eat."

His words snapped India out of her ruminations. She was about to ask if he was hitting on her when he extended a white business card.

"Call me any time if you have questions or... need anything else." Light color tinged his cheekbones. At least he knew he had no business hitting on her in the ER.

"Thank you," India said, taking the card. His first name was Simon. Simon Stone.

He cleared his throat. "It was a pleasure meeting you, Ms. Monroe. Lay off the spicy tacos, okay?"

She laughed in spite of herself. "I'll do my best."

Chapter Six

"Oh my goodness, are you okay?" Kiara swept into India's apartment, pulling her into a sisterly hug.

After India's mother died, she moved in with her grandmother, who lived a couple of doors down from Kiara and her family. The two became best friends almost immediately and had been close ever since.

A bundle of energy, Kiara was a few inches shorter than India, with almond-gold skin and sparkling hazel eyes.

India laughed, squeezing her friend tight. "I'm fine. I told you, it was heartburn. Not a real heart attack."

Kiara stepped back. "I know, but still, it was scary, I bet."

"Very."

Kiara held up a paper sack. "Mom sent you some oatmeal raisin cookies. Want me to put them in the cookie jar?"

They had known each other so long, Kiara knew her way around India's apartment, and when she was at Kiara's house, she moved through the rooms as if she lived there.

"Yes, please. Then meet me in the living room. I have the snacks laid out for us."

India had set out a tray of nuts, cheeses, and crackers. She sat on the sofa and poured Arnold Palmer from a pitcher into two glasses. It was their favorite drink as kids, and they both still enjoyed it together.

Kiara joined her on the sofa and immediately picked up her drink. She took a sip while eying the spread. "Is that brie?"

"Yes, and this one is Comté. It's French."

"Of course."

"Of course," India said with a laugh. "The flavor is kind of nutty, like Fontina or Gruyère. They served it at a conference I attended a while back. I remembered it when I was at the store and thought it would be a nice addition to our tray."

Kiara grinned. "It's nice having a wealthy friend to introduce me to the finer things in life."

"It's just cheese, and I'm not wealthy," India said.

Kiara blew a raspberry with her lips. "Stop being modest. You live in this great apartment, you make a ton of money, and you only have to take care of yourself. You're rolling in dough, and I appreciate the benefits of knowing you."

They laughed as her friend set down her glass and then looked directly at her.

"So, what's going on? Based on our conversation, you sound like you're going through a midlife crisis."

"Maybe not that bad, but I have to do something." India placed a couple of almonds on her tongue.

"Do something like what?" Kiara asked.

India shrugged, at a loss because she hadn't completely figured out what she wanted to do yet but knew a change was needed. "Expand my options."

"Your health scare was a false alarm. You said so yourself."

"I know, but it might not have been. I could have ended up like my mother."

"Your mother had an undiagnosed heart condition."

"It wouldn't have been undiagnosed if she'd gone to the doctor instead of working around the clock. She had lupus, Kiara, worked two jobs, then started working three. *Three jobs!*" Her mother had a full-time job, worked nights during the week, and then worked for a commercial cleaning company on the weekends.

"You're not your mother."

"I'm not so sure about that." Folding her arms over her chest, India frowned. "She worked herself to death. Literally. There's no other way to say it. Look at the hours I put in now. Some days, I'm at the office for twelve hours."

"Except Friday nights," Kiara pointed out with a smirk.

India ignored her. "What kind of life am I living? All those hours at work, for what?"

"Okay, I understand where you're coming from. You had a health scare, and you're concerned you might be on the wrong track."

"I am on the wrong track. I have all this"—she waved her hands around the room—"but no one to share it with. No kids. No husband. I don't even know anyone on my father's side."

That part hurt quite a bit, not knowing an entire half of her identity.

Though her mother never said, India figured she had been an unplanned pregnancy because her parents had been teenagers when she was born. Her father, Karl Monroe, had paid child support, what little he could afford on his meager salary. He was an artist, a dreamer, she'd once heard Grandma Selah say, while her mother, Giselle, had been practical. She had never pushed Karl for more or taken him to court, so they struggled most of India's childhood.

After India turned eighteen, she didn't hear from him much. The last time she saw him was two years ago. She recalled the pain of that moment, which proved beyond a shadow of a doubt he didn't care for her or love her.

Kiara studied her with a frown etched into her forehead. "Are you saying you want to have kids?"

She had never seriously considered them before because of her lupus, but children had been one of the fleeting thoughts that entered her mind as she lay on her back in the emergency room.

India shrugged. "Maybe. I don't know. I'd be a horrible mother. I can't cook. What would they eat—cereal and Pop-Tarts?"

Kiara smiled at her. "Cooking is not the only requirement for being a mother, and personally, I think you'd make a great mom—if that's what you want."

"What makes you so sure?" India asked, hating she sounded as if she were fishing for compliments, though she was.

"Because you're a perfectionist, and I imagine you treating motherhood like one of your projects. You'll study it inside and out and become the best damn mom on the planet, putting the rest of us to shame."

India groaned. "Bad answer. Being a mother isn't like being a marketing executive. There are rules and guidelines in my industry. Being a mother is like being tossed into the middle of the ocean with no life jacket or idea which direction land is in. You have to keep swimming and hope you're going in the right direction."

Kiara laughed. "Motherhood is tough, but it's not that bad, I promise. Listen," she said, leaning closer, "forget what I said about you being a perfectionist and treating motherhood like your career. You want to know how I know you'd make a great mom? You're a fantastic godmother to my kids. You're patient with them. I'll never forget the day Jayden spat up on your brand new silk blouse, which I know cost a small fortune. I was mortified, but you just laughed."

"He was a baby. How could I be mad?"

"Exactly. You showed patience and had a sense of humor about it, which is typical for you. Being a mother is not for the weak. You have to have patience because kids—whew, lord—they will test you. And embarrass you in front of other folks. There are so many ups and downs and challenges, and keeping your cool is essential. That sense of humor is important to get you through the rough patches. Not to mention, you're nurturing."

"I'm not nurturing."

"You're nurturing," Kiara insisted. "God forbid Thiago eats a protein bar after work. You feed him every time he comes to your house, though you can barely boil water."

"Hey, I can boil water." She playfully tapped her friend's hand.

Kiara smiled. "You've been nurturing with my kids. Jayden and Josiah love their Auntie India, and speaking as a mom, I appreciate the way you love them—unconditionally—as if they're your own. It puts my mind at ease, knowing that if anything ever happened to me and Josh, my boys would be well taken care of."

India pointed a chastising finger at her. "Don't you dare make me cry."

"All I'm saying is, if you want to have children, you'll be a great mom. But if you're really worried about being a good mother, I'm here for you to lean on. Anytime."

"Thanks," India said softly. "I'm not ready to have a child yet, but it's definitely something I'm considering. My head is full of a lot of ideas at the moment."

"Are you thinking about having a child on your own?" Kiara asked tentatively.

"I would consider it, but we're putting the cart before the horse. Having a child is a monumental change. I think what I'd like to do is start small and begin dating. I'm thirty-three years old, and the last time I was in a serious relationship was in high school."

"Damien Jones. He was so fine," Kiara said wistfully. "I wonder where he is now."

"Who knows, but the point is I was, what, sixteen? He and I dated until we graduated and went to separate colleges. I've had men in my life since then, but no one serious. In college, I was focused on my grades. Then I found out I had lupus, which threw me into a depression for a few months."

"Yeah, you almost flunked out of college."

"Until you had an intervention."

"You're my girl. I couldn't let you flunk out of college."

"Which I appreciated, but by the time I graduated, all I cared about was succeeding, and that's how it's been all along. Every job, every position, has been moving me toward promotions and more success. I don't have much of a social life."

"At least you have Thiago."

India eyed her friend. "Do I?"

"It's not the *best* relationship, but you said the sex is amazing, and he did buy you that gorgeous bracelet for Valentine's Day."

She had to agree with Kiara. The bracelet was stunning. It was a gold and platinum bangle with a huge diamond that sparkled when it caught the light. But she hadn't worn it yet since she suspected Thiago felt obligated to give her the gift because of the holiday. There was no sentiment behind it.

"He didn't give it to me, though. He had it delivered because we didn't see each other on Valentine's Day. If the holiday had fallen on a Friday, I would have seen him, but it fell in the middle of the week."

"Are you thinking of breaking things off with Thiago?"

India swallowed against the wave of pain that hit her. Truth be told, she needed to pull back a little. Not be so into him.

"I'll keep my relationship with him for now. It serves a purpose."

"Mhmm. You get your back blown out every Friday night."

"You're crass."

"I'm living vicariously through you."

"Whatever. You have two kids under five. You and Josh have a perfectly fine sex life," India said dryly.

"Well..." Pink color tinged the crests of Kiara's cheeks.

"I think it's time I expand my options. Thiago and I have never made any type of commitment to each other. We both know the score. This is a convenience thing because we're both busy professionals. When it no longer works for either of us, we can walk away with no regrets."

Kiara picked up a cube of cheese. "I wish I could be like you. I'm an emotional creature. I have sex and fall madly in love. That's how Josh got me. Bastard." She popped the cheese in her mouth.

India laughed. "And you love that man like nobody's business."

"Hard. Can't imagine my life without him."

India experienced a twinge of envy. "That feeling wouldn't be so bad to have—to love someone and know they love me. I want someone I can't imagine living without, and I don't have that with Thiago. He and I are placeholders for each other. Eventually, he's going to slow down and look for the perfect little wifey to host his dinner parties, and I'm going to find a man who won't be intimidated by my success and independence."

"How are you going to find this mystery man?" Kiara asked.

India sipped her beverage, using those few seconds to think. "I have an idea already."

Kiara's eyes widened. "You've been holding out. Who?"

"No, I haven't, I promise," India said with a laugh. "It's the emergency room doctor. I wasn't paying him any mind at the time, but I think he was hitting on me, and I have his card."

"A doctor. Nice. You know what, I can check with Josh and see if any of his guy friends are single and get back to you. What do you think?"

India didn't hesitate. "I'm open to all possibilities."

Giddy, Kiara clapped her hands and did a little dance. "I love playing matchmaker. Oh, do you need him to be in a certain income bracket? Because I just remembered one of Josh's friends is single and a really nice guy, but he doesn't make the kind of money you do. He does make decent pay, though. His name is Leo, and he runs a gallery on the north side of town, so you'd have your love of art in common."

"Definitely a plus, but to be honest, I don't care what he does. As long as it's legal, he's nice to me, and he's not intimidated by my career and the money I make, we can give dating a shot."

Kiara's grin widened. "Perfect. I'll talk to Josh."

Chapter Seven

Something was wrong.

Thiago sat at the head of the large table in the main conference room with executives from various departments. His father had been more hands-off, but he had implemented the meetings when he took over, using them to stay abreast of what was going on in the various departments and encourage inter-departmental connections and solutions.

Today, he could hardly concentrate, and the reason was India.

His eyes casually swept her form as Sam updated the group on technological advances in the logistics department.

It wasn't her hair. She'd had a haircut over the weekend, but he was accustomed to seeing her regularly cut her hair in a neat style and brush her curls flat to frame her face.

It wasn't her clothes. She was sharply dressed as usual, this time in burgundy pants and a matching jacket buttoned to the neck, with a burgundy belt tied around her waist. She looked as put together as she always did, but the difference wasn't her appearance. It was her interaction with him.

He knew her personality as well as he knew her luscious body, and her behavior with him was off. Granted, they were careful at work, and at the moment, they were in a room full of people, but she had been cooler than usual in her greeting this afternoon. She also hadn't looked at him once since the meeting started. Not even when he spoke.

What could possibly have happened between Friday night and today?

Thiago shifted in his chair, forcing his attention back to the vice president of logistics. After Sam finished, a few of the other executives complimented him on the rollout of the new software, which promised to save them significant time in the coming months. In business, every second counted.

One by one, the group went around the table, taking turns to give updates, and anyone with a problem received feedback and suggestions. Only one of three women in the room, when it was India's turn, she told the group about her marketing plan, which she said would be in Thiago's inbox by the end of the day.

After they finished, Thiago gave everyone an update on the company's health and the strides they were making as they expanded at breakneck speed.

"Our success is all thanks to you and the hard work you do. This company is nothing without its people. You're the heart and soul of this organization, and at the end of this quarter, your bonuses will reflect your contributions."

Soft, appreciative laughter rippled around the table. Only a faint smile from India. She finally looked at him, and he felt her stare pierce the depths of his soul.

"In a couple of weeks, about twenty members of the teams from our Argentina and Brazil offices will arrive for the executive coaching I mentioned a while back. After a discussion with

HR, we decided it would be a good idea to include the teams from South America. The consultants we hired are expensive. Everyone is expected to be here the entire week for the coaching sessions. You should not have plans because you have known about this for months, but if you somehow forgot and made plans, cancel them. No one is excused. Understood?"

Head nods all around. One man pulled out his phone and started typing.

Thiago continued, "There is something I need to tell you all, but it must stay in this room."

A hush fell over the group, and all eyes turned to him.

"I have made a decision, and I'm taking the company public."

Soft gasps fell from the lips of most of the executives, while others looked around the room at each other, as if searching for understanding about this latest development.

"Why?" asked Helen, an older woman. Concern was carved into her features.

"For the benefits. First, let me explain that I did not make this decision lightly. I made it after extensive research and consultation with the few people in the world who are smarter than I am."

Some of them smiled at his joke. What they didn't know, but India did, was that his father disagreed with his plans, one of the few issues they had clashed over.

He and his father held the majority of the shares in the company, but his siblings and other family members also had a minor stake. He could convince them easily enough, but his father was more difficult to persuade that the IPO was the right move.

Thiago understood his hesitation. He had built Santana International using the income from his movie career but was not as motivated by profit as Thiago. His father had expressed concern about the short-term thinking that often came with the pressure to show quarterly earnings. Thiago saw the big picture and understood that, through an IPO, they could achieve much more than they were currently doing.

"What are the benefits?" Sam wanted to know.

Thiago was prepared to answer the question. "Access to capital is a big one. Selling shares will help us generate more cash, which means we can expand into new markets, develop new products and income streams, and potentially acquire our competitors."

"Running a public company comes with a whole different set of pressures. Quarterly pressures, for one, and more regulations that we'd have to adhere to," another executive said.

"You're quality control, and you're concerned about regulations?" Sam asked.

A few people laughed.

"I don't have a problem with quality control," the man said, shooting an annoyed look at his colleague. "I'm concerned about regulatory requirements, such as SEC filings and audits. I worked for a publicly traded company before coming here, and believe me, it was a nightmare."

"I'm aware of all the requirements," Thiago said. "I weighed the public scrutiny against the potential benefits of increased capital and market visibility. The reason I am telling you this now is because I have already started working with a consultant to handle the change. Our meetings have been offsite, but we're moving to the part of the process where they will have to come onsite and inspect our records to get us up to speed. Staff may have questions, and I expect you all to allay their fears and keep the IPO quiet until we are further along in the process, with a set date for going public."

"How long does the process take?" Helen asked.

"Approximately two years in our case, but we're hoping to go public in a shorter timeframe. I have been working with the consultant for six months, and at most there are 18 more months to go. If we are lucky, it will be no more than a year." It was an aggressive timeline, but one he strongly believed they could meet.

"Is this something we *have* to do?" Helen asked, sounding less than enthusiastic.

"No, we do not have to do this, but it is in the company's best interest," Thiago replied.

He saw genuine fear and concern on the faces of Helen and some of the other executives around the table. In an effort to put their minds at ease, he said, "Becoming a publicly traded company will be good for us. We will ensure the transition is done right and benefits everyone in the company, from my position all the way down to the janitor. Any more questions?"

There were two more questions, but surprisingly, no more afterward.

"Thank you for your time, and I will keep you updated on our progress. Please remember that what I shared with you stays in this room for now."

There were nods all around.

As the executives rose from their seats, Thiago didn't move. "India, could you stay behind for a few minutes? I have questions about the marketing plan."

She appeared to be startled by his request but sat back down as the others filed out of the room.

When the door closed behind the last person, he let his gaze rest on her face. "Is everything okay?" Thiago asked.

"Yes, everything is fine," she replied. Her voice was extra cool. No, not cool. Guarded.

"You don't seem to be yourself today."

"It's a busy week so far." She smiled, but the expression appeared less than genuine.

"Do you need more help—"

"Everything is fine, Thiago. Really. This is business as usual for us, isn't it? There's nothing for you to be concerned about."

Her answer seemed reasonable. She was trying to placate him, yet he couldn't shake the feeling something was wrong.

"Are you upset I canceled on Friday night?"

She shot him a look, halfway between surprise and a glare. Then her face slipped into another fake smile. "It's not the first time you've canceled. If there's nothing else, I have a million tasks to complete."

Thiago wanted to demand she stay put and answer his questions—truthfully this time—because she was obviously hiding something.

Instead, he said, "You may leave."

India stood, but as she walked past, his hand whipped out and grabbed her wrist. The sudden, automatic movement took her by surprise. She stared at him in shock. They were both shocked because he had made a rule about not touching in the office. Forbidding contact made sense, but right now, he wanted to pull her onto his lap and demand to know what was wrong. Something was definitely wrong, whether she admitted it or not.

He released her. "I should not have done that," he said.

"It's fine," she murmured, rubbing her wrist. After a moment's hesitation, she left without another word.

Thiago remained seated.

She was not the woman he had slept with Friday night. She was not the woman whose legs had been wrapped around his thighs and whose pillowy lips had been stretched around the girth of his hard dick, draining him of energy with the same expertise with which she did her daily work.

He scrubbed his fingers across his bearded jaw.

What the hell was wrong? Was she simply in a bad mood, or had he done something to upset her?

Chapter Eight

Thiago straightened his tie as he walked into the conservatory at the rear of his parents' home. The hum of conversation hit him, along with the soft clink of glassware and the gentle swell of classic jazz from the string quartet on an elevated platform in the middle of the room.

He saw his sister, Monica, right away. She had recently cut her short, natural hair, and her makeup was immaculate. Both arms were locked around her fiancé's arm as they chatted with friends.

Andre Campos wore a suit and tie, but there was no mistaking the subtle roughness in his brooding appearance. Thiago was very protective of his sisters and hadn't been sure at first that Andre was the right man for Monica, but he had proved himself worthy by loving her openly and treating her the way she deserved to be treated.

Monica had a big personality, and Andre seemed content to let her shine in the spotlight—and shine she did tonight. Her shimmering, floor-length gold dress clung to her slender curves and brushed her ankles, only offering a glimpse of the bedazzled sandals on her feet. And that smile—well, she was glowing —had become a permanent fixture on her face.

The party room, as the family called it, contained a high ceiling and arched windows that let the moonlight pour in from all sides. Glass panels revealed the pitch-black sky dotted with stars, and chandeliers attached to iron rafters cast a warm glow on the party.

Guests were dressed in cocktail attire, milling around the room with glasses of wine or small plates containing canapés. Servers moved among them in crisp white shirts and black vests, while a photographer captured candid photos of the attendees.

His brother, Bruno, was near the bar with his pregnant wife, Marissa, talking to their other brother, Ignacio. Meanwhile, Ignacio's fiancée, R&B singer Delta J, was surrounded by what appeared to be a group of young fans.

Thiago strolled toward the long banquet table on the other side of the room, greeting family members and friends along the way. He stopped in front of the spread, lifted a mini beef Wellington from one of the silver trays, and added two of the phyllo cups topped with caviar.

Someone came up beside him. "You finally made it."

The comment came from Ethan, his older stepbrother. Ethan was a real estate mogul who was on track to complete his biggest project later this year—a mixed-use development named Horizon, located southeast of the city.

"Finally?" Thiago said.

"You're late," Ethan said pointedly.

Technically true. He had stayed longer at work than he should have. On the way out, he had swung by India's office to say good night, expecting to see her hard at work behind her desk since they weren't going to see each other later. Instead, her office was empty, and the lights were out, which meant she had already left.

"Fashionably late," Skye, Ethan's wife, interjected.

"*Gracias, hermosa*." Thiago pulled her into a hug, and her very pregnant belly pressed into his abs.

Stepping back, he took a good look at her. Her face was fuller, her tawny-gold skin glowed, and her eyes held a distinct sparkle. Though she and Ethan hadn't been married long, she'd practically been a part of their family for years, and he'd never seen her livelier or more attractive. Pregnancy looked good on her.

"Since you're having his baby, you know you're never getting rid of him now, yes?"

Skye giggled. "I know. But I kinda like this guy."

She placed a hand on Ethan's arm, affection in her gaze as she looked at her husband.

Thiago shrugged. "I tried to warn you."

"Go to hell," Ethan muttered, slipping an arm around his wife's shoulders.

As they continued talking, their youngest sibling, Maxwell, approached. A product of Thiago's Mexican father and Black stepmother, he had toasty-brown skin and longish curly hair.

"Did I miss anything?" he asked, scanning the room.

"Just the lipstick on the corner of your mouth," Ethan said dryly.

Maxwell's eyes widened. "Seriously?" He lifted a hand to his face.

"What have *you* been up to?" Skye asked.

"No good, apparently," Thiago said.

Maxwell swore, grabbed a napkin from the table, and wiped vigorously at his mouth. "Is it gone?"

"No."

"Here, let me..." Skye took the napkin and dipped it in the

glass of water in her hand. Then she carefully removed the lipstick evidence from Maxwell's skin. "Better."

"Thank you," he said with a sigh.

"Please tell me you're not balancing multiple women here tonight," Thiago said.

"Okay, I won't tell you. But if I were to tell you, I'd say there are two." Maxwell's eyes jumped around the room, searching.

"Why in the world did you invite two women to the engagement party?" Ethan demanded.

"I didn't. One assumed she was invited and showed up, the other one I actually invited." Maxwell frowned. "I'm screwed."

"In a manner of speaking," Thiago quipped, putting a phyllo cup in his mouth.

"Dr. Santana, care to tell me how you have time to date multiple women with your schedule as a resident?" Skye asked, looking genuinely perplexed.

Maxwell was almost finished with his medical residency and had already started his job search to have a position lined up when he completed his training.

"It's not easy, believe me. Oh damn." He ducked. "Gotta run," he said, darting away.

"This is going to be an interesting night," Ethan said, watching his brother disappear among the crowd.

Thiago and Skye laughed.

"Have you seen Audra?" Thiago asked.

"She was over near the bar earlier, talking to Ignacio and Bruno," Skye replied.

"I need to find her." She had promised to pick up a gift and put his name on it, but he hadn't had a chance to follow up with her.

He scanned the room. "There she is. Excuse me." He put down his plate.

Sidling past a few guests, he walked up to Audra. Unlike Monica, who was thin, Audra was short like his stepmother and had a thicker figure. She was chatting with Aunt Florence, a spunky older woman who never went anywhere without some type of headpiece. Tonight, she wore an elegant cream statement piece with a wide brim and structured crown, adorned with a delicate bow and layered fabric flower. It was the perfect match for her cream and gold ensemble.

"Hello, Aunt Florence," he greeted her.

"Hello, Thiago." She looked behind him, as if searching for someone. "You came alone?"

He groaned inwardly while Audra stepped back and covered her mouth to hide her laughter.

"Yes, I came alone."

"A handsome young man like you should have a lady on your arm to attend events. You do like ladies, don't you?"

"Yes, I do," Thiago said, fighting to keep the weariness from his voice.

"Thought I'd check. Things are different nowadays. There's no shame if you want to bring a young fella to the party. How old are you, dear?"

He didn't want to answer, but it would be rude to ignore her.

"Thirty-four."

"Thirty-four? Well, you're getting up there, aren't you? You have the job, now you have to get a family. Everyone else is getting married and having kids. You're a man, so you don't have the same concerns about your biological clock, but at least a wife—"

"Do you mind if I borrow Audra for a few minutes? I need to talk to her in private."

If he didn't cut her off now, she'd never stop. Aunt Florence had a habit of offering unfiltered, unsolicited advice, and he

54

couldn't handle her candid conversation at the moment. Marriage and babies may be preoccupying her mind, but he was more concerned with building an empire.

Thiago took his sister's arm.

"We can finish our conversation later," Aunt Florence said.

"Okay," Thiago muttered, and he dragged Audra into a corner.

She was busy laughing.

"Are you finished?" he asked.

"Now, I am."

"I'm leaving as soon as the toast is over. What did you buy for Andre and Monica?"

"A handcrafted keepsake box with both their initials on the top. It was only a few hundred dollars. The note says, *For your love story.*"

"Sounds perfect. Thank you."

"Why don't you hire a personal assistant?"

"Someone else had the same suggestion," Thiago said.

"Who?"

"India, my VP of marketing."

"Well, she's right."

"Why would I waste my money when I have you to add the personal touch?"

"One of these days, I'm going to say no. Or maybe I should start charging." She tapped her chin.

"Siblings should not charge each other for minor tasks."

She pursed her lips. "We'll see. How are things going at work? I heard about the Santiago Migos fiasco."

"We'll be rolling out our new marketing campaign next week to grab their market share." The revised plan India and her team proposed was a vast improvement.

"That's fast," Audra said.

"We cannot afford to wait, and our head of marketing is very good at her job."

"You always speak so highly of her," Audra said thoughtfully.

"Like I said, she is good at her job." Thiago kept his voice neutral.

"Huh."

He shot a sideways glance at his sister. "What does 'huh' mean?"

"I rarely hear you talk about anyone else at the office. India's the only person you consistently mention."

"Because she is good at her job."

"She's also very attractive." Audra arched an eyebrow.

"And you know this how?"

"I did a little research since you mention her so often."

"*Ay Dios*," Thiago muttered.

"All I'm saying is, if you like her, you should make a move."

"Yes, make a move on a subordinate. Great idea." Yes, he was being deceptive.

"Oops, you're right. Terrible idea. So do you have anyone you're seeing?"

"I do not have time to date."

"Too busy?" Audra asked.

"Exactly."

"Make time. Aunt Florence is right. Before long, you'll be all alone wondering where the time went. Crying yourself to sleep."

Thiago chuckled. "I will dry my tears with all the money I make."

Audra pursed her lips again. "Thiago, money isn't everything. Having someone to share your life with—"

A glass bell rang, pulling everyone's attention to the center of the room.

The band had stopped playing and left the small stage. His father was standing in their place with the bell and a drink in his hand.

"Now I have your attention, hello everyone," Benicio Santana said.

"Hello!" the crowd greeted back.

Like Thiago, Benicio had a beard, but his hair and beard were completely gray. Right now, he was in his element, the center of attention for a few minutes. His father loved to talk and was always the one they chose to make announcements and toasts at family events. He handed off the bell to a member of the staff.

"Servers will be coming around to make sure everyone has a glass of champagne. We are about to toast the happy couple. If you are not drinking, look for the servers with a green ribbon around their wrists to get a non-alcoholic drink."

Thiago and Audra took a glass from one of the male servers passing by.

Benicio surveyed the crowd, his gaze stopping at a point near the back. "Rosa, do you want to come up here?"

Thiago couldn't see his petite stepmother, but by the chuckles from that corner of the room, she must have vehemently shaken her head in refusal.

"I had to try," Benicio said with a shrug. As the laughter died down, he added, "Andre, Monica, please join me."

Monica and her fiancé stepped up on the stage and stood to his right.

Benicio smiled at Monica, who held a flute of champagne in one hand. Then he turned his attention to the audience.

"Many of you know Monica as my stepdaughter, but to me, she is simply my daughter. She was only four years old when I came into her life, and I have been trying to keep up with her ever since."

Scattered laughter came from the crowd.

"I remember one night, not long after Rosa and I were married, I told Monica to go to bed. The older kids had already gone to bed, and her mother had told her more than once that she needed to go to sleep, but she had a mind of her own. I was in the kitchen fixing myself a snack when she marched in wearing pink Mickey Mouse pajamas and placed her hands on her hips. She told me in a very serious voice, with a frown on her face, that she was going to be very important when she grew up, and she was going to stay up all night when she did."

As the group laughed, his face softened. Then he turned to Monica. "You were important then, and you are important now —to every single one of us here who loves you. And you can stay up as late as you want."

Thank you, Monica mouthed, leaning in for a hug.

Benicio briefly squeezed her and kissed her temple. Then he turned his attention to his future son-in-law.

"Andre, I remember you from her college days. I saw the way she lit up when she talked about you back then, and life or Fate brought you back together. You make my little girl very happy, and for that reason, you will always have my love and respect."

"Thank you, sir," Andre said.

Benicio lifted his glass. "So now I make a toast to Monica and Andre. May your days be filled with joy and laughter and may your love story endure, inspiring everyone lucky enough to witness it. I look forward to your wedding, and I hope and pray you have many, many happy years together. Cheers to the happy couple!"

"Cheers!" the group called out.

Thiago touched his glass to Audra's and a few friends nearby, then took a sip of the bubbly.

As he had told Audra, he left after the toast, but not before congratulating Monica and Andre and talking to a few family members.

He slipped through the front doors and jogged down the outer steps to his vehicle, sitting in the dark for a moment before making a decision. He scrolled to India's name. It was late, but not too late. If she were open to it, he could pop by her place. He had never gone to her home this late, but after their odd interaction on Wednesday, a visit might be the perfect way to end the night and get their relationship back on track.

As he was about to shoot off the text, he hesitated. He needed a good excuse to reach out at this hour, on a day he had told her they wouldn't see each other. He'd tell her that he wanted to discuss the marketing campaign for the company's retail stores.

Satisfied, he tapped out the message and hit *Send*.

Then he started the car and headed off the property, anticipating he'd be able to see India tonight after all.

Chapter Nine

India applied another coat of lipstick as she checked her appearance in the mirror behind the sun visor of her Audi. She pressed her lips together to evenly distribute the color and then flipped the visor back up to the roof.

Taking a deep breath, she let it out slowly, a little anxious because she hadn't been on a date in a very long time and didn't know what to expect from Dr. Simon Stone. Hopefully, they would have a good conversation, and if the night went well, they could plan another date in the near future.

Simon had gotten off work late, so they were having dinner later than she normally ate, but she didn't mind. The restaurant had great reviews, and she had looked forward to dressing up in something other than the pants she usually wore for work. She had taken a chance with a fuchsia sweater and fuchsia dress, but it was a fun color, so she decided not to over-think her outfit.

At the last moment, she left the sweater in the car and opened the door, stepping into the chilly air and tucking her purse under her arm. As she strolled toward the entrance of the restaurant, she saw Simon, casually dressed in a white shirt and gray slacks.

"Looks like we arrived at the same time," he said, a smile breaking out on his face. His wavy hair was brushed back from his forehead. Unlike in the emergency room, tonight he wasn't wearing glasses.

"A good sign," India said.

He nodded in agreement. "It means we're in sync," he said, opening the door.

India had made the comment thinking it was a good sign that they were both on time and respectful of each other's time. She merely smiled and didn't attempt to correct him, walking ahead of him into the warm interior.

They approached the hostess stand together, and after a few minutes were escorted to their table.

India sat across from Simon and looked around. "I've never eaten here before."

"This is one of my favorite restaurants, which is why I recommended we come here. If you like fish, the salmon is excellent."

"I do like salmon," India said, opening the menu.

Simon leaned across the table, catching her attention. "Can I say something?"

"Of course," she replied.

"You are an incredibly beautiful woman. I noticed in the emergency room, but you're even more beautiful this evening. The color you're wearing was made for you."

Her cheeks warmed at the compliment. "Thank you. You look pretty amazing yourself."

He sat back. "That wasn't a line, by the way."

"I didn't think it was," India assured him. With the evening already started on a positive note, she relaxed.

They both perused the menus until the waiter arrived, and

they placed their orders, India choosing the salmon and Simon selecting a chicken dish. Then they spent the next hour in leisurely conversation as they ate salads and then their meal, covering a variety of topics. India learned Simon had become a doctor because he wanted to follow in the footsteps of his grandfather. She also learned he was divorced, and his daughter and ex-wife lived in another state. He didn't go into details about the end of his marriage, but she sensed it was still a sensitive topic when his demeanor noticeably changed.

By the time they were sipping coffee and enjoying dessert, India had a good idea of the kind of man he was. Charming and humble were the adjectives that came to mind.

Simon placed his coffee cup in its saucer. "Okay, so you know I like to fish because it relaxes me," he began.

"And bike ride for cardio, which you would never convince me to do," India added.

He laughed. "Why not?"

"I'm a little embarrassed to admit this, but I never learned to ride a bike, unless stationary bikes count," she added with a hopeful lilt in her voice.

He laughed. "It does not."

She shrugged. "Oh well."

"I can't believe your dad never pushed you down the street on a bike with your little helmet on as you wobbled to stay upright. It's a rite of passage for every American kid."

"Not every single one. My dad never did it, and my mother was too busy working to worry about whether I could ride a bike." India took a sip of coffee.

"Oh." The smile evaporated from Simon's face the moment he noticed her reluctance to discuss her parents. "Enough about me. What do you like to do in your spare time?"

India finished chewing the piece of pie she had lifted into her mouth. "Well, you know I have lupus, and I took up yoga years ago to help with the pain. I worked with a trainer initially, and now I'm to the point where I can do it alone at home. I like walking, usually down the street outside my building a few days a week."

His eyes turned sympathetic. "You stick to low-impact exercises to avoid a flare-up."

"Exactly. For the most part, I've been lucky, but years ago, a bad one landed me in the hospital. My boss at the time was very kind and gave me all the time off I needed."

She would forever be grateful for Benicio Santana's patience when she was hospitalized. He had held her job for her. That's what made Benicio so special. It had taken more than two months for her to fully recover and get back to where she could work a full day. Even then, he insisted she ease into her schedule, starting with half days before allowing her to put in more time.

India's phone vibrated in her purse on the table. "Excuse me," she said apologetically.

"Go ahead," Simon told her.

She checked her phone and saw a text from Thiago.

On my way to your place. I wanted to review the numbers for the retail stores CPC campaign.

She couldn't believe what she was reading. He had left the engagement party and wanted to come by her place to work. Even more incredible, he thought *she* would be available and willing to do so with him.

"You're frowning. Bad news?" Simon asked.

"Sorry, this is my boss."

"On a Friday night? The same boss who gave you the generous time off?" Simon asked, sounding surprised.

India glanced up at him. *No, actually, his handsome son who makes my skin tingle with the mere brush of his hand against mine*, she thought.

"His replacement. His son. He's a bit of a workaholic."

An understatement. He was consumed with success and power and had been angling to take over his father's conglomerate for years. Truth be told, he was doing a helluva good job. His business acumen was one of the traits she admired about him, but she had no desire to work tonight. She was turning over a new leaf. Besides, she was busy.

"Let me respond to this text right quick, and we can get back to our conversation."

Her thumbs flew over the letters as she tapped out a reply: *Out to dinner. The review will have to wait until Monday. Talk to you then.*

"There." India shoved her phone back into her purse. If it vibrated again, she would ignore it. "Now, where were we?" She smiled across the table.

"You were telling me about your kind boss, and before that, you were telling me about the yoga and walking you do, which explains the great figure you have," Simon commented.

India laughed softly. "You're full of compliments, aren't you?"

He shrugged, grinning.

"Yoga and meditation were among the recommendations made by my rheumatologist, to minimize the pain and stiffness from the disease. And he was right, they do work—at least for me. He recently recommended a new medication, but I haven't decided if I want to try it yet. I'm still doing research." She gave him the name of the drug and asked if he'd heard of it.

"I'm not familiar. How is it different?"

India dabbed her mouth. "Instead of taking pills, I can give myself an injection once a week. He thinks that, working in conjunction with my other meds, my lupus could go into remission. But it has quite a few side effects, like all drugs, so, like I said, I'm still deciding."

Their conversation continued to flow without awkward pauses. At the end of the meal, they left the restaurant and strolled to India's car.

Standing beside the driver's side door, she said, "Thank you for a wonderful evening."

"Does that mean I get another chance to see you again?" Simon asked.

"Yes, it does. Assuming you have time in your busy schedule."

He blew out a breath of frustration. "I love my job, but it can be taxing on my time. I'm on call next Saturday, so would next Friday night work for you again?"

India opened her mouth to turn him down, but then she thought, *why should I?* Friday night was when she and Thiago had their rendezvous, but over the past seven months, he had canceled multiple times. Friday nights weren't sacred to him. She couldn't blame him for missing tonight for his sister's engagement party, but there had been other times when he had canceled on her. So next week, she would have to cancel on him.

"Friday night works," she confirmed.

"Perfect. Next time, I'm taking you to a spot where we can have dinner and then listen to a live band afterward." He rubbed his hands together and wiggled his eyebrows.

India laughed. "I love listening to live music. Sounds like a good time to me."

"Then I'll be in touch in the middle of next week with the details. Good night, India." Simon leaned in and gave her a kiss on the cheek.

His lips were soft and warm, but the kiss didn't ignite any heat in her body. Nothing like the rip-roaring fire she experienced when Thiago's fingertips barely grazed her skin. But that was to be expected. She'd known him longer and slept with him, while this relationship was brand new.

"Good night, Simon." India climbed into her car.

"Drive carefully," Simon said.

She flashed him an easy smile. "I will. You do the same."

He waited until she had closed her door before walking away.

Chapter Ten

India walked into the break room and placed two boxes of macaroons on the counter. About once a month, she stopped at a French bakery on the way to work and picked up the treats, leaving them in the break room for staff to enjoy.

As she was walking out, one of the admins walked in and spotted the pink boxes. "It's gonna be a great day," she sang, dancing over to the counter.

"Don't eat them all, LaNelle. Save some for the rest of the staff."

LaNelle shot her a look. "I'm not making any promises."

Laughing and shaking her head, India continued to her office. She had a lot of work to do, so she dove in right away. At nine-twenty-eight, her phone rang, and she saw Thiago's executive assistant was calling.

"Good morning, Ms. Monroe. Mr. Santana would like to see you in his office at eleven to review the cost-per-click reports for the retail stores campaign," he said.

India stifled a sigh. It wasn't his fault Thiago didn't understand the need for advanced notice.

"Sure, Amir. I'll be there at eleven," she said, which meant she had an hour and a half to prepare.

"Thank you. I'll let him know."

India placed her desk phone in its cradle and rolled her shoulders. She wasn't feeling particularly well. Her joints were rather stiff and achy today. Thiago's request for those numbers, in addition to everything else she had to do, was the last thing she wanted to deal with, but she didn't have a choice.

"That's why I get paid the big bucks," she muttered. It was her own fault for suggesting they touch base on Monday.

She tapped two tablets of painkillers in her palm and swallowed them down with a few sips of Fiji water. Then she called Beth Ann and asked her to print the data along with colored graphs and a short summary for her review. When she finished the conversation, she made a video call to her counterpart in Asia, and they spent an hour bouncing ideas off each other. The commercials they were showing weren't resonating in Japan, so they discussed alternatives and sketched out ideas for future marketing promotions.

By the time she finished the conversation, it was almost time to meet with Thiago. She pushed away from her desk and stepped into the hall, almost bumping into Beth Ann as she did so.

"You have those figures?" India extended her hand.

"I do." Beth Ann handed them over. "They look great."

India bent her head over the documents and retreated into her office.

"Is there anything else I can do to help?" Beth Ann asked.

India lifted her head. "No, this is all I need. You're right, the ROI is impressive. The cost-per-click price is low, and the conversion rate is higher than expected. Thank you."

"Yes, ma'am."

Sitting on the edge of her desk, she flipped through the material, familiarizing herself with the figures before she went into Thiago's office. She knew he'd start drilling her with questions and expect an answer.

When she felt prepared, she checked the time.

"Shoot," she muttered. The last ten minutes flew by. She was running late.

She rushed from her office to the other end of the building where he was located. In the center of the floor were support staff in cubicles. Some nodded and smiled as she passed by, and she returned the greeting, though she didn't have time to stop and socialize.

She breezed past his assistant, Amir, who barely acknowledged her as she went by. At the door, she knocked and then pushed her way in.

Thiago was standing at the window, staring out at the view. He turned around when she entered, and she walked across to him, very aware of his commanding presence. Despite her annoyance at him, she couldn't help but notice how amazing he looked today in a charcoal three-piece suit.

She especially liked him in three-piece suits. Something about the fit turned her on. His tie was perfectly knotted, and the cut was razor-sharp, tailored to his broad shoulders and muscular frame with almost unfair precision. The vest hugged his torso like it had been stitched onto him, emphasizing the flatness of his stomach, while the jacket added timeless elegance.

India's throat went dry. He always radiated power, but in this suit—basically lethal corporate armor—he exuded authority. She wanted to stay annoyed at him but hadn't had her usual Friday night fix, so her body was already betraying her, her nipples tightening at the sight of his sensual lips and big hands.

She physically ached, with a hunger that couldn't be satisfied until the next Friday night they met up. Dammit, but she'd already committed to seeing Simon.

"I have the numbers from the CPC campaign," she said, keeping her voice cool though her body was heating up.

"Thank you." Thiago took the blue folder and then sat behind his desk.

India awaited his response. He didn't have any guest chairs, so she stood quietly in front of his desk while he flipped through the pages.

After a few minutes, he asked, "This is everything?"

"Yes."

He continued flipping through the sheets, a fine line creasing his brow. "How was your weekend?"

The question took her by surprise. She had expected him to ask about the campaign, so she didn't respond, which prompted him to lift his gaze and look at her in a questioning way.

"Oh, um, I had a good weekend. Thank you. How was yours?"

"Fine." He returned his attention to the pages.

"Monica's engagement party went well?"

"Yes. A lot of people were there, of course—friends and family. Plenty of food, and my father made a very nice toast for her and her fiancé."

She hadn't seen Mr. Santana much since Thiago took over. He had taken on a consulting role with the company, so he rarely came to the office. She missed his presence.

"Afterward, the party continued at the club Andre, my future brother-in-law, owns."

"You like to dance, so I'm guessing you went?"

"No. I went home after the toast."

"You had an early night?" India asked.

"Not exactly, but I didn't go out partying with the rest of them."

The office fell silent again as he continued to review the papers.

"What did you do on Friday night?"

"I went out to dinner," India answered, suddenly uncomfortable, as if she had done something wrong by going out with Simon.

"So I understand from your text. Alone?"

They didn't have an exclusive relationship, but she wasn't exactly sure how in the world to answer his question. Would he have a problem with her seeing another man?

"No."

Thiago continued to look at the pages, but she had the distinct impression he was paying very close attention to her answers. He lifted his gaze, his dark eyes boring into her, almost demanding she divulge everything from this weekend.

"Who did you go out with?" he asked.

The conversation had officially become intrusive. Never before had they drilled each other on what they had done when they were apart.

"A friend," she replied.

She didn't lower her gaze, boldly looking at him in an unflinching way.

He gave her a long, thoughtful look. "A friend. Was it Kiara?"

"No."

Thiago lifted his right eyebrow in an inquisitive way. "Does your friend have a name, India?"

"Why are you asking about my plans from Friday night?" she countered.

He gave an elegant shrug. "I'm curious."

"I went out with a friend. No one you know. Do you have

questions about those numbers? We chose to compute five-year projections, but we could look further into the future if you prefer."

He stared at her, and it took all her willpower not to look away. She clenched the fingers of one hand into a fist behind her back to combat the urge.

"If I didn't know any better, I would think you were avoiding answering the question," Thiago said. He sounded pleasant enough, but she knew him well and saw tension in the way he held his body perfectly still.

"Why would I avoid answering the question?"

"I don't know. You tell me."

"Thiago, you went to an engagement party, and I went out to dinner with a friend. I'm not asking you specifically what you did on Friday night. I'm sure you had a great time with your family, and I had a great time at dinner. Was there anything else you needed?"

"No."

"Good," India said with immense relief. "I have work to do. If you have additional questions, you know where to find me." She turned on her heel and headed to the door.

"I'll see you on Friday?"

India paused and took a deep breath. Why did she feel as if she was doing something wrong? She wasn't doing anything wrong.

Slowly she turned to face Thiago. "Actually, I need to cancel this Friday night."

"Do you have plans again... with your friend?" he drawled.

He had probably guessed she had been with another man, but she wouldn't give him the satisfaction of admitting it. If he wanted to know, he'd have to ask her outright.

"Yes, I do. So, maybe next week?"

"Maybe," he said in a tight voice, an inscrutable expression on his face. "If *I* don't have plans."

His response set her teeth on edge, and she fake-smiled at him. "I guess we'll see when the time comes."

India marched out the door, feeling his dark gaze on her the entire time. In the hallway, she was able to breathe easier but was unsure of what had just occurred. Their relationship was changing. She supposed the change was partly her fault. Since the last time they slept together, her view on life had gone through a monumental shift, and perhaps Thiago was picking up on the difference in her.

Nonetheless, she was certain she had made the right decision. Though they had sizzling chemistry, she and Thiago were not in a committed relationship. They weren't in a relationship at all, and she needed to keep her options open.

Chapter Eleven

S he had lied to him.

Thiago lowered the folder in his hand and stared at the closed door where India had exited moments before.

She had lied, or at the very least was being deceptive.

He pushed up from his chair and shoved his hands deep into his pockets. Frowning, he stood in front of the window and looked out at the Atlanta skyline.

He suspected India was seeing someone else, which explained why she hadn't been willing to see him when he was free last Friday. It explained why she gave evasive answers and was going to be busy yet again this coming Friday. Too busy for him.

Am I losing her?

The idea of India with another man was deeply unsettling. His nostrils flared, and he experienced a rush of emotion he couldn't do anything to stop. It felt suspiciously like jealousy—a foreign concept—which gripped his body with harsh, sharp talons.

True enough, they weren't in a committed relationship, but he didn't like the thought of... sharing her. It sickened him to the core.

Thiago swung abruptly from the window, walked over to the bar, and fixed himself a whisky and Coke. He didn't usually drink this early, but he needed the liquor as he pondered a situation he hadn't considered happening—the possibility of losing India.

While his brothers believed he didn't have relationships, he did—sort of. He had lovers because, at this point in his life, his priority was work. As a result, the women he had slept with over the years had never held his attention for very long. When their time together ended, he had the concierge service send them a parting gift—a Van Cleef bracelet, Lorraine Schwarz diamond earrings, or a two-tone Cartier watch.

But India was different. He never once became bored with her, and they had fit together perfectly right from the start.

Thiago took a long sip of his drink, going back in time to when he was visiting from Brazil and had first seen India years ago. Back then, she had been working one floor below.

"Who's that?" he had asked his father.

"The new director of marketing, India Monroe."

Her hair was longer then. Hoop earrings peeked between the strands, which were parted on one side and framed her face in a neat arrangement of curls that touched her shoulders. He'd been mesmerized by her chocolate-brown skin, full lips, high cheekbones, and those dark-brown eyes looking at him with very little interest.

He could count on one hand how many times he saw her after the initial encounter, including after she received the promotion to vice president of marketing for the U.S. and moved to the executive floor.

She was an attractive woman. He wasn't blind. But he

hadn't had any intention of sleeping with her—until he came to town for Ethan and Skye's wedding last July.

One Friday night, by chance, he walked into the sports bar down the street, and India was there. She had removed her blue jacket, exposing a blue sleeveless top that showed off arms with a hint of definition.

He joined her at her table. They ate together and had a few drinks. They shared a few laughs. They talked about business. They talked about current events.

At the end of the meal, he told himself that he was simply escorting her to her car in the parking deck to be a gentleman. But on the walk over, he knew he had been lying. He wanted her. Badly. He was consumed with the possibility of relieving his aroused body by thrusting into hers.

She was sharp, sexy, funny. If he had been reading the signals correctly, the attraction was mutual.

"Thank you for walking me to my car," she had said, looking up at him with fuck-me eyes.

Desire crackled between them. There was no way he could walk away. He didn't remember what he said to her. All he remembered was leaning in, and she didn't put up a hand to halt him. She never whispered the words *No* or *Stop*.

When he kissed her, the pavement beneath his feet shifted. He became consumed with need. He unbuttoned her pants right there in the parking deck and finger-fucked her until she spasmed uncontrollably. As he sucked her neck, she panted through her orgasm, her cries soft and broken as her fingernails dug into his shoulders.

Afterward, he realized how dangerous their behavior had been. Anyone could have seen them, but at the time, he had only cared about making her come. All he could say in his defense was, "Goddammit. I didn't plan to do this here, but you..."

Another passionate kiss followed his declaration, prompting her to invite him back to her place. They almost didn't make it to the bedroom.

When she tried to lift off her blouse, he held her hand.

"No," he said, his voice sounding guttural and hoarse. "Let me."

Then he lifted the top over her head and tossed it to the floor. He pulled down her pants and surprised her by lowering to his knees and using his teeth to drag her blue cheeky below her hips.

They spent the rest of the night screwing each other's brains out. His tongue and hands came to know every inch of her body. Her soft, walnut-tipped breasts. Her smooth thighs that spread wide to welcome him, and the sweet wetness between them that he never wanted anyone else to have the pleasure of tasting.

When he finally left, he was walking on clouds, but when he saw her the following Monday, she acted as if nothing had happened.

It drove him crazy, and he wanted her again. He'd spent the entire rest of the weekend thinking about her and the irresistible softness of her mouth, the scent of her skin, and the way she felt in his arms.

Then his father asked him to stay indefinitely, and he invited himself to her apartment on the following Friday night, and their Friday night hookups became the norm. They didn't make any promises to each other, but meeting up became the perfect way to end the work week and de-stress.

Taking over Santana International would have been a lot more challenging without her to talk to. And of course, he enjoyed making love to her. She satisfied his appetite for sex and was just as unrestrained and devoted to pleasure as he was.

The shape and press of her slender fingers were permanently engraved on his skin.

Bottom line, Thiago couldn't afford to have another man come between them. He wouldn't tolerate it. He had to figure out who the hell this man was.

And get rid of him.

Chapter Twelve

"So, what do you think? I can pick you up on Friday, and we can go from there."

India and Leo had been playing phone tag all weekend, and he'd finally caught up with her as she was walking back from lunch.

"I love the idea, but since this is the first time we're going out, how about we meet at the comedy club instead?" India asked, side-stepping a man coming toward her on the sidewalk.

"No problem, but I promise, I've been vetted by Josh and Kiara," Leo told her.

"I love Josh and Kiara to death and know they would never risk my safety, but since I don't know you, I'd still like to be careful. Does meeting up work for you?" She hoped her insistence didn't turn him off. She had enjoyed talking to him and looked forward to finally meeting.

"Listen, I want you to be comfortable, so meeting up is not a problem. I'll see you Friday?"

"See you Friday. Text me the location."

"Done. I'll touch base with you on Thursday to make sure nothing's changed."

After the call disconnected, India dropped the phone inside the pocket of her blazer as she briskly walked the few blocks to the Santana International building, hurrying back to work so she wouldn't be late. She'd had to wolf down her sandwich earlier because she had taken part of her lunch break to run to the bank, and the line had been long. As an executive, no one would bat an eye if she returned late, but she liked to set a good example for the staff.

The phone buzzed in her pocket, and she removed it to find that Leo had texted the information, as promised. He was taking her to see a stand-up comedian on Friday since he had to work Saturday and Sunday because a big artist was in town for an exhibition. She had contemplated canceling but decided she wanted to meet him right away—if for no other reason than to determine if she wanted to keep him on her list of prospects.

She hated canceling on Thiago again, though. Hopefully, he'd understand, but she dreaded telling him.

Speak of the devil, she thought.

Up ahead, a driver held open the door to a limo in front of the building, and Thiago emerged from the back seat. Her pulse jumped at the sight of him, tall and imposing as he adjusted the cuffs of his navy blue jacket, which he'd paired with a pale yellow shirt today. His neatly coiffed hair glimmered under the rays of the midday sun. Once again, she thought he looked handsome enough to be a model.

When he saw her, his footsteps slowed. "India," he greeted her, his voice crisp and professional as he opened the door to the building.

"Thank you." She slipped in ahead of him.

Employees and visitors milled around the lobby, entering and exiting, their footsteps echoing on the ceramic tile. One of the security guards at the desk nodded respectfully as they passed by.

After a short wait at the bank of elevators, they entered the cabin with three employees. Thiago's hand briefly brushed hers as they made their way to the back, and a tremor of awareness went through India. It seemed like forever since they'd touched, and the brief contact ignited her skin, sending a spark all the way to her core.

The doors closed, and the employees whispered softly to each other in front of them.

"Nice lunch?" Thiago asked in his cultured, accented voice.

"Yes. Did you have a good one?"

They sounded stiff and formal, far removed from the teasing banter they engaged in when he came to her apartment. Granted, they weren't alone and were always careful at work—except for the tense seconds the other day when he grabbed her —but their conversations had never been this stilted. The difference saddened her.

"Yes. It was a working lunch, very productive."

The elevator doors opened, and the employees filed out, going in different directions on the floor. The doors closed, and India and Thiago were alone.

"We ate at Garlique," he added.

She shot a look at his strong profile. "Your brother's restaurant, right?"

He nodded. "The very first one he opened. Last year it won the James Beard award for outstanding restaurant."

No mistaking the pride in his voice at his brother's accomplishment.

"Impressive."

Not that India was surprised. Benicio and his wife Rose, Thiago's stepmother, had done an excellent job with their children. They were all accomplished in their own way.

"How was your weekend?" Thiago turned his dark eyes on her, and the air in the elevator contracted.

"Nice, thanks. And yours?" India purposely shifted the conversation back to him.

"Fine," he said shortly.

The cabin stopped on the executive level.

"I assume you're free this Friday?" Thiago asked as the doors slid open.

He asked the question she had hoped she wouldn't have to answer for at least another day or two.

Tension tightened her belly as they stepped onto the top floor. The receptionist hadn't returned to her desk yet, so the lobby was thankfully empty.

"Unfortunately, I won't be able to see you on Friday."

His eyebrows snapped together. "Again?" There was a massive amount of incredulity in the single word.

"My schedule is crazy right now." The explanation sounded vague and flimsy to her ears. "I should be free next week Friday, though."

A muscle in his jaw jumped, his irritation evident in the firm set of his features. "I see. Is this going to become a habit?"

"No. Like I said, my schedule is out of control right now, and I've had to... move some things around—our Friday night appointment being one of those things."

Admittedly, she really was having a hard time juggling two additional men, and she'd only recently started. Surely the situation would get easier. She couldn't go out during the week, which left the weekend, but both men had jobs that sometimes required weekend hours.

After her date with Leo on Friday night, she had another one with Simon on Saturday. She had invited him over to her apartment for a low-key, relaxing evening of pizza and movie-watching with the hope they'd get to know each other better and she'd perhaps develop more romantic feelings for him.

After their second date last week, he kissed her before they parted ways. The experience had been... underwhelming. No spark. No fire. She liked him well enough and hoped the situation would improve.

"Appointment." Thiago repeated the word she had used with distaste, as if it soiled his mouth.

India smoothed the hair at her nape. "We've never given what we do a name. I didn't know what else to call it," she said.

"I suppose calling it the night we screw would be crass," he said.

"Crass, but accurate, don't you agree?"

He stepped closer, but she held her ground.

"You're different." The words sounded like an accusation.

"I'm busy."

"You've never been this damn busy."

"It's very simple, Thiago. Things change, and we learn to adjust," India said lightly, longing to end the conversation.

"Are you seeing someone else?"

India hesitated then lifted her chin higher. "Yes."

His eyes flashed with emotion. He definitely didn't like that bit of information.

"If there's nothing else..."

"There is nothing else—for now," Thiago said ominously.

She opened her mouth to demand to know what he meant, but the elevator pinged and the doors opened. The receptionist and one of the admins exited the cabin.

"Good afternoon," they said in unison.

India smiled in acknowledgment as they walked past, the admin going down the hall and the receptionist stepping behind the huge desk.

Thiago kept his gaze on India, and the air vibrated with tension. Then, as cool as you please, he turned and walked away.

She released the breath she had been holding. The receptionist was making a big show of working, which looked more like she was simply moving around items on her desk to avoid looking at India and Thiago.

India took off in the opposite direction of Thiago, relieved he now knew she was seeing other people. When all of this started several weeks ago, she hadn't intended to pull back from him. She had simply wanted to explore her options, but a little distance might be good.

Self-preserving. Heart-protecting.

Because she'd had plenty of time to think and acknowledged she was dangerously close to falling for Thiago. She wanted to see him on Friday nights and every night, which was a problem. She had spent all this time with a man she had no future with—a situation she hadn't squarely faced until she thought she was literally going to die.

She needed to wean herself off her need for him and squash the feelings threatening to overrule her common sense. Dating other men was the perfect mechanism by which to accomplish her goal.

Now she had to convince her heart she was making the right decision.

Chapter Thirteen

Thiago pounded his fist on India's door. He had never shown up at her apartment unannounced before and wasn't certain she was home, much less if she would let him in. But they needed to talk.

He glared up at the camera above her door. "Let me in," he said.

He kept his eyes locked on the lens and waited.

Moments later, the door swung open from the inside, and his eyebrows shot higher when he saw India's appearance. She wore light sweats and a T-shirt, and on her face was some type of green goop.

"What is that on your face?" Thiago asked.

She glowered at him. "It's called a mask. What are you doing here?" she asked irritably.

"I came to see you," he replied.

"Obviously, but why?"

"We need to talk."

"About?"

He rested a hand high on the door frame and leaned closer. "Are you going to allow me inside or not?"

"Now is not a good time. If you have something to say, say it and leave."

Something inside him snapped. She was treating him as if she didn't want him there, and he had never experienced that before. He shoved the door wider and marched in, brushing past her.

"What do you think you're doing?" India demanded.

Thiago stopped at the edge of the living room. Now he understood why she didn't want him there. A box of pizza sat on the table beside a decanter of red wine. Two glasses were also on the table, along with silverware and two plates stacked on top of each other.

Slowly, he turned to face India. "Do you have a date tonight too?" he bit out.

She folded her hands across her torso.

"Answer the question!" Thiago barked.

"This isn't the office," she retorted. "You can't boss me around in my own home."

"Do you have a man coming here tonight—yes or no?"

She sighed, and her shoulders dropped like someone at the end of her rope. "I have plans with someone, yes."

"Plans? Oh, really? Who is he?"

"You don't know him."

"Of course I know I don't know him, India, but who is he? And how long have you been fucking other people?"

"I'm not fu—why are you making such a big deal about this?"

He didn't miss what she had been about to say. Perhaps she wasn't screwing the man yet.

"Because you canceled on me the past two weeks, and now

I know why. There is another man in your life, and I feel blindsided."

"I'm sorry, but what do you want from me? Am I supposed to sit at home every night waiting by the phone for you to call?"

"I didn't think you would be doing that, but I certainly did not think you would be doing *this*, either." He stabbed a finger in the direction of the food. "How serious is your relationship? How long have you been seeing him?"

India closed her eyes, took a deep breath, and released it. "Woosah," she said softly.

"Hoo-saw? What the hell does that mean?" Thiago demanded.

She opened her eyes. "He and I started seeing each other in the past few weeks, okay? He's a doctor I met when I had to go to the emergency room a while back."

"You were in the emergency room?" Thiago exclaimed. "Why didn't you tell me?"

"Why would I tell you? I went there on a Saturday."

She answered in such a flippant manner, he was appalled to realize she believed he wouldn't care she had been in the hospital because her visit didn't occur on a Friday.

"Why did you have to go to the doctor?" Thiago asked.

"It was a false alarm," India said dismissively. "I thought I was having a heart attack, but it was heartburn. The whole episode was embarrassing."

Thiago relaxed. His entire body had locked up with tension when he thought something had been seriously wrong.

"Is the good doctor the only other man you're seeing?" he asked in an overly pleasant voice.

India averted her eyes.

Thiago let loose a stream of Spanish curses. "How many others are there?" he demanded.

"You make dating sound awful, and it's not. Kiara set me up with a friend of her husband's, and we went out last night. Why do you care?"

"How could you ask such a question!" Thiago bellowed, blistering rage shooting through him. "Friday night is *my* goddamn night. Do you really think I want another man—" The chime of the doorbell cut him off.

Maybe it was for the best because he had been about to say, "Do you really think I want another man spending time with *my woman?*" But in reality, she wasn't his woman, was she? They had made no formal declaration regarding the status of their relationship, so technically she was allowed to see other people.

Which he hated. He hated the idea of her with another man, especially since her apartment was the space he escaped to one night a week. Right now, it was being sullied by a fucking stranger whose fucking face he was tempted to bash in the minute he walked through the fucking door.

"He's here, and you need to leave," India said.

Thiago caught her by the upper arm. "Are you sleeping with him?" He hated asking the question but had to be sure. Wondering would eat him alive.

"Not that it's any of your business, but no."

Relief flooded him.

"Not yet," she added.

Her words were like a fist to the chest. He didn't move a muscle. Was she trying to drive him *insane?*

"Do not sleep with him tonight."

Her eyes widened. "Why should I listen to you—"

"Promise me you won't sleep with him," he said urgently.

The doorbell rang again, more insistently this time.

"You can't tell me what to do in my personal life. Go to hell." India yanked away her arm.

She marched over to the monitor, checked the screen, and then opened the door. The man in the hallway looked as surprised as Thiago had been when he saw her with the mask on her face.

"Hi," he said slowly. "Am I early?"

He caught sight of Thiago in the background, and his eyebrows raised. He peered at Thiago with curiosity from behind a pair of glasses. His hair was slicked back a little too deliberately. Thiago instantly disliked him.

"You're not early. I'm running late." India stepped aside so he could enter.

Quietly seething, Thiago watched him walk into the living room. *His* living room, as far as he was concerned.

"Hello," the man said.

India stepped up to the two of them. "Thiago Santana, this is Dr. Simon Stone. Simon, this is Thiago. My boss."

Boss? The word landed like a slap.

Thiago's jaw tightened. He extended a hand with minimal enthusiasm.

Simon shook his hand with a weak and forgettable grip. "Nice to meet you."

Thiago's smile was tight. "Yes."

India softly cleared her throat. "I believe you were leaving...?"

A beat passed.

"Actually, we were talking before Dr. Simon arrived, and I didn't get confirmation on the idea I presented. Maybe we could all sit down and have a nice little chat." Thiago rounded to the other side of the sofa.

"I don't think that's a good idea," India said, a hint of panic in her voice.

"No? You do not mind, do you, Doctor?"

"I... uh..." Glancing from one to the other, Simon appeared bewildered.

Thiago poured himself a glass of wine and swirled it before lowering his nose to the rim to breathe in its spicy notes.

"What vintage is this?" he asked India.

She glowered at him, clearly furious he was refusing to leave. "Amarone della Valpolicella, from Italy," she bit out.

"Excellent choice," he said, taking a slow sip.

Simon cleared his throat. "Should I—"

"Simon, please have a seat. Thiago, may I speak to you for a moment, please? Over near the door?" Her voice was sweet, but her eyes shot daggers at him.

"Certainly."

Thiago carefully placed the glass on the table. "Excuse us," he said to Simon before following India out of the living room.

"You win. I won't," she said in a low voice.

"You won't... what?" Thiago prompted.

She inhaled slowly and exhaled slowly. "I won't sleep with him tonight."

His gaze skated down the length of her body. He believed her. She looked comfortable, not dressed in the sexy attire she usually wore when he came over. Of course, she could be wearing a G-string and one of those demi-cup bras under her sweats. For a moment, he imagined peeling off her clothes to uncover such a delectable surprise underneath.

"Good. I'll see you next Friday night." He wasn't asking, he was telling her.

He couldn't see her face below the mask, but her eyes were blank and emotionless. "Okay," she replied in a wooden voice.

Okay? *Okay?*

He held his tongue. Someone somewhere should nominate him for sainthood. Perhaps he would nominate himself.

Feeling Simon's gaze, Thiago glanced over his shoulder to get another look at his enemy before he said to India in a lowered voice, "Remember your promise. I am holding you to it."

Then he opened the door and walked out.

Chapter Fourteen

T hiago's leather chair squeaked as he leaned back, his head angled toward the window, his left hand tapping a restless beat on the glass top of his desk.

He had work to do but had an issue to deal with—his very distracting VP of marketing. Considering he was not known for his patience, he had exhibited a monumental amount since Saturday.

He hadn't called India, giving her space and trusting she had kept her word about not sleeping with her date. Dr. Stone did not impress him. He couldn't see what she saw in him. There was something else too. Something he couldn't quite put his finger on. The man seemed nice enough, but he couldn't help but wonder if the nice guy act was simply... an act.

Then there was the friend of her best friend's husband. He didn't have a name, but the shadowy image of the second man lurked in the corners of his mind like a stalker disrupting his thoughts and worrying him.

He had to do something. He had to eliminate the competition.

Sitting idly by was not his style, especially when he saw his perfect arrangement with India falling apart. There was also the odd tightness on the left side of his chest that had appeared and remained since Saturday. He couldn't get rid of the irritation, and the more he dwelled on the situation with India, the tighter his chest became.

For two Friday nights in a row, India had canceled on him, and on Saturday when he had suggested they get together this Friday night, she had been rather indifferent. Nonchalant. Apathetic. Detached.

All words he hated but which basically meant the same thing. She wasn't excited about seeing him. She wasn't looking forward to their time together, which could mean she liked the doctor a lot. She had invited him into her home, and if Thiago hadn't arrived, she might have had sex with him.

His woman—well, not his woman. He had no hold on her. His... what was she? Lover was the best way to describe her role. His lover had spent Saturday night with another man in her apartment, eating pizza and drinking wine and might have enjoyed herself immensely.

But she always had a good time with Thiago, didn't she? The sex was incredibly hot and passionate. They were comfortable with each other and talked, though admittedly their work and personal lives were carefully delineated. Did she want more?

Thiago shifted in the chair, a frown creasing his brow.

Was that the issue? If so, he could fix the situation easily enough. She mentioned going on dates with those other men. Maybe she wanted to go out to dinner or something. He could give a little, especially if his actions got rid of the goddamn doctor and the other man, whoever he was.

Maybe India wanted courting along with the sex.

Thiago pushed to his feet with resolve and exited his office.

As he marched down the hall, employees scurried out of the way. One woman did a one-eighty when she saw him and hurried toward her cubicle, leaving her conversation partner standing awkwardly in the middle of the floor. The employee dipped his attention to a bunch of papers in his hand, trying to look busy after he'd been abandoned.

Two members of the staff gave Thiago uneasy, close-mouthed smiles as he passed by, which he didn't return. He was on a mission. He had a plan, and he didn't have time to play smiley face with the staff.

When he arrived at India's office, he knocked loudly on the door.

"Come in," her voice called from inside.

He stepped in and shut the door behind him. She shot to her feet, like a soldier about to salute a commanding officer.

Her eyebrows drew together. "Thiago, what are...?"

"Have a seat." He waved her toward the chair with his hand.

"I'd rather stand," she said carefully, tension in her shoulders. Obviously, his unannounced visit had caught her off guard. She seemed rattled.

He stepped closer to the desk, which allowed him to catch a hint of her sweet perfume. For the thousandth time, he thought about how she always smelled so incredibly good. She hadn't been wearing perfume on Saturday night, but did she spritz some on for Simon after he left?

"How did your date with Dr. Simon go on Saturday night?"

Her right eyebrow arched higher. "Are you asking me if I had sex with him?"

"Yes," Thiago bit out.

She inhaled deeply and let out a silent breath. "No, Thiago, I didn't have sex with him. I made you a promise, and I kept it."

Relieved, he tapped his finger on the surface of her desk. "Good. Did you have a good night?"

"This is a very strange conversation. I don't think it's a good idea for me to give you a review of my evening with Simon."

"Why not? I should know who my competition for your attention is."

"Competition is an interesting word."

An awkward silence filled the room.

"Do you plan to continue seeing him?" Thiago asked.

She picked up a pen and turned it over in her hand. "I'm not sure. He's a nice man."

Thiago heard the unspoken "but," which gave him hope. "Sounds exciting," he said sardonically.

India frowned at him. "Did you just come down here to ask me about Simon?"

"No, I had another motive for coming to see you. We're still on for Friday night?"

"Yes. Sure."

There it was again. The lack of enthusiasm.

"We're going to do something a little different this time."

"Oh?"

"We're going to dinner."

"*Going* to dinner?" India repeated, confusion on her face.

"Yes."

"You mean out somewhere? Not dinner at my place?"

"Yes," Thiago answered.

"Okay." She still looked confused, her eyes narrowing. "Why?"

"Because I want to take you to dinner. Is that a problem?" Thiago asked.

"No, of course not, but we don't do dinner—out, I mean. Usually I b-make dinner."

"You don't have to this week. I am taking you to dinner. Is. That. A. Problem?"

"No. Going out is fine," she insisted.

"Good. I will make all the plans. We're going somewhere nice, so wear a pretty dress."

"Yes, sir," she said sarcastically.

Had she used those specific words on purpose? A low current of electricity stirred in his blood.

"You know I like when you say that," Thiago said, a dark, husky quality to his voice.

Sometimes they role-played. Boss and employee. Doctor and nurse. Cop and suspect. Nurse and patient.

Her expression changed, softened a smidge, and he caught a glimpse of the old India, the woman he bantered with, the woman who flirted with him, the woman who gave as good as she got.

"Was there anything else?" she asked in a cool voice, as if trying not to slip into the comfort of past behavior.

"Why haven't you worn the bracelet I bought you for Valentine's Day? Do you not like it?"

"I do. It's lovely."

"But...?" Thiago prompted.

She shifted uncomfortably, as if she didn't want to say what was on her mind, a rare occurrence for India. "How much thought did you put into it? You probably had your concierge service pick it out." She shrugged.

"Wrong. I picked it out myself."

Her eyes widened a fraction. He had definitely surprised her with that bit of information.

"I didn't know," she said in a low voice. She gave him an odd look, as if seeing him for the first time.

"Now you do. I will pick you up at seven o'clock from your place."

Straightening, India nodded. "I'll be ready. I'll wear a pretty dress... and the bracelet."

His mouth twitched in the faintest smile. He hadn't had much reason to smile lately and hoped this was the beginning of a change in their relationship, back to where they used to be.

"Good."

Without another word, Thiago left her office, and the fist-like tightness on the left side of his chest, over his heart, loosened somewhat. On the way back down the hall, he nodded at a few employees. He didn't return their uneasy smiles, but he almost did.

Almost.

Chapter Fifteen

"What about this?" India held up a red dress so Kiara, who was watching her from FaceTime on her iPad, could see.

Her friend scrunched her nose. "Ehh."

India dropped her arms in defeat. "You haven't liked anything I've shown you. He said to wear a pretty dress."

"Did he use those exact words?"

"Unfortunately, yes. He's about as charming as a bull." And yet she was crazy about him and doing her best to satisfy his ask, her pulse beating with the promise of something new and exciting.

"Sweetie, that's a pretty dress—*if you were going to the Oscars*, but I know he has family in the entertainment industry. Is he taking you to the Oscars?"

"Sarcasm is ugly on you." In a huff, India tossed the dress onto the pile on the bed. "I have nothing to wear!" she exclaimed.

"Now I know that's a damn lie. I can't believe how difficult you're making this."

"He and I have never gone on a date before. I'm nervous!" She blurted out the truth unexpectedly.

Suddenly, Kiara lowered her gaze and whispered, "Yes, you can show her, but you have to hurry, okay? We're having a very important conversation."

Three-year-old Jayden squeezed into the frame by climbing onto his mother's lap. "Auntie India, look what I find. A sparkly rock!" Jayden held up his treasure, eyes bright and excited.

India leaned in close as though inspecting a rare jewel. She gasped. "Oh my goodness! It's very pretty and so sparkly. What a find! That's a special rock, Jayden, and only the best explorers find those."

Grinning, Jayden's little chest puffed out, and he looked at his mother. Kiara kissed his cheek.

"Good job, pumpkin. Go put it on the shelf with the others, okay?"

"Okay. Bye-bye, Auntie India!" Beaming, Jayden hopped down and took off.

"He has not stopped talking about his sparkly rock since he found it this afternoon," Kiara said, amused. "I guess that's his favorite now. Where were we? Oh, you said you were nervous. Nervous about what? You've been putting your tongues down each other's throats for months. This should be easy. It's just dinner."

"It should be easy, yes, but it's not. It's different. It's a *date*. We're past that stage. It's like going backwards. As you pointed out, we've put our tongues down each other's throats for a while now." Not to mention he'd stuck his body parts in her various holes.

"You have to relax. You're going to eat a nice dinner and have some conversation, that's all," Kiara said in a soothing voice.

"We've never done that. That's not true. We've done dinner

and conversation, but not like this. It feels strange. *Official.* He's changing the parameters of our relationship, and I don't know how to act. Dating is for normal people, not Thiago Santana. We're supposed to have amazing sex, talk for a bit, and then go our separate ways." India marched into her walk-in closet and yanked the hangers left, searching for another dress.

She pulled one from the closet and held it up. "What about this?"

Kiara squinted. "Bring it closer."

India walked over and held it pressed against the front of her body. "What do you think?"

Kiara tilted her head to the left. "I like it. I like it a lot, actually. It's sexy without being over the top, and the apricot color looks good against your skin. It'll be a nice date outfit. That's it. That's the dress." She grinned and clapped.

"Finally," India said with a sigh.

"What does this mean for my boy, Leo? He liked you."

"I liked him, but..." India sighed. "How do people cheat? I'm trying to juggle two men and a lover, and I'm already exhausted."

Kiara laughed. "Maybe you need more vitamins."

"Something's gotta give. Honestly, Kiara, I liked Leo, but the spark wasn't there. He's a nice guy, but I think someone better is out there for him."

Kiara stuck out her bottom lip. "Too bad, but I understand."

"I called him before I called you and talked to him. I didn't want to waste his time. He took it well."

"You're right, he's a nice guy, and I'm sure he'll find someone else. What about your doctor friend, Simon?"

"I haven't decided yet. I'll make a decision depending on how tonight's date goes with Thiago. I better go. I still have to shower and get dressed, and if there's one thing I know about Thiago, he's never late. Matter of fact, he's often early."

"Before you go, I have something to tell you," Kiara said.

"Okay, what's up?" India examined the dress from arm's length away.

"I'm pregnant."

She dropped the dress to stare at her friend. "Again?"

Kiara burst out laughing. "Stop."

"You stop. Have you two ever heard of birth control? Hell, the pull-out method?"

Kiara giggled shamelessly, looking content and happy—as she should. "Listen, I don't want to be old and gray running after these children, okay? I'm already tired, and I'm only in my thirties. God bless anyone who has a kid after forty. Josh and I are getting them out of the way, right the hell now."

"I don't blame you. Is this the last one?"

"If we have a girl, yes. If not, we're going to try one more time."

India shook her head, her face breaking into a smile. "You know I'm happy for you."

"I know."

"When are you due?"

"September. The boys are less excited than I had hoped they'd be."

"Because they told you they wanted a puppy, not a baby sister or baby brother."

"Well, they're getting another sibling, at least for now. Until I can convince Josh that we should let them adopt a puppy. He said the boys aren't old enough to take care of a pet yet, and he doesn't want the responsibility. When they're older, they can have one." Kiara rolled her eyes.

"I'm on Josh's side, but I'll let the two of you figure out how to proceed. Whenever you're ready for the puppy, Auntie India will take Jayden and Josiah shopping for a dog bed, toys—the works."

"I know you've got us. Okay, girl, I'll leave you alone so you can enjoy your first date with your boss, the man you've been swapping body fluids with since last year." Kiara smiled sweetly.

"Thank you for putting it so poetically."

"You're welcome. Have fun!" Kiara blew a kiss before she disappeared from the screen.

India turned toward the pile of clothes on her bed and groaned inwardly. Her OCD wouldn't allow her to leave them there. She had to put them away before she left on her date with Thiago.

She moved quickly and hung each article of clothing back in the closet. As she stepped into the bathroom, she recalled her friend's words.

I don't want to be old and gray running after these children, okay?

India pressed a hand to her flat belly, happy for her friend but also envious. From the time she received her diagnosis, she'd known nothing in her life would be simple when it came to the disease living in her body. Once, a doctor had told her, quite bluntly, "You have to plan very carefully if you ever want children. You need to be in remission first—at least six months. Pregnancies are already risky on their own, but in your case, it's worse because you have lupus. You could have a flare, and your kidneys could fail, your heart or lungs could become inflamed. You could *die*."

He had scared the crap out of her. The message was clear: women with lupus had babies all the time, but they took a big risk.

Perhaps that's why she'd worked so hard all these years. Not only because she wanted to have a better life than the one she'd grown up in. She knew, deep down, she might never have a family like other people. So she adjusted, making her world revolve around work and climbing the corporate ladder. Like she'd adjusted when she lost her hair five years ago.

After the big flare hospitalized her, her hair started falling out for months afterward. Her thick, beautiful, curly hair was no more. Her edges were gone, and her hair growth stunted. She touched her head now, the phantom weight of her old curls pressing on her shoulders, cruel in their absence. A lump rose in her throat, sharp and unexpected. She swallowed hard to push it back down.

For a while, she had mourned the loss, wearing wigs, visiting trichologists, hoping for a miracle. Until she finally swallowed her pride and accepted her fate. One Saturday, she walked into a barber shop and asked for a fade. Leaving the shop, she had been a little uncertain about the new style until an older man stopped her on the way to her car.

"Excuse me, honey, I don't mean to be disrespectful, but I love that cut. You are stunning."

"Thank you," she had said, her face blossoming into a smile.

The compliment warmed her from the inside out and chased away the last of her doubts. The fade had become her standard hairstyle ever since.

The new drug her rheumatologist had told her about could put her lupus into remission and change her life. Maybe it was worth trying. Maybe it was the answer she'd been hoping for.

Energized by the positive thought, she stepped into the stall. After her shower, she started getting ready.

The apricot dress had a ruched waist with short sleeves capped at her shoulders. She was ultimately pleased with this choice. The dress was elegant without being overdone. She slipped on a pair of gold heels and an ankle bracelet, added large gold hoops to her ears, and then checked her appearance in the mirror.

Using her pick, she gave her curls a little lift on top and then turned her back to the mirror. Looking over her shoulder, she smoothed a hand down her hips. No panty lines, and her butt looked round and firm.

Minutes later, she picked up her purse as the doorbell rang, announcing Thiago's arrival. She was on her way to the door when she remembered the bangle and rushed back to the bedroom. She removed it from her jewelry box and snapped it onto her wrist. The stunning piece of jewelry was sleek and elegantly made of gold and platinum with diamond clusters meeting in the center at a diamond halo. Knowing he had picked it out himself was a pleasant surprise and made the piece more special.

The doorbell rang again, and India turned off the light and made her way down the hallway. After a quick check on the monitor, she opened the door.

Thiago stepped inside. His gaze slowly trailed down her body, pausing briefly at the bracelet on her wrist. Her skin prickled under his scrutiny. Then without saying a word, he stepped forward and placed a hand at the back of her neck. The warmth of his touch had been sorely missed, and she welcomed the possessive way he held her.

"Hello," he said in his deep, accented voice, which sounded sexier than ever. He dropped a kiss on her parted lips, and a little electricity danced under her skin. "You look exquisite, but I'm sure you know."

She practically melted. "Thank you. You look nice," she said, eyeing his outfit.

He had obviously gone home to change, which was a surprise. He must have left work early before coming to pick her up, and there was no doubt he did because instead of a suit, he wore a long-sleeve powder blue shirt and dark slacks.

He also smelled incredible. A mix of his cologne and the

fresh, clean scent of soap, reminiscent of a sea breeze. The combination was dangerously tempting. They hadn't made love in weeks, and she could feel her core tightening as she imagined him sliding between her thighs later tonight.

"Are you ready?" Thiago asked.

India nodded and followed him, experiencing an unusual, overwhelming amount of emotion. Tonight was so different from how they usually interacted outside of work.

"Where are we going for dinner?"

"Someplace exclusive, where it's typically hard to get a reservation," Thiago said as they entered the elevator.

"Not hard for you, I imagine," she replied, casting a glance at his profile.

There was a satisfied, smug expression on his face. "No, it was not," he admitted. "It might be difficult for your doctor friend, though."

"If I didn't know better, I would think you were jealous," India remarked.

"Why would I be jealous? I have the upper hand."

"How so?" India asked as the doors eased open on the first floor.

He smirked, this time meeting her gaze. "I know you, better than the doctor does. And I'm going to make sure that when this evening is over, you do not even remember his name."

Chapter Sixteen

At first, Thiago had considered taking India to one of his brother's restaurants but changed his mind. Too easy.

He decided to put forth a little effort and chose Wine & Bone for their night out. The high-end restaurant was known for its extensive wine list and succulent steaks. Their popularity meant a long waiting list for reservations, but he had paid a hefty sum for another customer's private room reservation, which meant he and India could enjoy their meal without distraction.

The hostess led them into The Ember Room, cozy and hidden away from the main dining room. As she politely waited beside the table, she mentioned in a hushed voice that the waiter would arrive soon.

Thiago helped India into her chair.

"Thank you," she murmured.

As the hostess departed and he sat down, she looked around. The unlit fireplace must make for a great atmosphere during colder months. Lowered lights cast a warm golden glow on the table, which was covered with a white tablecloth. They had a good view of the street outside through one-way glass allowing them to see out, but no one could see in. Colorful artwork lined the walls, and a bottle of wine was decanting on the table—a Bordeaux he had ordered ahead of time.

There was a discreet knock on the door, and then their waiter entered, a bearded young man with a short ponytail. After introducing himself as Griffin, he briefly went over the menu and told them about the specials. He then took their orders and poured them each a glass of wine before disappearing.

"I have to say, you did good for our first date," India said, placing her cloth napkin across her thighs.

Thiago briefly smiled across the table. "You sound surprised."

"I'm not. You do everything to the best of your ability."

"Exactly," Thiago said.

She laughed a little and shook her head. His confidence could be a turn off for some people, but he always had the distinct impression that she appreciated his self-assurance and possibly saw it as one of his more attractive qualities.

At first, they talked about surface topics, steering clear of anything personal, but during the salad course, India asked, "I've always wondered, why did you decide to work for Santana International? Your other siblings didn't. As an angel investor, you're an equity partner in a number of businesses, and you have partnerships with family members, like the olive grove in Spain with Ethan and Bruno. You have plenty of money on your own."

"I've never seriously considered working anywhere else before," Thiago admitted. "None of my other siblings were interested in taking over my father's company, and I naturally gravitated toward working with him. I admit, though, for a long time I didn't know what I wanted to do. Bruno had cooking, and Ignacio was obsessed with acting and modeling, and I had... nothing."

Since then, his investments and ownership shares in multiple companies had made him a billionaire. He had become known as someone who took big risks, and luckily, they had mostly paid off, especially in the technology sector where he concentrated, which had the greatest risks but the greatest rewards.

"You suffered from middle child syndrome," India remarked in a matter-of-fact voice.

"No," Thiago said, shaking his head.

"There's no shame in it. It affects a lot of people. Middle kids often feel invisible or overlooked because they're not the youngest or the oldest. They tend to become independent overachievers."

"So what's your excuse? You are an overachiever."

"I'm an only child, and well, we have our own issues," she said with a slight shrug.

"Care to elaborate?" Thiago asked, lifting his wine glass to his lips.

Using her fork, India punctuated the words. "Perfectionism. Independence. Overachieving because of pressure and high expectations. Not wanting to ask for help."

"Not good," he said.

"I know."

"I hope if you need help, you won't hesitate to ask *me*."

She seemed surprised by the statement and didn't respond right away. "I didn't know that was an option."

"Now you do."

He could tell she was digesting the information in the silence.

"Thank you," India finally said. "Growing up as an only child wasn't all bad. I had my friend Kiara, who lived in the neighborhood. We were as close as sisters." She laughed, as if remembering something from the past.

"Now you have to tell me why you laughed," Thiago said.

"It's silly."

"I still want to know."

She bit the bottom corner of her plump lip, which she often did when she was in deep thought.

"Like I said, Kiara and I were very close, and I used to spend a lot of time at her house. When I moved in with Grandma Selah, she went back to work, so I'm sure she was happy for the break from having to take care of me and help with homework when she got home. Anyway, Kiara and I were inseparable in school. Everyone knew if you saw one, you saw the other. I'm dark-skinned, but Kiara is light-skinned. The kids had a running joke, calling us salt and pepper." She laughed again.

"The nickname never bothered you?"

India rested her chin on her fist, fully engaged in the conversation and forgetting her meal. "No, because we didn't believe they were being malicious. We kind of embraced it. To be honest, we were like night and day. Kiara is funny and never really wanted to work. She shamelessly admits she went to college to find a husband. Meanwhile, I was the serious one, working hard and getting good grades."

"Did you always want to be in marketing?" Thiago asked.

She cut a cucumber round in half. "I actually wanted to be an artist."

"Really? I would have never guessed."

"There's a lot you don't know about me."

She fell quiet, and he chose not to fill the silence because he suspected she wanted to say more.

India fiddled with the napkin on her lap. "The charcoal sketches in my apartment... I drew those."

Thiago almost dropped his fork. "The three framed ones hanging on the south wall above your desk in the living room?"

She nodded, and he saw something he had never seen on her face before. She appeared bashful, as if embarrassed to admit her secret talent. "I—I have a ton more in a box in my closet."

He leaned forward, completely enthralled by this revelation. He had assumed they had been done by a professional artist. "I had no idea."

"I stopped drawing about two years ago," she said, looking uncomfortable as she shifted in her chair.

He was about to ask why, but she continued talking.

"I've drawn all kinds of images. Landscapes, still life, portraits. I started out drawing people. The first one was a boy I had a crush on in middle school." As she shared more, she seemed to relax.

"He must have been something special," Thiago remarked.

"He was a decent guy."

"Your first love," Thiago guessed.

"My first crush," India corrected.

The correction took him aback. "Don't tell me you have never been in love."

She paused, swirling her wine as she looked at him across the table. "This might surprise you, but I don't think I've ever been in love. I've been in deep like. In lust. But in love?" She shook her head. "Never."

"I'm surprised. You're a beautiful woman. I imagined you fighting off male attention all your life."

"Male attention has nothing to do with love," India pointed out.

"True."

"So what about you? Have you ever been in love?" she asked.

"We do not want to go down that road." Thiago placed some lettuce in his mouth.

"Why not?" India asked with a laugh, her eyes sparkling with amusement. "You started us down this road."

"Because I wanted to find out more about you, not divulge my innermost secrets."

"Too bad, I want to hear all about your secret love. Were your feelings unrequited? Was there pining? Who was she?"

He took another sip of wine and then carefully placed the glass on the table. "I don't know if it was love, but there was a girl in high school who I was certain I would marry. Her name was Kimberly. Her father was in the military, and one day they arrived, and then they were gone again. I was devastated. We stayed in contact for a while but eventually lost touch."

"Maybe you should find her."

"Years ago, I found out she is happily married with two children. I don't think her family would appreciate me coming back into her life."

She laughed lightly. "Probably not. What did you like about her?"

Thiago pondered the question for a few moments. "She was smart and never took shit from anyone. She stood up for other kids who were bullied, which told me that she was compassionate. And she was beautiful. Full lips, cinnamon brown skin, and long braids falling to her waist. She would put these gold sparkly things on individual braids. She was... magnetic. A goddess."

"Do you have a thing for Black women, Thiago?" India asked in a teasing voice.

He chuckled. "One could say that, yes. I suppose that's why I enjoyed my time in Brazil so much."

His biological brothers had both ended up with Black women but over the years had dated women of all races and backgrounds. He, however, except for one relationship in distant memory, had always been drawn to darker-skinned women.

"By the way, it is not a fetish. It's a preference," he added.

"Interesting..." India said, tipping her glass to her lips.

The waiter arrived with the main course. Thiago had chosen a steak with a side of vegetables. India had opted for steak as well, along with the restaurant's famous roasted carrots with harissa and yogurt.

"Remind me of your Mexican and Colombian background again," India said.

"Born in Mexico, moved to Colombia after my parents split, and my mother took us back to her country. I was glad when she sent us to live with my father permanently. My mother is not a bad woman, but she is not very maternal. I missed my *abuela* most of all when we moved. She was more like a mother to us. She passed years ago, but I can still taste her *arepas con queso*. They were..." He kissed his fingertips. "The smell of cornmeal dough and the taste of the gooey cheese is a fond memory."

"We were both lucky to have our grandmothers in our lives. I've never had *arepas*, though. I'll have to find a restaurant that makes them," India said.

Thiago paused from eating. "No, absolutely not. You will not go to a restaurant. You need to taste the homemade version. I cannot cook, but I will ask Bruno to make some. His are delicious."

"You don't have to do that."

"I insist. Do not argue with me."

She smiled. "Yes, sir."

Had she said that on purpose?

He watched as she continued eating, calm and composed, while need uncoiled in his gut.

Chapter Seventeen

After their conversation at the restaurant, India had new insight into Thiago.

He talked about his home life and growing up in a blended family after he and his brothers moved to the States and his father met and married his stepmother. The transition had been difficult at first, mixing cultures, and of course, there was his struggle with the language when they started school. But eventually, he grew to love his stepmother, his new siblings, and the life they had embarked on in Georgia.

As they strolled through the main doors of her apartment building, Thiago placed a light hand at the base of her spine. The ride up in the elevator was quiet, but India sensed tension in him. There was tension in her too—sexual tension which started as he drove closer to where she lived.

She unlocked and opened her front door. "Did you—"

Thiago pushed her against the wall, and she immediately forgot what she was about to ask. The door slowly eased shut and enveloped them in darkness, with only the twinkle of lights from the surrounding buildings coming in through the living room windows.

Seconds before they kissed, her lips parted. His head lowered to hers, and she let him into the soft interior of her mouth. Inviting him to plunder. To take. To devour.

His hand slid up her dress and between her legs, stroking her swollen clit. She moaned, angling her body against his palm. At the same time, she ran her hands up his chest, over his shoulders, and then locked both arms around his strong neck. Lifting one leg to his waist, she ground her hips harder against him.

She had missed him. Missed touching him and feeling his hard body pressed into hers. She had missed the way he caressed her body, as if she belonged to him and him alone.

Thiago released her mouth, but with his body flush against hers, his hard flesh probed between her thighs, an exquisite torture reminding her of the pleasure she'd had to forgo the past few weeks.

"You seem impatient all of a sudden," she whispered shakily in the darkness.

With each arm flat on the wall on either side of her head, he spoke in a low, husky voice close to her ear. "I have been impatient for weeks and all night, two seconds from losing control. My body is used to having you on a schedule, at a certain time on Friday nights. I would have made love to you on the table in Wine & Bone, but I didn't want to shock the restaurant staff."

Thiago spun her toward the wall, and she flattened her hands against its cool surface, holding her breath as he lifted her dress, crushing the fabric in his fists. Lowering to his knees behind her, he pushed the dress higher and curled his fingers into the strips of fabric on her body. With a sound of irritation, he ripped the thong from her hips, as if its very presence had offended him.

"At this rate, you're going to have to give me a lingerie allowance," India panted to the wall. She waited impatiently for the sensation of his lips and the brush of his beard—elegant and masculine, soft and rough—like the man himself.

"Done," he said in a husky growl.

When he pressed his lips against her ass, her blood heated to boiling. She arched back, angling for more of the gentle scraping of his facial hair against her soft skin.

Thiago sank his teeth into the flesh of one ass cheek and gently sucked, as if taking a bite of a piece of succulent fruit. India let out a low moan, the sound echoing against the walls of the small entryway.

"The past three weeks have been torture. I needed you so much..." Thiago said in a hoarse whisper.

She didn't understand another word he said because the rest of the sentence was spoken in Spanish.

He turned her to face him and kissed her mound. "I missed my girl," he whispered.

Watching from above, India released a breathless laugh. "She missed you too."

His moist tongue stroked her slit, and a trembling groan fell from her lips as she tossed her head back in abandon.

"Thiago," she whispered, sinking her fingers into his soft hair.

"*Dime.* Tell me what you want," he whispered, lifting her right leg onto his shoulder.

He pressed his lips to her lower lips and then penetrated her body. She knew it was coming but was still unprepared. The shock of the intimate contact had her head spinning, and Thiago was relentless with his assault—sucking her clit and probing her folds with his stiff, wicked tongue. He started gently but then applied more pressure until the wet stimulation became almost unbearable.

"Please... *please*," she begged as his mouth devoured her and his hands traced the curves of her hips and ass.

When she couldn't possibly handle any more, he inserted two fingers into her core, and she broke apart. His name flew from her lips in a rough chant, over and over as her body convulsed.

Finally, she collapsed against the wall, and he straightened to his full height. Cupping her face in his hands, his dark-brown eyes glittered down at her.

"I have missed doing that to you." He nibbled on her bottom lip.

"I can't move," India said, feeling absolutely drained.

Thiago kissed the corners of her mouth and then fully claimed her lips again, and she melted against his hard frame as desire rippled through her. Her body was behaving as if he hadn't already given her an orgasm. Her appetite for him truly knew no bounds.

With their mouths locked together, Thiago lifted her from the floor and marched them back to her bedroom, her dress still hiked above her hips in a wanton display of desperate need.

They fell onto the bed and fumbled with each other's clothes. The warm glow of the pendant lights dangling from the ceiling gave her a good view of the determined set of his handsome face.

India undid his pants and the buttons on his shirt while Thiago yanked the zipper on her dress and pulled it down her arms to expose her breasts.

She clutched the fabric of his open shirt and rubbed her breasts against the hairs on his chest, reveling in the sensation of its roughness against the taut sensitivity of hers. She was desperate for the full force of his arousal between her legs. She had been suffering through a famine and was finally allowed to gorge in a wild and ravenous way.

Thiago sucked a nipple into his mouth while his hand smoothed down her collarbone and cupped her right breast. He teased both nipples, pinching one with his fingertips and stroking the other with the tip of his tongue.

She buried her fingers in his black hair and arched her back, forcing more of her breast into his mouth. He squeezed the other, his torturous caress making her bite down on her lip to keep from crying out loud.

India savored their lovemaking, but she wanted him inside her. She longed for the thrust of his deep possession. Sliding her hand inside his pants, she circled his thick length with one hand and caressed him with squeezing strokes.

A guttural sound hummed from his throat—a sound that let her know he was nearing the edge.

"Are you ready for me, India?" he rasped.

"Yes," she whispered.

"Yes, what?"

"Yes, sir."

He groaned. Holding his erection in hand, he guided the tip to her entrance and thrust inside her. He filled her wet body, which stretched to accommodate him. Their coupling felt different this time. She couldn't explain why, but the sensation of naked flesh against naked flesh was more than erotic. There was something... something deeper in the joining of their bodies.

But India didn't want to think. She let her mind drift as Thiago plunged in and out of her. She wound her arms around the trunk of his body and lifted her gaze to the lights above while she concentrated on her pleasure.

Thiago's fingers curled around her throat. He applied

gentle pressure as his body moved inside hers. "Do not look away. Look at me," he commanded, his voice rough and hoarse.

She met his gaze and matched his furious pace, unable to look away now he had demanded her attention.

"Good girl," he whispered.

She held on tight, sinking her fingernails into his back, their bodies rocking together on the mattress in perfect sync. Then a tight sensation appeared in her lower belly.

"I'm coming," India said in a trembling whisper.

The words barely left her mouth before another explosion —more intense than the one he'd given her with his mouth— roared through her body like a runaway freight train. As she contracted around his stiff flesh, the hand around her neck tightened, deepening her orgasm as she soared into the stratosphere.

Thiago's entire body tensed, and he dropped his head to her shoulder, his roar of pleasure mingling with her cries as they tumbled into ecstasy together.

* * *

As India's uneven breathing returned to normal, she noticed Thiago was still fully clothed. As for her, her dress was a crumpled mess around her hips, and she still wore her heels.

Slowly, Thiago lifted off her. "Do you see what happens when you deny me? I turn into an animal."

Smiling, India lifted onto her elbows. "Water is wet."

A devilish grin graced his sculpted lips. "Come here, let me help you get undressed."

She pushed off the bed and stood in front of him, and he helped her out of her dress and shoes. His movements were careful, gentle, and solicitous. Compared to how he had moments before pounded her into the mattress with his hand around her throat, the contrast was almost comical.

Then she helped him undress, taking great pleasure in tossing his clothes into the dark corners of the room.

The second time they made love was slower, more sensual. Thiago commanded the pace. His movements were no longer frantic. He made love to her with gentle reverence, caressing her heated skin and licking her taut nipples. Their hands explored each other's bodies, touching all the intimate places and pulling soft groans from each other's vocal cords.

When he entered her, he slid in with devastating slowness, pushing her onto her stomach and forcing her shoulders low to keep her ass in the air. Her back arched deeply to take every inch of him. Gripping the pillows, she rocked in time with each of his thrusts.

"Oh god, Thiago," India breathed, her voice muffled by the pillow.

She squeezed her eyes shut as he pushed his knees wider and spread her thighs for deeper penetration.

"You feel so good... incredible," he whispered in a hoarse voice.

His fingers fastened like handcuffs around her wrists as he continued to drive into her with sensual, languid strokes. It was almost unbearable, and whenever she was close to coming, he purposely slowed down, extending her pleasure to the point of suffering.

She came again, with her ass in the air and Thiago's hand at the back of her neck. This time, when she collapsed, she knew it was the end for her. She couldn't possibly endure another orgasm tonight. He came right after, and soon they both fell asleep, his body curling around hers in the dark.

India woke much later, unaccustomed to Thiago spending

the night. The arm thrown across her waist and his soft snoring must have cut her sleep short.

She didn't want to think, but the thought she'd brushed away while they made love came back. How different their lovemaking was this time. Deeper.

Had he ever been the same with his other lovers? Somehow he had managed to keep his relationships under lock and key, avoiding having his name linked with certainty to any specific woman.

With a start, she realized *she* was like those other women. Every single one. Hidden. In the shadows. No commitment. No... nothing.

She also recognized what was different. *She* was different. Her feelings were different. Her perception of their relationship had transformed from casual to meaningful.

India closed her eyes again, knowing she should sleep but unable to. Not with his heart steadily beating against her spine.

She wanted more, but wanting more from Thiago Santana was the most dangerous emotion she had ever allowed herself to feel.

Chapter Eighteen

I n the darkness, Thiago had his arm thrown across India's back, and his thigh sliced between her legs.

He shifted, and she moaned in her sleep, also shifting, her soft body moving sensually against his. Her bottom pushed into his pelvis, and a familiar hunger stirred in his blood. Slipping his hand beneath the sheet, he gently caressed the length of her thigh before sliding the same hand up her stomach and stopping to cup one of her breasts.

He knew he should get up, but he was extremely comfortable in this position. Leaving her bed was the last thing he wanted to do. Ten more minutes, and then he'd get up.

His body relaxed, and his breathing became even.

Ten more minutes, he thought.

Then darkness overtook him as he sank into the arms of sleep.

* * *

As Thiago woke up, he knew immediately he wasn't in his own bed. Rolling onto his back, he squinted against the sunlight streaming through the sheer curtains at the window.

"Good morning, sleepyhead."

His attention shifted to the doorway, where India was holding a steaming mug of coffee. She wore a long white robe, the silky material clinging to her body and highlighting the fullness of her breasts and nipples.

"What time is it?" Thiago asked.

"A little after eight."

"After eight!" He lifted onto his elbows.

He never slept late. Ever. He couldn't remember the last time he had slept past six a.m., even on the weekends. He was simply wired to rise early. When he went to bed late, he still woke up by six.

What the hell was wrong with him? Was he sick?

"I made coffee. Would you like some?" India asked.

"How long have you been awake?" Thiago asked.

She leaned against the doorframe. "About an hour."

He sat all the way up and ran a hand down his face. "I cannot believe I slept so late," he muttered.

"You probably needed the rest."

"Doubtful."

He had functioned perfectly fine for years with the amount of sleep he normally received. He worked a lot but didn't often stay up late. He believed in restorative rest for the brain and body, which was important for overall health and operating at peak performance.

"You should have woken me when you woke up," Thiago said, swinging his legs over the side of the bed.

"You were sleeping so peacefully, I didn't want to bother you."

He stared at her in disbelief. Not because she didn't want

to bother him, but because he had enjoyed uninterrupted, peaceful sleep until *after eight* in the goddamn morning.

"I need to use the bathroom."

"You know where it is," India said.

Thiago slipped from under the sheets, and India brought her mug to her lips, her gaze following his movements. She posed nonchalantly against the inside of the door, but her eyes betrayed the hunger consuming her at the sight of his naked body.

"You did not get enough last night?" he asked with a smirk as he walked past her.

"There he is," she said sarcastically.

With a laugh, Thiago continued into the bathroom and flipped on the light. After he relieved himself, he washed his hands and then stared at his reflection. He raked his fingers through his tousled hair and then smoothed the strands.

He wasn't simply bothered by oversleeping. He was also disturbed by the normalcy of waking up in India's bed and seeing her first thing in the morning. The casualness of her drinking coffee, looking relaxed and perky, had him wondering —what would it be like to experience this on a regular basis?

Such a ridiculous thought. He shook his head. Then he paused, frowning at his reflection.

Was it ridiculous? Why couldn't he spend the night on occasion? Maybe he and India needed to reevaluate the parameters of their relationship. Spending the night should be on the table. Also, he had never invited her to his home. He had never invited any woman to his home. It was his sanctuary, and he didn't want them to get the wrong idea about their role in his life. But he could bend the rule for India.

He exited the bathroom and found her seated on the settee by the window, legs crossed, holding the cup of coffee in one hand and her phone in the other. She didn't look up when he came out. He picked up his boxer briefs and pulled them on, all the while watching her.

India lifted her gaze from the phone's screen. "Why are you staring at me?"

"I was thinking about how absolutely stunning you are. You have bewitched me with your personality and beauty."

"We already had sex. No need to butter me up," she said in a teasing voice.

Thiago lifted his shirt off the dresser where India had tossed it in last night's haste to get naked the second time they had sex. "You don't think you're beautiful? Stunning?"

"I'm attractive. Stunning might be a stretch."

"You underestimate your appeal. Isn't that why you have such a busy dating calendar now?"

She arched an eyebrow at him. "I don't have a busy dating calendar."

"No? Last night was the first time you and I have been together in three weeks." Thiago shoved his arm forcefully through the sleeve of his shirt, the thought of her with other men grating.

"One of those weeks was because you went to your sister's engagement party, remember?"

He ignored the question. "How many men are you seeing now?" he asked.

"Let's not do this," India said, sounding tired.

"That many?" The tightness in his chest returned, like iron bands around his torso.

"It's not that many," she said carefully.

"Two? Three? Five?" The tightening of his chest increased as he waited for her answer.

"I'm seeing the same two men I told you about. There's Simon and a friend of Kiara's husband, Leo. Actually, I've already broken things off with Leo."

"I also want you to end your relationship with Simon. Today."

"Oh really? And why would I?" India asked in an overly pleasant voice.

"Because I am asking."

She laughed. "I know you're used to telling people what to do, but this is my house, and it's my relationship. So, no, thank you, I need a better reason than 'Because I said so.'"

"You want another reason? I don't like the idea of another man putting his hands on you."

"Do you plan to piss a boundary around my apartment to mark your territory?"

"Do I need to?"

"You have really lost your mind."

"I don't see what you see in him anyway."

"What's that supposed to mean?"

"He looks like a weasel," Thiago remarked.

"He does not look like a weasel," she said.

"With his pointy nose and his beady fucking eyes."

"He does not have beady eyes! Again, the way you're talking, I'd think you were jealous."

"Why would I be jealous of a beady-eyed weasel?"

She glared at him. "You've gone too far."

"Call him and end it now, India." His voice brooked no argument.

"Or what?"

"Or else." He kept his voice low and threatening.

"Or else what? You have no power over me."

"Don't I?"

India shot him an incredulous look. "Are you threatening me?"

"You have left me no choice," Thiago said, ignoring the twinge of guilt in his chest.

Her mouth fell open. "So you would fire me if I don't do what you say? You *asshole!*"

"I'm glad we understand each other."

"Why do you think you have the right—"

"Because you're *miiiine!*" Thiago's fist clenched at his right side as he dragged out the last word for so long it turned into two syllables.

Silence filled the room. His words shocked her as much as they did him. Good. Maybe now she would stop acting so nonchalant about seeing other men.

He waited in the silence for her to respond. Finally, she stood, straightening to her full height.

"I am not the property of any man—"

"Spare me the feminist bullshit. I'm not sharing you, and that's final."

Her lips pressed together. "All right, Thiago, you want me to stop seeing him. Fine. But I'm confused because you and I don't have that kind of relationship. We sleep together, but we barely know each other. Last night was literally the first time we went on a date."

"What do you want to know? Ask me anything," Thiago said.

"Really?"

"Yes. Really."

"Okay." She carefully placed her phone and the coffee on a side table. "Why are you so mean?"

"Is that a real question?" he demanded.

"Yes. When you walk down the halls, staff tremble when they see you. They're terrified of you."

"You are exaggerating," he said, pulling on his pants.

"I've seen their reaction with my own eyes. I'm not exaggerating."

"You are one to talk," he muttered dismissively.

"I'm tough, but I don't make people tremble in their shoes."

"Because you bribe them with macaroons," Thiago said, looking around for his socks. Where were they?

"You also don't take criticism well," India added pointedly.

His head snapped up, and his eyes narrowed at her. She looked right back at him, a challenge in her direct stare.

He resumed the search for his socks and found them in a corner. He picked them up and sat on the bed with his back to her. "I change my mind. I don't like the direction of this conversation. We should change the subject."

"That went well," India said sarcastically.

"If you were not such a smart ass, the conversation would have gone better." Thiago slipped on his shoes and faced her across the bed. "So what are we going to do now?"

"About what?"

"Your boyfriend."

"I don't know what you mean."

Silence cracked between them. She was purposely provoking him. Trying to drive him insane.

Thiago studied her for a moment. She had definitely bewitched him because he was about to offer something he hadn't offered the opposite sex since Kimberly in high school.

He walked over to India, and she eyed him warily, her body going visibly still.

"Did you sleep with the good doctor?" he asked.

"I told you I didn't."

"Then it will not be difficult for you to stop seeing him. Cut him off. I will be the only man in your life moving forward."

"You understand you're talking about monogamy?"

"Yes."

She didn't immediately reply, looking at him as if the words he'd spoken were so foreign to her, she had to ascertain if they were real. "You're serious."

"I want you to myself. You want to go out, we will go out like we did last night, and you should wear more dresses like the one you wore to Wine & Bone."

When her jaw hardened, Thiago guessed she didn't like what he'd said.

"Please," he added.

"Was that so hard?"

"Excruciating."

She shook her head in disgust, but the corners of her mouth twitched upward.

Thiago kissed the right side of her neck and took a deep breath, inhaling the intoxicating fragrance from her skin. "The thought of another man touching you..." He couldn't finish the sentence. "You *are* mine, India."

She lowered her gaze.

"You are going to call him?"

She swallowed. "Yes."

"Do I need to—"

She lifted her gaze. "You don't need to be here for the conversation."

"Let me know when it's done." Placing a hand on the back of her neck, he drew her flush against his body and kissed her. Her soft mouth yielded beneath his, and the irritating tightness in him loosened. His mouth moved over hers in fiery possession, fierce at first and then softening to unmistakable tenderness that conveyed his deep affection and desire to hold onto her.

When he finally lifted his head, he gazed down at her, reluctant to leave. His fingertips sifted through the soft hairs at her nape. "I better go."

She rubbed his chest. "Yes, because I have errands to run, which I can't complete during the week because I work for a man who's a slave driver."

"Sounds like a real bastard," Thiago said, catching her wrist.

He kissed her again, deeper and more thoroughly until his body awakened, and she was practically fused to him, her fingers caressing his hair with gentle strokes.

Finally, with more reluctance, he stepped back from her embrace, but not before double-tapping her bottom. "I'll see you later." He walked away.

"Thiago."

He paused at the door.

"Don't ever threaten my job again."

He watched her in silence, weighing his words. Normally, he didn't give a damn what anyone thought, but India was different. She held more power than she realized. More power than he liked.

His threat had been an empty one, simply made to get his way. While he appreciated she was no pushover, he needed to make sure she understood *he* was no pushover.

"Do not give me a reason to," he said.

Then he strolled out of the room.

Chapter Nineteen

"He what?" Kiara's voice came through the Volvo's speakers in high-pitched disbelief.

"You heard me," India said, flicking on her indicator and waiting for oncoming traffic to go by. "He insisted we should be in a monogamous relationship. The whole conversation took me by surprise."

She didn't tell her best friend the whole story—that Thiago had threatened her job. If he had asked her nicely—like a normal human being—to stop seeing Simon, she would have done it without a fight. She didn't have deep feelings for Simon, and they weren't in a relationship. They had seen each other a few times, so walking away was easy.

But the conversation with Thiago brought home the precarious situation she was in, and she needed to weaken the power he held over her.

"Did you agree?" Kiara asked.

"I did. I called Simon and told him I couldn't see him anymore." She waited for Kiara's rebuke.

Instead, her friend said, "You probably scared Thiago's ass

by dating other men. Unfortunately, some men like to play the field until someone else wants you and then decide they can't live without you."

"Maybe, but I'm not sure that was the case with Thiago. He has an insane work schedule, so I don't think he's been seeing anyone else. I could be wrong, but I don't think I am."

Not to mention, every Friday they didn't spend together, he explained why he couldn't come see her. He had never canceled their Friday night hookups without an explanation.

India pulled into her executive space in the parking deck and cut the engine.

"Whatever the reason, you're no longer a free woman. How did Simon react when you told him you couldn't see him anymore?"

"Surprisingly well," India said with a laugh. "Seriously, though, he expressed disappointment and wished me the best with my new man."

"Very mature of him. Don't tell Josh I told you this, but Leo was disappointed the two of you didn't hit it off. He really liked you."

"I liked him too, but..."

"Believe me, I understand. Sometimes the spark isn't there. Did you feel a spark with Simon?"

"Honestly, no, but I enjoyed his company. I assumed those feelings would eventually come."

"I think it's hard when the competition is a man like Thiago Santana. He is one sexy, sexy man."

Yes, he is, India thought.

She stepped out of her car. "I have to go. I'm about to walk into work. I'll talk to you later?"

"Sure, we can catch up another time. Have a good day," Kiara said before hanging up.

With Thiago's words ever present in her mind, India

considered her options and decided to put a plan in motion to protect herself. She had accepted they were now exclusive, but she had to be smart. She searched online for the number for the company Spencer Boyden. She then called them and spent the next fifteen minutes on the phone, satisfied after she hung up.

Then she analyzed results from various marketing campaigns, including a digital rollout Beth Ann had worked on. She critiqued the plan, offering suggestions for improvement, and then spent the rest of the morning reviewing the marketing budget, checking that their ROIs remained within the strict range put in place by Thiago. He held them to a high standard, but she had to admit the added pressure had forced them to think outside the box and improve their reach and sales with minimal increase in dollars spent.

Satisfied with the results, she told her assistant to order lunch, which she ate at her desk. After lunch, she locked her door and rolled out a mat on the floor. Putting wireless earphones in her ears, she listened to soothing music as she sat cross-legged on the floor during her afternoon meditation.

She hadn't been a natural at meditating, her mind constantly racing with tasks she had to check off her to-do lists and keeping up with the many objectives required in her role heading up the largest marketing department in the company. However, despite her skepticism, her teacher had been adamant mediation was not only achievable, it would be extremely beneficial in helping her control the effects of lupus that could be exacerbated by the demands of her job.

She had been in a constant battle of needing to rest but not wanting to succumb to the limitations of her body. It took time, but she learned to relax her mind, which helped tremendously, and meditated for fifteen minutes each afternoon.

By the end of the day, she felt drained but was satisfied with all she had accomplished and went down the hall for a bathroom break. She was washing her hands when Blanca Garcia walked in, an executive visiting from the office in Argentina. She had arrived a week early for the executive coaching scheduled for next week, allegedly to spend time gathering information on the U.S. operations and to work on the Buenos Aires expansion with Thiago.

India sincerely doubted her explanation but smiled briefly at her in the mirror. She didn't care for the woman but knew how to be polite.

Blanca briefly smiled back and pulled a tube of lipstick from her designer bag. She took her time applying the crimson color to her full lips.

"I'm about to go to dinner with Thiago," she announced, talking to her reflection.

India stiffened. "Oh?"

"He insisted. He wants to go over the details of the Buenos Aires expansion. Just the two of us." Her lips curved upward slightly as her eyes met India's in the mirror.

This was why India was suspicious of her early arrival. She had noticed how Blanca fawned over Thiago.

She snatched a paper towel from the dispenser. "You're very lucky to be able to spend time with him one-on-one. He's a busy man."

"Not too busy for me."

India let out a short laugh.

Blanca placed a hand on her hip. "Why do you laugh?"

"Sounds like you think you're special."

"I am. Very special. Thiago and I understand each other. We are both hardworking and come from similar cultures. We are also both single."

"What does being single have to do with work?" India asked.

Blanca dropped the lipstick in her purse with a knowing

smile. "As you said, he is a busy man, yet he has made time for me."

"You might be jumping to conclusions," India said in a saccharine voice.

One perfect eyebrow arched upward. "*¿Perdóneme?*"

"I'm just saying, it's obvious you're interested in more than going over the details of the expansion, and if that's the case, you'll probably get your feelings hurt."

Blanca laughed throatily. "You know him so well, do you? I assure you, I know him very, very well. Before I leave this continent, I plan to know him better."

India was fairly certain the dark-haired beauty didn't stand a chance. "Don't say I didn't warn you," she murmured.

"Why are you so certain?"

She paused, trying to think of a diplomatic way to explain. "Because you're not his type."

The comment earned her another throaty laugh as Blanca threw back her head, as if India had said something outrageously funny.

When she stopped laughing, she looked directly into India's eyes. "I am every man's type."

Okayyyy, India thought.

"Oh, I understand now," Blanca said.

"What do you understand?"

"You want him, no? I do not blame you. Who wouldn't? You would have to be blind not to be attracted to such a handsome and virile man, but you should probably let go of that idea because, by the time I leave Atlanta, I intend to find out if what I've learned is true—that he is an amazing lover with an insatiable appetite for sex." Resting a hand on the counter, she leaned closer and dropped her voice. "One of his exes is an acquaintance and should not have been talking about him because of a strict NDA. But...." She shrugged. "You did not hear that from me."

I can confirm what she said is true, India thought. Interestingly enough, Thiago had never asked *her* to sign an NDA. Men of his stature often had such requirements, so why didn't he require her to sign one?

"Tonight I will make my move. I will let you know how it goes. Wish me luck." Blanca slipped her clutch under her arm and swept out of the bathroom with her head high and hips swaying.

India took a deep, calming breath.

Women like her really got on her nerves because she was so confident in her physical appearance that she didn't stop to consider a man might want more substance. She obviously had plenty to offer since she was an executive in the company.

India wished she could be a fly on the wall when Blanca made her move and Thiago rejected her. At least, he better reject her.

She tossed the paper towel she had crushed in her hand and exited the bathroom. When she caught sight of Thiago and Blanca walking in the direction of the elevator, she temporarily froze. They didn't see her, but, as usual, Blanca was laughing enthusiastically at something Thiago had said, her hand brushing his arm.

They disappeared from view, and India continued toward her office, her stomach knotting traitorously with anger and jealousy though she told herself she had nothing to worry about.

When she stepped into her office, she was surprised to see a bouquet of summer flowers on the edge of her desk, among them sunflowers, marigolds, and dahlias.

"The bouquet arrived while you were in the bathroom."

Her executive assistant was standing at the door.

"What a surprise," India said.

"Maybe you have a secret admirer," Tonya remarked.

"Maybe."

Could they be from Thiago? India smiled slightly at the thought that he might have performed such a sweet gesture right after they agreed to be exclusive.

Tonya continued to hover at the door, and India shot her a look. "Thank you, Tonya."

With an embarrassed grimace, her assistant scurried away.

India closed the door and checked the card. They were *not* from Thiago.

She blinked twice, as if hoping the sender's name would change. Her shoulders sagged with disappointment as the excitement drained from her posture.

If the situation changes between you and your new man, let me know. - Simon

The bouquet was beautiful, but because the sender wasn't who she had expected, the gesture seemed hollow and the colors not as vibrant.

She replaced the card in the holder with more care than necessary, as though afraid her disappointment would shatter the lovely vase and spill petals and stems across the surface of her desk.

Sitting down, she crafted a text to Simon: *Thank you for the flowers.*

He responded in less than a minute.

You're welcome. I hope they brightened your day.

She was about to confirm they did but changed her mind. It was best not to go back and forth.

She didn't want to encourage him.

Chapter Twenty

India paced her office restlessly. She hadn't heard a peep out of Thiago except for an email he sent to all executives. She wasn't accustomed to having one-on-one time with him during a typical day, but considering he'd had dinner with Blanca Garcia—a woman who made no effort to hide her attraction to him—India's lack of interaction with him was particularly disconcerting today.

She couldn't help but wonder what had happened during his dinner with Blanca last night.

"Only one way to find out."

Squaring her shoulders as if preparing for battle, India left her office and started down the hall with purposeful steps. Half the floor was empty because most of the staff had left at a reasonable hour. She, however, was working late and knew Thiago would be too.

She swept past the empty desk where his executive assistant usually sat and marched up to the double doors of his office. She knocked twice and waited.

"Come in," Thiago's deep voice called from inside.

India entered and closed the door behind her.

He leaned back in his leather chair and looked at her with a curious expression. "This is a nice surprise."

"Working late as usual, I see," India remarked.

"So are you," Thiago returned.

His face had turned expressionless, so she couldn't tell what he was thinking.

"I heard you had a business dinner yesterday. How did it go?"

One of his eyebrows lifted higher, and he studied her in silence. "You are concerned about my dinner?"

"I was wondering if you had an enjoyable meal, that's all. Who accompanied you? Where did you go to eat?"

Slowly, he rose from behind his desk and walked toward the bar. "I had a very interesting dinner with Blanca Garcia. The food was good, but the company was a bit... odd. Drink?" He gestured toward the options.

India declined the offer with a shake of her head. "What was odd about your dinner companion?"

"She is interested in me," he said in his usual straightforward Thiago manner.

"Is she?" India asked innocently.

He shot her a look. "You would have to be blind not to notice she's interested in me. She is annoyingly obvious about it, and I have ignored her behavior for the most part because we rarely interact. Unfortunately, she came early for the training, and last night the situation became awkward. I should have known better than to accept her invitation to dine alone." He dropped clear ice cubes into a glass and poured water over them.

So Blanca had invited him to dinner and not the other way

around. The information gave India a sense of immense satisfaction.

"What happened?" she asked, fighting the giddiness threatening to overtake her at the newfound knowledge that Blanca's plan to seduce Thiago had fallen flat.

He sipped his water, eyeing her suspiciously over the rim of the glass. "She propositioned me."

"Nooo," India said, feigning surprise.

"I turned her down."

"You poor man. Does this happen often—women throwing themselves at you?"

"Very often. Why do you think I have a male assistant?"

She pursed her lips. "Really, Thiago?"

He shrugged, as if he didn't need to explain further.

"Women just find you so irresistible?"

"It is a curse," he said in a mockingly forlorn voice.

"I think people call your statement a humble brag."

"No matter. What I said is the truth. But why do I have the feeling you knew all about Blanca's plan to seduce me?"

"She might have mentioned her intentions when I saw her in the bathroom yesterday, before you left for dinner."

His eyebrows inched higher in surprise. "Is that why you came down here? To make sure I didn't succumb to her feminine charms?"

India averted her eyes. "Maybe. It's nice to know you didn't give in to temptation."

"There was no temptation."

"There better not have been," she said, not bothering to hide the smile on her face as she strolled toward him.

This time, Thiago's raised eyebrows were accompanied by a short laugh. "I see. Now you're the one making demands," he said, sounding rather pleased.

"She'll be here until the end of next week. I hope the situation won't be uncomfortable for you," India continued.

"I don't foresee a problem. I sent her home."

"Ouch. Too bad." India had been looking forward to asking Blanca how the evening went.

She sidled up to Thiago and gazed into his smoldering dark eyes. She was trying to seduce him but was already mesmerized by the intensity she saw in their depths.

Slipping a hand inside his pants, she felt his stomach muscles tighten.

Thiago didn't move. "What are you doing?" he asked in a strained voice.

"What do you think I'm doing?" she whispered seductively, massaging his length, feeling him harden beneath her palm.

Slowly, he placed his glass on the bar but didn't remove her hand. "We are at work. We do not—"

A knock sounded on the door, and one second later, it was pushed open.

India yanked her hand out of Thiago's pants and quickly stepped away from him.

"Oh!" His assistant looked surprised. "I didn't know you were in a meeting."

Brown-skinned, tall, and in his early thirties, Amir was brilliant and tough enough to handle Thiago's personality. He also did a good job of protecting his time from interruptions, which was probably why he appeared so taken aback by India's presence. She was not on the calendar, so she should not be in here taking up the boss's time.

"What do you have for me?" Thiago asked in a gruff voice, talking over his shoulder.

He couldn't risk facing Amir and having him see his erection. India turned away to keep from laughing.

"I printed out the reports you asked for and had them

bound. I picked them up from downstairs a few minutes ago."
Amir pointedly lifted the stack of red folders in his hands.

"Put them on my desk," Thiago said, pretending to be busy
at the bar.

What is he doing? India barely contained her amusement.
"Yes, sir."

Amir walked across the room and dropped the folders on
Thiago's desk. As he turned in the direction of the door, he cast
a quick glance at India. Did he sense the tension in the room?

She smiled disarmingly at him, and he smiled back.

At the door, he paused. "Do you need me to do anything
else?"

Thiago turned his head toward him. "No. You may leave
for the evening."

Amir nodded and left.

As soon as the door shut, India doubled over with laughter.

Thiago glared at her. "That was not funny," he said.

She wiped the tears from her lashes. "It was a little funny.
Come on," she said.

"You need to keep your hands to yourself."

"That's new," she said in a cocky voice.

"We have always been hands-off in the office." Thiago
strolled over to the door and turned the lock with a decisive
click.

India's breath caught. "What are you doing?" she asked.

Thiago shrugged out of his jacket as he walked toward her
at a leisurely pace. "Before Amir came in, you were doing
something."

"A second ago you told me to keep my hands to myself,"
India reminded him as she backed toward the desk.

"I did, but I didn't say anything about keeping *my* hands to
myself."

"Oh, I see. Rules for me but not for you."

She tried to run, but he caught her from behind with one arm and lifted her off the floor. Breathless and laughing, she twisted around to face him, the back of her thighs hitting the edge of his desk.

"You understand perfectly." Thiago tossed his jacket on the desk. Then he reached behind her and picked up the remote. With the press of a button, the window shades started lowering.

"Are you trying to take advantage of me, Mr. Santana?" India whispered.

He looked down at her with a heavy-lidded gaze. "Sometimes I think you are taking advantage of me." He spoke in a grave voice, as if he wasn't joking.

Did he really think she was somehow using him? "I would never..."

He caught her chin between his finger and thumb. "No, you would never. Nor would I use you. But you drive me crazy, you know that, don't you? Crazy with need." His eyes blazed down at her, reflecting the storm of emotions his lips had confessed to.

"You do the same to me, Thiago. It's impossible to think when I'm around you," India admitted in a soft voice.

He dipped his head and took her mouth, and she immediately opened to him. She tugged on his tie until the Windsor knot was undone, and she could continue undressing him by opening his shirt.

"No, not here," he said huskily.

Without warning, he scooped her up and tossed her over his shoulder.

India squealed softly, laughing and kicking her feet. "You're a barbarian," she said.

He marched over to the conference table and nudged the chair at its head out of the way with his foot. Then he carefully placed her on the cool glass surface.

"I'm going to Brazil on business in a couple of weeks. I want you to come with me," he said.

India leaned back on her hands, watching with interest as he finished unbuttoning his shirt. "Why?"

"Because we could stay a couple of extra days and spend the weekend together."

The unexpected invitation made her heart race. After her disappointment about the flowers yesterday, his offer excited her.

"Is that a request?" she asked to toy with him.

"It is an order," Thiago replied, tossing his shirt on the chair he'd moved aside. "Say yes."

"So I don't have a choice?"

He stepped between her open legs, and she held her breath in anticipation of their lips touching.

"No," Thiago said, looking down at her with arrogant confidence.

"This is what I'm talking about when I say you're mean." Her fingers fisted in his undershirt to keep him from moving away.

He laughed softly, and his warm breath feathered across her face, causing a throbbing ache between her thighs. She wanted him desperately. Perhaps because they'd been so careful in the past, making sure not to touch to avoid getting caught or raising suspicion. Now, here they were, about to have sex in his office—an act so forbidden, she was practically panting with lustful excitement.

"I need an answer, *mujer*," he said in a low tone. His authoritative voice sent thrills up her spine.

"I'm open to the idea, but I have nothing to do with the Latin American region. If we're both gone at the same time to Brazil, it might look suspicious to the staff."

"Who cares what they think? No one would dare comment about our trip to our faces."

Good point.

"*You* are going to take time off and enjoy the weekend?"

"When was the last time you went on vacation?" Thiago asked, placing his hands on either side of her hips.

"It's been a while," India admitted.

"For me too, and though this is only a few days, it is better than nothing. Unless you don't want to join me." Consternation creased his brow.

"No, I absolutely want to. I love the idea."

"But?"

"No but. I admit to being surprised by the offer, but I want to go. It will be nice to get away, and I've never been to Brazil."

Thiago's tongue teased her bottom lip. "You are my woman. This should not be a surprise."

You are my woman. Were there any sexier words in the English language?

"We will not think about work for a few days," Thiago added.

India smoothed her hands over his muscular biceps. "Is that really possible?"

"We can try," Thiago said.

She desperately wanted to try, and a change of scenery would be nice.

She tugged his undershirt from his pants and slid her hand underneath to explore his hair-rough muscles. "I can't wait," she whispered.

"I cannot wait to make love to you in every corner of my penthouse," Thiago said huskily. He removed his shirt and tossed it aside.

India lifted up so he could pull down her pants and panties. Seconds later, he was inside her, sliding into her aroused body with ease, his hands cradling her bottom as he thrust into her on top of the table.

As she barreled toward an orgasm, she knew meetings at this table would never be the same again. They would remind her of Thiago's ragged breathing, his rough kisses, and the way his hands gripped her as he claimed her body with each demanding thrust.

Chapter Twenty-One

Thiago entered the plane's cabin and settled on the soft, cream leather seat. He and India were flying to Brazil on the company jet, and he was early, so India hadn't arrived yet.

They would first go to São Paulo, where the Santana International offices were located, and stay at his penthouse for a couple of days before flying to Rio de Janeiro on Friday after lunch.

"Mr. Santana, can I bring you a drink while you wait?" a pleasant-looking flight attendant asked.

"Not right now. I will have one when my colleague arrives —a Yamazaki 18, neat. You can start steeping the tea I requested. She should be here shortly."

"Yes, sir." The woman nodded briefly and then left him alone.

Spending more time with India, he had noticed she enjoyed drinking tea and had made note of the brand he saw at her apartment the other day—a blend of ginger, turmeric, peppermint, black pepper, and cinnamon.

He gazed idly out the window, thinking about the potential minefield their affair could set off. Being a female executive who was sleeping with her boss could be problematic for India. If people found out, he could well imagine the rumor mill speculating about how long they'd been together and whether she had earned her current position on her back. Never mind that his father had promoted her to VP of marketing before Thiago took over as CEO.

So he'd made sure to arrange for her to have real work to perform in the São Paulo office, but he had also arranged for her to have time off. While he worked full days, her schedule consisted of half days, which meant time for sightseeing. In the evenings, they would spend time together, and he could show her some of the nightlife of the city.

São Paulo was known as the financial capital of Brazil and had a diverse population, which included Europeans, Arabs, and the largest concentration of ethnic Japanese outside Japan. In addition, there was an impressive culinary scene and plenty of museums.

India had seemed most interested in the art scene, so he'd recommended several museums. Her excitement for the trip had been palpable, and he'd felt gratified he was the reason for her pleasure, beyond making her toes curl and her thighs tremble as they clenched around him. Their relationship had certainly changed in the past few weeks. He had never hidden his relationships, but he was good at compartmentalizing. With India, the two worlds—business and personal—were bleeding together.

While they continued to meet in secret, they spent more time together and touched base much more often during the week, during which he had learned something shocking, which he teasingly told her almost made him want to break up with her. She believed oatmeal raisin cookies were superior to chocolate chip cookies. Appalled, he had threatened to end their relationship, to which she had put her foot down.

"You can't change my mind," she had said, an obstinate set to her mouth.

He promised if she ate his stepmother's chocolate chip cookies with macadamia nuts, then he could change her opinion, and made a mental note to have Rose make some for her.

He shared more stories about his childhood, opening up to her in a way he hadn't to other women, and after a particularly annoying business luncheon the other day, he'd called her on the way back to the office just to hear her voice. She had instantly calmed him.

The woman had even turned him into a texter! He had never been one to text much, using the option sparingly. But every day he found a new reason to send her a message.

I like that color green. It looks good against your skin.

I'm missing a cufflink. Did you happen to find it at your place?

He had also taught her Portuguese words in preparation for their trip:

"To say thank you, women say *obrigada* and men say *obrigado*, regardless of the gender of the person they are speaking to. Informally, you can say *brigadão*, which means thank you very much."

They had also begun sharing weeknight meals more often. Several times they had dined out. One night he had Amir pick up dinner and bring it back to the office before he left for the day. If his assistant thought the bags contained a ridiculous amount of food for one person, he gave no indication.

After everyone had left, India came down the hall. Thiago locked his door, and they ate at the conference table. Then he fucked her against the wall, his blood running hot from her cries of passion, stifling the sounds with a hand over her mouth in case someone was in the office or had come back for some reason. Then they took a shower together in his bathroom, the first time they had ever shared such intimacy.

Twice they had eaten dinner at his home...

Thiago shifted in the chair. He hadn't wanted to analyze his feelings, but the truth was, those two nights were extra special because India had spent the night.

The first time had been on a Friday night, two weeks ago. That particular day, he had told her they would eat dinner at his place. She followed him home in her car, and upon arrival, discovered the delicious spread his chef had prepared for them. They talked until late, made love, and then fell asleep.

He had enjoyed waking up to her in his bed. So of course, when he invited her to come over Monday night, he told her to pack an overnight bag. They had left his house at the same time in the morning to go to work. His only regret was that they couldn't ride to work together.

Thiago's peripheral vision was snagged by a flicker of movement, and he turned to watch the limo he had sent for India ease to a smooth stop beside the plane. When she exited the vehicle, his body came alive at the sight of her.

One corner of his mouth lifted higher when he saw she had done as he had asked. April was early autumn in Brazil, and the climate was temperate. Last night, she texted him a picture of a sundress.

Thinking about bringing this on the trip. Too much? she'd asked.

He'd immediately picked up the phone because a simple text could not properly convey his feelings. "It's perfect. Wear that tomorrow for our flight."

She had laughed, insisting she had already picked an outfit for the plane, so he hadn't been sure if she would wear the dress. But he watched with heat flickering in his veins as it billowed in a soft breeze. She wore a light jacket over it because the temperature had dropped lower than usual for an April afternoon, but he would promptly have her remove the jacket when she came on board.

As she approached the stairs leading up to the plane door, he got to his feet to greet her.

When she saw him, a smile spread across her face.

"Hi," she whispered.

Thiago immediately pulled her into his arms and kissed her soundly. It was impulsive. He couldn't stop himself. Traveling together had added another dimension to their relationship, cementing their couplehood.

"You look amazing. Thank you for wearing the dress," he said.

"You were so insistent, I didn't want to disappoint," she replied.

Thiago became momentarily lost in her eyes before he realized the chauffeur was standing at the door with her bags, his eyes politely averted as he waited.

"I will take those," Thiago said.

"Have a safe flight, sir—ma'am." He nodded and left them alone.

Minutes later, they were seated beside each other in the middle of the plane when the flight attendant approached with a steaming cup of tea and his whisky on a tray.

"We will be in the air shortly," she said, placing their drinks before them.

After she was gone, India turned to Thiago. "Tea for me?"

"It's the herbal tea you drink," he answered.

Her eyebrows lifted higher. "How did you... you ordered the tea I like?"

"Of course. I saw the box in the cabinet at your apartment."

"You didn't have to do that, but... thank you," she said quietly.

"You're welcome."

A moment passed between them. Something indefinable. Something heavy. He knew she felt it too because she suddenly focused on her cup, lifting it to her lips.

"Good?" he asked.

"Perfect," she confirmed. "What are you drinking?"

"Yamazaki 18, whisky made in Japan's first and oldest malt distillery. Would you like a taste?"

Thanks to the large Japanese community in São Paulo, he had been introduced to Yamazaki whisky and had fallen in love with its delicious flavor, reminiscent of blackberry and dark chocolate.

"Sure." India lifted the glass to her lips. "Mmm, that's really good. I'll need a glass of that later with dinner."

Thiago chuckled. "There's plenty," he said, as the captain announced they were preparing for takeoff.

Moments later, they were in the air.

Chapter Twenty-Two

India eyed Thiago in the private elevator shuttling them to his penthouse suite. They had just returned from dinner, and tomorrow they had an early flight to Rio de Janeiro, where he had reserved a room for them at the luxurious and historic Copacabana Palace on Copacabana Beach.

While India was excited to go to their next destination, the trip had been magical so far.

On the ten-hour flight south, they had slept on the company jet, so Thiago was refreshed when they arrived and went into the Santana International offices the next morning. She had spent the morning in a museum before visiting the company. She met with the marketing team, including the vice president of marketing for Latin America, whom she'd spent time with when he had participated in the coaching sessions last month. Though they served different markets, they were able to learn from each other and promised to stay in touch to further exchange ideas.

In the evening, they took a taxi to Vila Madalena, an artsy

neighborhood known for its nightlife. Atop the Unique Hotel, they sipped caipirinhas and ate dinner at the Skye Bar with locals and tourists while admiring the city view.

The next day, India went into the office first and took the afternoon off for sightseeing. She joined a tour group, which included a return to Vila Madalena and a walk down its famous winding pedestrian street called Beco do Batman, or Batman's Alley, where the walls were covered in breathtakingly beautiful murals. On the excursion, she made friends with a fellow tourist from Colorado, and they acted as photographers, snapping photos of each other in front of the impressive works of art.

Later, she explored a few other places Thiago recommended, including the Museu de Arte de São Paulo Assis Chateaubriand. She spent over two hours there, admiring the work of well-known European artists like Gauguin, Goya, and Gainsborough, as well as the museum's collection of Brazilian and other Latin American artists.

That night, they went dancing after dinner, and Thiago showed he had the same dangerously sexy moves on the dance floor as he did in the bedroom.

"You look tired," Thiago remarked, cupping her cheek.

"I might be, a little bit. I've packed in a lot the past couple of days."

The constant physical activity, more than she was used to, had taken its toll on her body. She was also suffering from a bout of nausea. Last week, she'd experienced the same thing and had thrown up after work. She'd had fish for lunch then and had wondered if the meal could have been the culprit, but here she was, feeling very much like she wanted to throw up again after eating chicken. She had a sneaking suspicion she knew what was causing her to be sick two weeks in a row.

Thiago pulled her into his arms, and she laid her head on

his chest, reveling in the comfort of his embrace. "Then you need to rest tonight," he said, kissing the top of her head.

Their situationship was long over, and the Thiago she had known had been replaced. There were so many moments of tenderness and playfulness in this new man, which made her believe their relationship could develop into something more. Something longer-term, perhaps.

India kissed his bearded chin. "I'll make it up to you tomorrow, once I'm good and rested," she promised.

They exited the elevator, which opened into the entryway of his penthouse apartment. The space was adorned with walnut floors, and a dramatic painting in an ornate gold frame dominated one wall, the image showing Brazilian farmers of all skin tones tending the land. Recessed lights reflected off the dark floor, and a vase containing a royal blue orchid provided an eye-catching pop of color against the room's warm earth tones.

In the bedroom, the view was spectacular, with floor-to-ceiling windows giving an unobstructed view of São Paulo's glittering skyline of high-rises and skyscrapers. The king-size bed in the middle of the room had an upholstered headboard and appeared small in the expansive space. The decor in general was all about texture and warmth, with thick rugs covering the floor, and tables and chairs in solid colors and floral prints, including a sitting area perfect for moments of quiet reading.

India surreptitiously watched Thiago as he removed his jacket, leaving on his long-sleeved shirt that clung to his frame, pulling a little at his biceps and emphasizing his strong, wide shoulders.

It should be illegal for a man to look so good, she mused.

Not only did he have an incredible body, his features were arranged in such a way that the average person was forced to stop and stare. She had seen plenty of people—women, especially—ogling him as they walked to their table this evening, as if each person was pulled in by his square jaw, smoldering dark eyes, and dangerously sensual lips.

"That's new," India remarked, nodding at the watch on his wrist as she slipped off her heels.

"It is a vintage Omega Seamaster." Thiago flicked his wrist so she could better see its gold face, which matched the gold link band. "They gained their reputation as dive watches and have a strong association with the James Bond character, believe it or not. This one belonged to my grandfather. My father's father. He wore it every day, and when he passed, my father handed me the watch. He said Grandfather had wanted me to have it."

There was no arrogance or steel in Thiago's voice. Just quiet pride that he had been chosen as the one to inherit the watch from his grandfather, someone he obviously admired.

"How old were you when you received it?" India asked.

"Twelve." He paused. "Because of this, I started collecting vintage watches. I became obsessed."

"Where are the others? Here or in Atlanta?"

"Here." He paused again, appraising her with a thoughtful look. Then he seemed to come to a decision. "Would you like to see my collection?"

"Yes. Please."

India recognized right away that sharing this part of himself was monumental, and anticipation fluttered in her veins as Thiago entered his dressing room and she followed behind him.

Past the island in the center and toward the back, they arrived at a door built into the wall. He keyed in a code and then pressed his thumb to the biometric pad. She heard a soft *whoosh*, and then he turned the handle. Her mouth fell open when she saw the interior. More dark wood and recessed lights, but also rows of watches, each nestled in a velvet box on a shelf.

There were dozens, a literal who's who of luxury watches— Patek Philippe, Rolex, Audemars Piguet, Cartier, Jaeger-LeCoultre. Some with leather straps, others with linked bands made of gold or platinum. They were elegant and masculine, many of which sat behind a small plate attached to the shelf with an engraved date and text explaining the significance of the watch.

India walked slowly into the room. "There's a small fortune in here. How in the world did you get your hands on all these watches?"

"It was not easy, believe me," Thiago said with a low chuckle. "That is not entirely true. Some are easier than others to acquire. Auction houses are a good place to find them, and so are private collectors who want to sell quietly. A few people have approached me directly, and I have bought others after the owner passed away and their family wanted to liquidate their assets. I have gotten some very good deals that way."

He placed the Omega in its box and picked up another watch. "This Patek Philippe was made specifically for the FIFA World Cup in 1962 and gifted to the Brazilian team captain after they won. It took me four years to convince the family to part with it." He placed the timepiece back on the shelf and pointed to a Rolex with a black face. "In the 1950s, those were given to Italian navy divers. Many were lost at sea, and of the ones available, few are in good condition. I was lucky to find that one at an auction house."

"Why watches? Why not cigars or coins or something else?" India asked.

He pondered the question for a moment before he spoke. "Many of these watches have been on the wrists of men who helped shape history, and they all have a story. When I wear one of them, I like to think I am bridging the gap between history and the future. Like my grandfather, these men are gone, but their memories live on, and their legacies endure for generations."

"You're different when you talk about this," India observed.

He acknowledged her comment with a nod. "Do you know how some people like to go hunting at thrift stores to find hidden treasures? It's the same for me. Finding a piece, learning the history behind it, and then adding it to my collection gives me a great sense of satisfaction. One day, I plan to move them to my house in Georgia, but I need to have a climate-controlled vault built first. Bigger than this one since I'm almost out of space here but plan to continue collecting for a long time."

Thiago pointed out a few more of the watches and explained their significance before they finally exited the room.

"Few people have seen my collection," he said, confirming her thoughts as he closed the door and twisted the handle back in place.

Her pulse skipped at being granted entry to such a private part of his life. "Thank you for sharing your passion with me."

"This is a hobby. *You* are my passion."

He looked at her as if he wanted to eat her up then and there, but instead of her body responding with desire as usual, the nausea she had been experiencing for almost an hour worsened.

India placed a hand against her stomach, as if she could force her insides to behave.

"What's wrong?" Thiago looked at her with a deep frown on his face.

Oh crap, she was going to throw up. "I don't feel so good." India lifted her other hand to her mouth.

"You don't look very good, either," Thiago remarked, his frown deepening.

India wrapped an arm around her midsection. "I think I'm going to be sick. No, I'm definitely going to be sick." Nausea bubbled from her stomach into her chest.

Thiago reached for her. "Are you—"

India turned quickly away and made a mad dash for the adjoining bathroom.

Chapter Twenty-Three

S tartled, Thiago stared after her for a few seconds. Then he shot out of the dressing room, but those few seconds of delay had cost him, and India had moved fast. By the time he arrived at the bathroom door, she had already locked herself inside.

He wiggled the doorknob. "India?"

Then he heard her retching.

Thiago pressed his palm flat against the door, helpless in the wake of her obvious distress.

When she stopped, he tried talking to her again. "India, should I call a doctor?"

"No. Give me a minute," she replied, her voice sounding weak and strained.

He heard her throwing up again.

Thiago stood uncertainly outside the door. He didn't know what to do. It pained him to hear her suffering. He wanted to fix this. Should he ignore her and call a doctor anyway?

Backing away from the door, he went to the kitchen, filled a glass with room temperature water, and returned to the bedroom. He stood outside the bathroom again, listening. It sounded like she was throwing up a lung.

What the hell was wrong with her? They had both eaten the same meal, so it couldn't be—

Thiago stilled. He knew exactly what her throwing up meant.

He sat on the edge of the bed, letting the idea sink in. India must be pregnant, and he was going to be a father.

A *father*.

The word echoed in his head as his thoughts raced. There was so much more he wanted to do with the company. He had a five-year growth plan mapped out, and of course there was the IPO, which he hoped to launch in less than two years.

Was he ready for the responsibility of a child? Of course.

He was Thiago Santana, and he loved a challenge. He would tackle fatherhood the same way he had tackled other challenges in his life—by seeking out knowledge so he could be the best. By honing in on fatherhood, he would become the best damn father possible. And India, well... he already knew she would excel at motherhood.

Beneath the cool logic of his assessment, something stirred in his chest he hadn't expected. He smiled at the idea of her carrying a piece of him inside her. An image of India with his child in her arms sent a sharp surge of emotion through him. She wouldn't simply be the woman who shared his bed. They would have a permanent connection, and the thought filled him with... a possessive sense of satisfaction.

Thiago heard water running in the bathroom, and then the door creaked open. India leaned against the frame.

"Sorry about that," she murmured, avoiding his gaze. One hand fluttered to her stomach while the other gripped the frame as if she needed the support.

Thiago stood and approached. "Are you all right?" he asked gently.

"I'm fine, but I need a new stomach." Her voice sounded small and pained, so the joke didn't land.

She looked up at him with baleful eyes, and he handed her the water.

"Thank you," she said gratefully.

After she had drunk half of it, Thiago asked, "Do you care to tell me what is going on?"

"There's nothing going on."

"Nothing at all? Nothing you want to tell me?" Thiago prodded.

India stared at him in confusion.

"India, we were having a conversation, and then you ran out here to throw up. Do you think I don't know what this means?" No point in beating around the bush. He'd go straight to the point if she didn't want to broach the subject herself.

"I got sick. What do you think this means?" India asked slowly.

Thiago straightened his shoulders, slightly annoyed at her fake display of confusion. "Do not play dumb with me. When were you going to tell me?"

"Tell you what?" she asked.

Thiago stepped closer. "That you're pregnant."

Her mouth fell open. "What?"

"Are you carrying my child?"

She pressed a hand to her forehead. "Oh my goodness, I'm not pregnant, Thiago!" She moved past him.

"You can deny it all you want, but I know the signs," he said in a firm voice, following her.

"Do you now?" She tossed the question over her shoulder as she continued toward the kitchen.

"What are your plans?" Thiago asked.

India drained the water from the glass and then dropped it with a heavy hand onto the island. She swung to face him. "I'm not pregnant."

"I do not believe in abortion. I am Catholic."

"When was the last time you stepped foot inside a church?" she demanded.

"That doesn't matter."

"It matters to me since you obviously think you have a say in my decision about *my* body."

He stepped closer and jabbed a finger at her belly. "That is *my* child you're carrying."

India sighed. "Before either of us says something we'll regret, let me tell you again, for the third time. I. Am. *Not*. Pregnant."

Not. Pregnant.

This time, the words landed like a roundhouse kick to the jaw, knocking the wind out of him. The earlier rush of anticipation bled from him like an open wound, leaving him feeling drained and empty. He had leaped so far ahead, already making plans for the son or daughter who would carry his name and both their DNA. The dream dissolved as quickly as it had arrived, leaving a hollow ache in its wake.

"Not pregnant." Repeating the words didn't take the sting out of them as he'd hoped.

His jaw tightened as he forced his face into neutral lines. This was better anyway. The timing was off. He had big plans, and a child would derail them and preoccupy too much of his time.

"If you're not p—" He couldn't bring himself to say the word again. "If you're not, what happened back there?" Thiago demanded in a gruff voice.

"I was sick," India answered.

"We ate the same meal, so it was not the food."

"You're not going to let this go, are you?"

Thiago folded his arms across his chest. "What do you think?"

She sighed, as if the world had been placed on her shoulders. "Fine, I don't feel like arguing, and I know you won't stop until you get an answer. I have lupus, and I started a new medication a few weeks ago, where I have to inject myself once a week. One of the side effects of this new medication is nausea, though I had no idea it would be this bad." She rubbed her belly as if trying to eliminate the remnants of her nausea. "I thought I would only feel queasy, but apparently not."

Slowly, Thiago unfolded his arms and examined her. She looked more exhausted than before. "You never told me you had lupus."

Why had she never shared such an important piece of information about herself? Had he not pushed, it was obvious she wouldn't have told him now, either.

"The topic never came up in conversation." India shrugged in a nonchalant manner. "So anyway, what were we talking about before?"

"You cannot tell me you have lupus and then change the subject, India. I don't know much about this disease, but I know it can be very debilitating."

"My lupus has been under control for years."

"If it is under control, why are you taking new medicine?" Thiago asked.

"I was trying a new drug my rheumatologist suggested, and we hoped it would work in conjunction with my other meds so my lupus would eventually go into remission. Then I'd be off prescription drugs. But this is the second time I've been sick and thrown up, and the only change is I started injecting myself with the new medication. It doesn't agree with me, I guess." She looked defeated.

Thiago was angry at her for not telling him sooner and angry at the medication for not working the way she needed it to.

He swore softly, running his fingers through his hair, and India eyed him warily.

"I cannot believe you never told me this," he said in a low voice.

India wrapped her arms around herself. "We don't—didn't have that kind of relationship." She spoke in an equally low tone and looked away first.

"You said your lupus has been under control for years. When was the last time it was... out of control?"

"About five years ago. I was in the hospital for about a month."

"I remember you took a leave of absence around that time. I believe you were gone for two months or so?"

She nodded. "A total of ten weeks. Your father was very kind and gave me time off to recover. He held my job for me, and I'll forever be grateful."

"Well, this conversation has been eye-opening. I certainly did not know you had lupus, and I have been pushing you and pushing you." He shook his head.

She touched his forearm. "I'm fine, Thiago. I'm not solely dependent on my medication. I've learned to minimize the symptoms in other ways. I meditate in my office. I do yoga, get massages, drink herbal tea with anti-inflammatory properties. There are so many options to help keep it under control. I'm obsessed, really, because that's how my mother died. She also had lupus, and it damaged her heart."

"I am so sorry." Thiago had heard her talk about her mother and grandmother but never her father. "What about your father?" he asked tentatively.

He saw an immediate change come over her. "My father

and I haven't had much of a relationship since I turned eighteen and he was no longer responsible for my support. He barely provided support anyway. Eventually, we fell out of touch."

Pain flitted across her face, so fleeting, he almost missed it. She stared at the fingers of her left hand spread out on the island countertop. When she spoke again, he could tell by the lack of emotion in her voice that she was in another world—a world filled with pain and disappointment.

"He was an artist. My mother said that's where I got my talent from because she couldn't even draw stick people." She smiled faintly. "As an adult, it made me feel connected to him, though... though we didn't have much of a relationship. Two years ago, I saw my father at a gas station, and he didn't recognize me, Thiago. He walked out of the convenience store and walked in my direction, where I was pumping gas. He had an unlit cigar hanging from the corner of his mouth. I was about to greet him when I received the shock of my life. He used to call me Indy, but he never said a word. He... he nodded and walked by me to his truck. So much time had passed he didn't recognize me, his own daughter."

He couldn't bear to hear the thick pain in her voice. "And then you stopped drawing."

She nodded, and he pulled her into the safety of his arms to shield her from the horror of the memory.

"*Dios*, I'm sorry, *mi amor*," he whispered.

"His own daughter," she said again, her voice quivering.

Thiago easily lifted her from the floor and walked back to the bedroom with her cradled in his arms. Under the covers, she remained curled up against him, her tears leaving damp spots on his shirt.

When she finally stopped crying, she lifted her head from his chest and wiped at her wet cheeks. "Sorry."

"No need to apologize." Thiago swept his thumb across her jaw to remove a teardrop she had missed.

"I've never told anyone about that incident. It's so embarrassing." She kept her gaze lowered.

"You could still have a relationship with your father."

Thiago and his father didn't always see eye to eye in business, but he couldn't imagine not having a relationship with him at all, and it was clear India wanted to be closer to her father. One of them needed to make the first move.

"I will never have a relationship with him," India said with iron in her voice.

Thiago propped up her chin, forcing eye contact. "Never say never. You don't know what the future might bring. Reach out. It is not too late."

"He'll have to make the first move. I'm not setting myself up for any more hurt."

By the resolve in her voice and the firm set to her jaw, Thiago didn't doubt she meant every word.

Chapter Twenty-Four

As Thiago dealt with the bellman and their luggage, India walked across the carpeted floor of their suite at the Copacabana Palace on Copacabana Beach in Rio de Janeiro. The iconic hotel opened in 1923 and was a well-known landmark, famous for being one of the most luxurious hotels in South America.

Thiago had booked them a top-floor suite that included daily champagne, butler service, and a breathtaking view of the beach from their private veranda. Stepping outside, India leaned against the railing, shielding her eyes from the warm sun as she surveyed the beachgoers splashing in the waves or lounging on the sand.

Thiago slipped his arms around her waist from behind and nuzzled her neck, and she leaned back against his solid frame.

"I assumed there'd be more people on the beach," India remarked.

"It's the time of year. The beach is much more crowded in the summer months with tourists and *cariocas*," he said, referring to residents of Rio. "But the weather is still perfect for us to enjoy ourselves. We're going to take it easy today. I don't want you to overdo it," he said.

"Thiago, we're in Rio. I want to see everything since we don't have much time."

He was worried about her health, and while she appreciated his concern, she knew what her body could handle and didn't want to miss out on sightseeing since she didn't know when she'd ever have the chance to return.

"Tomorrow. Today, we relax and enjoy the beach," Thiago said firmly.

India sighed loudly, though she secretly liked how he was insistent on taking care of her. "Yes, sir."

He groaned, gripping her hips and pressing his pelvis against her bottom.

Giggling, she twisted out of his arms and held his hand, leading the way inside. "Come on. You promised me a relaxing day, so let's get started."

The hotel provided them with loungers and an umbrella so they didn't have to rent any from the vendors on the beach. As protection against the effects of the sun, India wore a large hat and a long-sleeve cover-up over her aqua-blue one-piece since skin flares could cause her to break out in rashes or hives.

They crossed the street to get to the beach and settled in their spot on the sand. At the same time, a young woman sped by in a string bikini, screaming as she was chased by a young man in a speedo. One thing India immediately noticed—Brazilians were not shy about showing off their bodies.

She leaned over and covered Thiago's eyes. "Don't look."

He chuckled, taking her hand and kissing the palm. "I did not see anything," he promised, reclining in the chair and slipping on a pair of dark shades.

India lay back too, placing her hat on her stomach as she observed the scenery. Slowing down and taking time to relax made her realize how long it had been since she had done this very thing.

The steady rush and retreat of the Atlantic was music to her ears. Each swell of the waves was like the ocean inhaling and then releasing a breath.

"I could get used to this," she said, scanning the sea of bright umbrellas dotting the landscape like flowers on the sand.

Thiago folded his arms behind his head. "Coming here was my escape from São Paulo. Sometimes I would drive instead of fly."

He wore navy-blue swim trunks that showed off his slim hips, thick thighs, and sculpted chest. He blended in perfectly with the bronzed bodies lounging nearby.

"How long is the drive?" India asked.

"A little more than five hours. One day we'll come back and take the drive. It was not practical this time."

The way he casually mentioned them returning meant he saw a future with her. In fact, his reaction last night when he thought she was pregnant had been eye-opening. He had clearly wanted the imaginary baby. If she read him correctly, he had been... dare she use the word... *disappointed* she wasn't pregnant?

She couldn't see his eyes behind the sunglasses, so she guessed they were closed. Her gaze rested on him for a moment. He would be a good father—firm, but playful, with high expectations, no doubt. He would be the disciplinarian, while she would be the big softie.

The shrill laughter of children farther down the beach caught her attention. A group of boys and girls were kicking around a soccer ball in the sand, clapping and cheering for each other.

India closed her eyes and at some point drifted off to sleep. She was awakened by Thiago, who was standing above her. He had removed his sunglasses and extended a hand to her. "Let's go in the water and then eat lunch."

After rubbing on sunscreen, they made their way down to the cool water.

"How do you like your trip so far?" Thiago asked as they waded in.

"It's heaven," India replied.

He grinned at her, and her heart raced. She never stood a chance, did she? Not from the moment she left the sports bar with him last July. She had fooled herself into believing Thiago would be nothing more than a fling, but the truth was undeniable. Their Friday nights together had been her oxygen, and she had lived for every moment in his presence, looking forward to one of these rare but sexy smiles that captivated and dissolved her under its weight. Despite her best efforts, she had fallen for him.

I'm in love.

"Are you all right?" Thiago asked. "You are staring at me in an odd way."

India laughed, her cheeks hot with embarrassment. "I... I remembered something I needed to do back at the office—"

"You are not supposed to be thinking about work. We are taking a break, remember? Whatever you have to do can wait until Monday."

"You're right." She forced a smile to her lips.

Thiago sent a spray of seawater in her direction, and she squealed, averting her face. Then she splashed him back, but he scooped her up, and she laughed, clinging to his broad shoulders and wrapping her legs around his waist as the ocean swirled around them.

Thiago's smile slowly faded, and for one long, charged

moment, they stared at each other. When he kissed her, India clung to him, opening her mouth to accept his tongue. She succumbed to the moment—the roar of the surf, the hum of beach activity, the distant call of the seagulls. For a few minutes, nothing mattered but the two of them. The world narrowed to the heat of his skin, the salty taste of water on his moist lips, and her overwhelming happiness at being in his arms.

* * *

Today was Saturday, their last full day in Brazil.

"Are you ready yet?" Thiago called from outside, sounding impatient.

"Two minutes!" India yelled, applying lip gloss to her nude lips.

She wore wide-legged white linen pants, a powder-blue loose-fitting shirt, and comfortable shoes. With her straw hat, she looked like a true tourist.

Yesterday, when they finished at the beach, she had been tempted to buy lunch from one of the hotdog carts. Beyond the usual condiments, there were options to add corn and peas, tomato sauce simmered with onions and bell peppers, quail eggs, or *batata palha,* crunchy shoestring fries. Instead, they ate a filling meal at one of the kiosks on the boardwalk. Afterward, they ordered acai bowls from a street vendor, enjoying the cold, delicious treat as they strolled back to the hotel. India's was covered in granola and honey while Thiago chose granola and condensed milk.

Back at the hotel, he had arranged for them to have massages and spa treatments, which filled the rest of their afternoon before they went out to dinner. Today was all about sightseeing, and she was excited because Thiago had hired a private driver so they could hit the major attractions. The tour would last all day and included lunch.

Satisfied with her appearance, India exited the bedroom. "You're so impatient," she said.

Thiago grumbled something in Spanish.

"What did you say?" India asked.

"I said you look beautiful."

"And I was worth the wait?" she asked.

"Let's go, shall we?" Thiago extended his hand.

She curled her fingers around his. "I'll take that as a yes."

"Believe whatever you like," he said.

India rolled her eyes and let him lead the way out the door.

As they strolled down the hall to the elevator, Thiago's phone rang. "Hello?" he answered.

Pause.

He came to an abrupt stop. "When?"

India searched his face for a clue as to what was going on. His eyes locked with hers, and a faint smile broke out on his face. "How are Skye and the baby?"

He listened for a moment.

"Well, congratulations. When Skye wakes up, tell her I said congratulations too. Make sure you send me a picture, but I'll stop by to see my new niece when I return to the States." Thiago hung up and resumed walking. "My brother Ethan and his wife Skye had their little girl a few hours ago. They named her Angel."

"Mother and daughter are fine?" India asked.

He nodded. "Both are sleeping. Ethan is going to send a photo of the baby."

"Congratulations, Tío Thiago. How many nieces and nephews do you have now?"

"Audra has five, and Ethan's makes six. When Bruno and Marissa have their baby next month, that will be seven." He frowned, suddenly realizing how much his family had expanded. "If this keeps up, I'm going to need a spreadsheet to keep track of birthdays."

India burst out laughing. "If you can handle running a multi-million dollar company, you can keep up with those birthdays."

Chapter Twenty-Five

B efore India and Thiago reached the lobby, his brother sent a photo of the newest member of the Connor-Santana clan—a red-faced little girl, eyes closed and swaddled in a white blanket.

"She's adorable. She has the right name. She looks like an angel," India said, returning Thiago's phone to him.

"Yes, she does," he agreed, taking one last look before tucking the phone in his pocket.

Their driver, Bernardo, was waiting in the lobby. He was a tall, slender man with chestnut-brown skin.

"*Bom dia,*" he greeted them.

Then he led the way to a white air-conditioned vehicle and opened the door so they could slide into the back.

On the way to their first destination, India took photos of Rio de Janeiro in all its colorful, noisy glory. She captured bougainvillea spilling over balconies in public and private spaces, entrepreneurs selling street food under bright umbrellas on the sidewalks, and the art painted on the sides of buildings.

Their first stop was the Christ the Redeemer statue atop

Corcovado Mountain. Bernardo dropped them near the ticket entrance, where vendors were selling inexpensive souvenirs. India purchased a few items before she and Thiago took the tram to the top. It transported them through the Tijuca National Forest, one of the largest urban forests in the world.

When they arrived at the summit with the other passengers, the statue loomed high above them, impossibly tall with its arms stretched wide. Beneath the clear blue sky, the white stone appeared to glow. With visitors milling around, India tipped back her head and stared up at the magnificent structure. Excluding the pedestal, it was 98 feet high and was the largest Art Deco-type sculpture in the world.

Thiago stepped up beside her. "Incredible, no?"

"Incredible doesn't begin to describe it," India replied.

"Stay there. I'll be your photographer."

He took her phone and crouched down to capture the monument above while she struck a pose. They took additional photos with her near the railing, with Rio sprawled behind her, and then it was time to move on.

Their next stop was Escadaria Selarón, a tiled staircase in the Lapa neighborhood, whose popularity exploded after the music video "Beautiful" by Pharrell Williams. The design was a gift from Chilean artist Jorge Selarón to the Brazilian people. The steps blazed with color, each riser decorated with mismatched tiles in bright reds, yellows, and blues. Some were painted with flags, while others contained faces or patterns.

India's artistic eye appreciated the complexity of the project. Trailing her fingers along the cool ceramic, she marveled at how chaotic yet harmonious the combination of colors appeared.

"The design reminds me of a quilt. I want a couple of photos on the steps," she said, handing Thiago her phone.

She waited for a couple to finish snapping their pictures and then sat on the step they had abandoned.

Thiago crouched low, capturing her against the rainbow of colors. After several clicks, he showed her the images.

"I like these better than the ones at Corcovado Mountain," he commented.

"I do too," she agreed.

Taking her hand, Thiago then led her around the artsy neighborhood, where they browsed the small stores lining the streets. India spent extra time in one shop in particular where they sold unframed art and handmade jewelry. She bought rings and bracelets for herself and Kiara and a couple of prints to hang on the wall at home. She purchased souvenir T-shirts for Josh and her godsons at another location.

Their leisurely walk took them to the Metropolitan Cathedral of Saint Sebastian. Completed in 1979, it was the seat of the Archdiocese of Rio de Janeiro, and its majestic design was inspired by the Mayan pyramids.

When they stepped inside, Thiago dipped his fingers in the holy water at the front and traced the sign of the cross over his forehead, chest, and shoulders, quietly adding, *"En el nombre del Padre, del Hijo, y del Espíritu Santo."*

India was struck by his reverent tone—in stark contrast to the clipped precision of his business voice—and the humility demonstrated by his bowed head. He was different. Still powerful but softened by the ritual. She was witnessing yet another facet of his personality and felt a twinge of shame at how she had casually dismissed his faith two days before.

When they ventured deeper inside, she gasped at the gorgeous stained glass windows that stretched from the floor to the ceiling.

"This is huge," she said in a hushed voice, looking around in wonder at the vast open space.

"The sanctuary holds up to 20,000 people," Thiago said, keeping his voice equally low and respectful.

They didn't take photos there, and after they left, they walked to a nearby restaurant for lunch. Afterward, Bernardo picked them up for the final destination on their day-long tour —Sugarloaf Mountain.

Located at the mouth of Guanabara Bay, a trip to the top offered panoramic views of the city and the water beyond. As the cable car carried them to the granite peak, India clutched the railing, a little nervous when the ground fell away beneath them.

From behind, Thiago placed a hand on either side of her on the railing. "You're not afraid of heights, are you?" he asked, his voice a low rumble in her ear.

"I never thought so until this very moment." India laughed nervously, her fingers tightening on the steel bar.

"Don't worry. Thousands of people take this trip every day. It is perfectly safe," Thiago said, amusement lacing his voice.

When the cable car stopped, and they stepped out, India decided the view at the top was worth her accelerated heartbeat. As the wind whipped around them, she inhaled a deep breath and sighed. "Wow."

Thiago slipped an arm around her waist. "*Esto es Rio.*"

India lost track of how much time they spent up there. As they admired the view, Thiago pointed out Copacabana Beach, Christ the Redeemer, the blue water of the Atlantic, and the jagged mountains rising in the distance. They took plenty of photos and then had drinks at one of the restaurants before heading back down the mountain.

As Bernardo drove them back to the hotel, India nestled against Thiago in the back seat, scrolling through the pictures on her phone. Each image held a piece of the day—her smiling beneath Christ the Redeemer, sitting on the tiled steps, and finally holding tight to the hat on her head as the wind whipped around them on Sugarloaf Mountain.

This short trip had been exactly what she needed, and she wished they had more time.

At the hotel, they showered and changed clothes, then went downstairs to the poolside bar and enjoyed pre-dinner drinks while people-watching. Later, when they caught a taxi to a restaurant down the beach, the sun had dipped low, painting the city in amber and fiery red.

Like a typical churrascaria, the establishment was bustling with servers in crisp uniforms moving between the tables with skewers of sizzling meat. This particular location, however, featured a buffet with an incredible array of seafood, such as *moqueca*, a Brazilian fish stew, grilled fish, huge shrimp, mussels, and more. They ate until full, with Thiago teasing India after she surrendered her plate while he went back for thirds.

Night had fallen by the time they left, the strip along Copacabana Beach lit up by street lamps and the glow of lights from cars and buildings running parallel to the water.

"Let's walk back," India suggested.

Thiago frowned. "Our hotel is more than a mile away," he said, concern in his eyes.

"So? It's our last night in Rio, and I want to walk along the beach." Instead of waiting, she took off without him.

"A mile is too much after such a long day," Thiago called after her, following at a slower pace.

India glanced over her shoulder. "I can handle it."

After a few feet, she looked back again. Thiago was strolling along, his hands tucked into his pants pockets.

"Can't keep up?" she teased.

"I'm enjoying the view," he replied, his eyes sparkling.

India pouted. "I don't want to walk alone."

He quickened his pace to walk beside her. "If you get tired, I'll carry you."

"Deal."

They removed their shoes and let them dangle from their fingers. Side by side, they strolled the length of the beach, the cool grains sliding between India's painted toes. The breeze rustled Thiago's hair and whipped the hem of her dress around her calves.

Along the way, they encountered other pedestrians—a couple walking their dog on a leash, friends laughing and talking animatedly, kids running toward them ahead of their parents.

Nearing the Copacabana Palace, India remarked, "See, we're almost back at the hotel. You were worried for no reason."

"I am still worried," Thiago said without hesitation. "If you so much as stumble, I will throw you over my shoulder."

She laughed. "Like a caveman?"

He gave her a half-smile, his eyes glinting with humor. "You would complain the whole time, but I would ignore you because I know you'd secretly love it."

She sighed dramatically. "Your arrogance knows no bounds."

"Am I wrong?" he asked, his voice carrying easily over the roar of the surf.

"I'm not answering."

"Then the answer is yes," he said with confidence, taking her hand.

His gaze swept over her face, sending a flutter through her chest. Her body knew what was coming and wanted it.

They put on their shoes and, hand in hand, walked onto the boardwalk. At a lull in the traffic, they hurried across the street to their hotel. The elevator was almost full of guests when India squeezed in, followed by Thiago. The throbbing between her thighs heightened now they were almost to the room.

Thiago's fingers brushed hers, a quietly intimate move no one else saw, which turned the throbbing into a deep-seated ache.

The ride up seemed to take forever, the cabin stopping several times to let passengers off on lower floors. By the time she and Thiago arrived at their room, heat had spread throughout her limbs, and her stomach clenched.

Thiago lifted her from the floor and sank into an armchair. India straddled his thighs, his hard length pressing against her core, deepening the aching need to be taken by him.

"Are you sure you're okay? Are you sure...?"

India undid his belt. "I'm fine. I promise."

She pressed her lips to his, and Thiago held her face, kissing her long and deep. His lips slipped hungrily over hers, his tongue delving into her mouth to dominate and possess.

As the fingers of his hand slipped into her hair, India lowered the zipper on his pants. Lifting up on her knees, she shoved aside the crotch of her panties and settled onto his hard dick, moaning her relief.

Her body stretched around his girth, and she began to ride him in a desperate race to ecstasy. Thiago groaned in response, gripping her hips and undulating his pelvis beneath her so their bodies moved in time to a silent, erotic rhythm.

Wrapping her arms around him, India moaned louder, squeezing her eyes shut as his soft mouth and the drag of his beard caressed her sensitive throat.

Her lips parted on breathless pants as she pumped harder. This was the closest she could come to telling him about her true feelings without actually whispering words of love.

She was an ambitious, independent woman who had fallen in love with her boss—not her brightest move to date. She had surrendered her heart to a gruff, arrogant man who didn't even want it.

But until he pushed her away, she would savor every moment in his arms, including this one, where he had her body on fire. Where his lips stoked desire and made every inch of her ache for relief.

When she came, it was sudden and forceful. His name fell from her tongue in a husky scream of surrender. Thiago's mouth covered hers. He swallowed her cries as their bodies bucked against each other.

Finally, India buried her face in his neck, her arms squeezing tight as spasms rocked through her in the aftermath of her orgasm.

Every time with him felt like the first time. This was where she belonged—wrapped in the arms of this man, Thiago.

No one else would ever do.

Chapter Twenty-Six

"Are you okay?" Thiago asked India.

Since their return from Brazil last Sunday, he had been keeping an eye on her. She and her team had met in his office that afternoon, and the meeting had already wrapped up, but he had asked her to stay behind under the pretense of needing to discuss some of the marketing figures. The truth was, he suspected she wasn't well.

"I'm fine."

"You don't look fine." He had become attuned to the changes in her voice and heard the subtle strain.

"Nothing major. My joints are a bit stiff."

She rolled her shoulders and laughed to minimize the weight of her words, but now that he knew she had lupus, there was nothing funny about her answer.

"Go home. You're done for the day," Thiago said, rising from the chair and walking away from the conference table.

"Excuse me?"

He turned to see the expression of disbelief on her face.

"I have way too much work to do—"

"You're done, India." He hated having to repeat himself.

Slowly, she rose from the chair and clasped her hands together. "Thiago, you're being ridiculous."

"*I* am the one being ridiculous?" he scoffed.

When she opened her mouth to protest, he stepped forward, staring into her eyes and daring her to argue with him. He didn't mind their verbal sparring. He appreciated that she was no pushover, but he was not going to tolerate her stubbornness when it came to her health.

India sighed resignedly. "Fine. I'll go."

"Thank you."

"I'm not an invalid," she muttered with a pout, like an adorable, petulant child who hadn't gotten her way.

"I know." He dropped a soft kiss on the middle of her forehead. "Go. I will check on you on my way home."

"All right, I..." Her voice trailed off, and she looked down at her phone, a frown emerging on her brow.

"What's wrong?"

"Nothing. I received another text," she said.

"What do you mean *another* text? From who?" Thiago moved closer, but she covered her screen. Considering their newfound closeness, he was sorely offended. "If someone upsets you, they upset me," he said.

"There's nothing for you to be upset about."

"Yet your expression tells me otherwise."

India eyed him as though struggling with the decision to divulge what was on the phone. Finally, she said, "Promise me you won't get upset."

"Whenever someone says those words, I am certain I will be upset. Therefore, I will not be making any such promise."

She blew out a breath of frustration. "Why are you so difficult?"

"I could say the same to you. What are you hiding from me?"

"I'm not exactly hiding anything from you, but I... It's a text from Simon."

"Simon? Why is he texting you? You did tell him—"

"Yes, of course I told him that I was seeing someone else seriously. I told him weeks ago."

"Then why is he texting you?" Thiago demanded.

"He seems to be having a little difficulty accepting the break."

"I know exactly how to make sure he accepts the break," Thiago said in a menacing way.

"Your reaction is the reason why I didn't tell you, but I don't want there to be any secrets between us. Please, let me handle Simon," India said.

"You mean how you have handled him thus far?"

She rolled her eyes. "I have the situation under control. Don't stress me out more than I already am. You know I have lupus." She smiled.

Thiago narrowed his eyes at her. "How convenient. Now you want to use your disease to shut me down, to protect another man."

"I'm not trying to protect him, but I don't want his messages to be a big deal. I will talk to him, okay?" Her eyes pleaded with him to understand.

"How many times has he been in touch since you told him you were moving on?"

"I haven't counted. He sent flowers one day, and he's texted a handful of times."

Now was the time to come clean about what he had done. "There is something you should know about your doctor friend. I hired a private detective and had him investigated—"

"You had him investigated? Oh, this should be good." She crossed her arms, her face settling into firm lines.

"Do you remember how two minutes ago you told me you didn't mention he was contacting you because you were concerned about my reaction? Well, for the same reason, I didn't tell you that I had him investigated. I didn't see the point since you had ended your relationship with him. Now I see he has been keeping in touch, that changes everything.

"The investigation uncovered a couple of parking tickets and a speeding ticket from two years ago. All minor. What interested me were the accusations made by his ex-wife. After their marriage ended, he continued to text her and send flowers. Then, according to her, shortly after he saw her with another man, he became violent. One day, he smashed her car windows. Another time, he flattened her tires and threw a rock through the window of her home. The good doctor denied the charges, and the restraining order his ex-wife requested was denied since there was no proof he had done any of those things. Fortunately for her, a few weeks later, he moved to Atlanta to work at the hospital."

India's eyebrows drew together. "He doesn't give off stalker energy. I'm genuinely shocked."

"Which is why I should be the one to talk to him."

"No," India said immediately.

"Why not?" Thiago demanded.

"From what you said, it sounds like the behavior escalated when he saw his wife's new man, and if you talk to him, I *know* you'll piss him off. It's better if I handle the situation. I'll give Simon a call and politely but firmly ask him to stop contacting me."

"Politely and firmly sounds like the right way to deal with a stalker," Thiago said in a dry tone.

India pursed her lips at him. "If my method doesn't work, then you can get involved."

Thiago didn't like her plan, but at least she lived and parked in a secure building. He also knew her well enough to know she wouldn't budge. He locked eyes with her to ensure she understood the gravity of his next words.

"You have until tomorrow to talk to him. If he gives the slightest hint that he will not accept what you say, let me know. Then *I* will talk to him. I will walk right into the hospital where he works and make sure he understands you are off-limits."

"Got it, but I doubt you'll have to get involved. Now, I'm going to take your offer and go home."

Thiago captured her chin between his fingers. "I know you are accustomed to taking care of yourself, but you have me now. If this man gives you any problems, or if anything seems out of the ordinary in the coming weeks, you let me know right away. Am I clear?"

Her face softened with appreciation. "Yes, and thank you. I promise I'll let you know if my car is vandalized or anything else odd happens."

"I hope so. And do not take any work home. Get some rest. I will stop by later."

"I'll see you later."

He kissed her briefly and watched as she walked out of the office. When she was gone, he rounded the desk and sat in his chair.

They'd had a wonderful time in Brazil, and since they'd been back, their relationship was stronger than ever, but he didn't like that Simon continued to reach out to her. As a man, he knew what that meant. Simon hadn't accepted she had moved on, and being nice only encouraged the doctor, making him think the door to their relationship was still open. India would have to put her foot down hard to make sure he understood he didn't stand a chance with her.

As for Thiago, he meant what he had said. He would go to speak to Simon if he didn't leave her alone. He would check in with India to make sure she did talk to him. In the meantime, he wanted to ease her burden at work.

He hadn't known much about lupus before their conversation in Brazil, but since their return to the States, he had done his research.

While the average person's immune system helped them fight infection and disease, for people like India, the immune system actually attacked the body, causing inflammation and leading to lupus flares and potential long-term damage. The disease destroyed the body's organs and was completely unpredictable.

In addition to learning more about the disease, he also understood how the steps India took helped minimize her symptoms. He wanted to help her but couldn't let her know. She was proud and independent, but he already had ideas.

Picking up the phone, he called his assistant into the office.

Amir arrived with his iPad and an electronic pen in hand, stopping in front of Thiago's desk.

"I need you to work on a couple of projects that I think will boost morale and increase productivity. Here's what I want to see happen." Swiveling his chair to the right, Thiago crossed his ankle over his left knee. "I want to institute a new program in the company. It will be a wellness program, and we need a name. If the program works here at our U.S. headquarters, we will roll out the idea to the entire company. First, we're going to start offering in-house massages to staff as a way to help with stress. Anyone who needs a break can book a massage."

"Will there be a limit to how many massages staff can get in a week?" Amir asked, his pen poised above the tablet screen.

"No. If they need one, they can have one."

Amir raised his eyebrows in surprise. "Aren't you worried some people will abuse the policy?"

"There is always the possibility for abuse, but I trust staff to use their judgment and will not make everyone suffer because a few may take advantage. Second, we'll have some kind of wellness room. We'll also need a name for that. It will be a place where staff members can go to meditate or get a mental reset. The room has to be quiet and away from the chaos of work so they can take a true break."

"Yes, sir."

"Third, find a company that specializes in ergonomic workstation consultations. I want everyone to have their workspace checked to make sure it's comfortable and reduces physical strain. They need the right chairs, wrist support, proper monitor height—that kind of thing. There should be enough money in the office equipment budget to cover any purchases. Have operations contact me if there's a problem."

"Yes, sir."

"Finally, we're going to implement yoga sessions."

Amir looked up. "Yoga, sir?"

Thiago stared at him. "Yes, yoga."

"Right," Amir murmured, going back to writing.

"Find a qualified yoga instructor who can come in several times a week for anyone interested in taking classes. There is an unused room in the gym downstairs that could probably be used for the classes, but I'll let you and operations figure out the details. I want a rollout of the wellness program by the end of the week."

"So soon, sir?"

"Is that a problem?" Thiago asked.

"No. Not at all. The end of the week is plenty of time."

"Pull in anyone you need to help. Make sure they understand the request is coming from me."

"I most certainly will, sir."

Thiago tapped his fingertip on top of the desk. Was he missing anything? "That's all for now," he said. He could always implement additional ideas as they came to him.

"Got it," Amir said with a nod. He left and quietly closed the door behind him.

Chapter Twenty-Seven

"Come on in," Bruno said, stepping aside so Thiago could enter.

Thiago had driven to the outskirts of Atlanta to visit his older brother, a restaurateur and famous chef. He followed him into the kitchen, a bright, spacious showpiece with stainless steel appliances and all sorts of equipment.

"Where is Marissa?" Thiago asked, switching to Spanish to talk to his brother. He took a seat on one of the stools in front of the nine-foot waterfall island in the middle of the kitchen.

"In bed. She's not feeling well," Bruno replied, moving over to the stove.

Bruno had met Marissa when, ironically, he had contacted the matchmaking company where she worked to find him a wife. None of the women she chose for him worked out, and she and Bruno ended up falling in love.

"She's almost due, isn't she?" he asked.

"Overdue," Bruno corrected. "The doctor suggested they might have to induce labor."

Thiago didn't know what the process entailed, but it didn't

sound good. "Mother often complained you were a late baby," he reminded his brother.

"Like father, like son," Bruno replied with a shrug and a laugh.

"And where's Theodore?" Thiago asked, referring to Marissa's son from a previous relationship.

"At his father's for the weekend."

"Do you and his father still get along?" Thiago asked.

"We have an okay relationship, which is the best we can hope for at the moment. He wasn't pleased when Marissa told him about her pregnancy. As you know, before I came along, he had hoped they would get back together."

"He shouldn't have cheated on her, then," Thiago remarked.

Bruno hummed his agreement and placed a plate of food in front of Thiago. "I hope you're hungry. I made plenty."

"I'm starving," he replied.

Bruno fixed himself a plate and sat down while Thiago poured them each a glass of wine. "So, what brings you out here?"

"I wanted to see my brother and sister-in-law," Thiago said.

"Nice try. I know you, remember?"

Thiago chuckled and tasted the wine. Replacing the glass on the counter, he asked, "Have you ever met India Monroe? She's the vice president of marketing at Santana International."

Bruno took a moment to think. "Once, I believe, when I went to Father's office. Did she take a leave of absence a long time ago?"

Thiago nodded. "She's the one. Happened five years ago, and I found out why recently. India has lupus, and she was hospitalized for a while, and when she left the hospital, she needed time to recover. Father held her job for her. She's fully recovered now but still has the disease, of course. There's no cure."

"Is there a problem with her?" Bruno asked, slicing into the chicken breast on his plate.

"She and I are in a relationship."

Bruno lifted his gaze from the plate and stared at him. "Tell me you're kidding."

"I'm not."

"For how long?"

"We started sleeping together almost a year ago, and recently we've become serious."

"This is a surprise. I always believed you were married to your work."

His singleness was a running joke in the family. Before India, he had slept with plenty of women but had the same arrangement: no commitment, no promises. Just sex.

He wasn't a complete jerk, but he was never seen with anyone on purpose. Out-of-the-way dining spots, vacations on private yachts—those were the norm. He also had the women he slept with sign NDAs that prohibited them from disclosing any information about him or their relationship.

Most women couldn't tolerate such an arrangement for very long, so the excitement fizzled after a while, and eventually, they moved on if he didn't end the relationship first.

"I took her to Brazil a couple of weeks ago, and she had a great time. We started in São Paulo and spent a couple of days in Rio. I showed her my watch collection."

Bruno raised an eyebrow as he chewed but didn't comment. He didn't have to say a word. Thiago understood his surprise because his watch collection was not something he shared with many people—certainly not a casual lover.

"Sleeping with India was not my best decision, but I don't regret it. There's something about her. She's tough, smart, and doesn't put up with my crap. She's also sexy as hell." He shook his head at that last part.

"I sense a but coming."

"Not a but. More of a hesitation. I'm thinking about asking her to take our relationship public at Monica's wedding next month."

He was tired of hiding. He wanted to walk into the church with her on his arm and introduce her to his family and friends. He longed to spend time with her in public, dining in the open instead of private rooms. He had even suggested they return to Brazil next year for Carnival, telling her it's the greatest show on Earth and that she needed to see it.

Every time they went out or sneaked a kiss at work, they risked being discovered. As the CEO and the man in the relationship, he would be fine. She, however, could have her reputation tarnished.

"How do you think she'll feel about letting others know about your relationship?"

"I have no idea. We've never discussed it, but I know it could be problematic for her."

"Female subordinate sleeping with the boss kind of thing?"

"Exactly. There's also another hiccup. She was dating another man for a short period before I told her I wanted exclusivity. She broke things off, but he continued contacting her. She recently told him in no uncertain terms that it's over and that she has moved on. According to her, he took the conversation well, and she hasn't heard from him since."

"How long has it been?" Bruno asked.

"Only a few days."

"Not very long."

"I agree, and I have concerns. My gut tells me this guy isn't done yet, and I'm worried going public will make him resurface and cause problems." He told his brother about the accusations Simon's ex-wife made.

"What's your plan? I know you have an evil plan," Bruno said with a smirk.

"I'm thinking of breaking his neck."

"Don't joke like that."

"Who says I'm joking?"

Bruno stared at him in a disapproving big brother way. "Isn't martial arts supposed to teach discipline and self-control?"

"It does. It also teaches how to break necks."

"Set aside Plan A, breaking his neck. What's Plan B?" Bruno tore off a piece of bread and popped it in his mouth.

"She and I go public and deal with the fallout." Thiago ate a baby corn.

"I like Plan B better, and you can control when and where you make the reveal."

Thiago ate more of his vegetables. "Maybe. I know we can't continue like this. I find myself doing things for her I haven't done for any other woman. She's been to my house and spent the night. For some reason, I want this relationship to be normal and out in the open."

Bruno studied him for a moment. "You know why," he finally said.

"What do you mean?"

His brother sat back and let the silence speak.

Thiago laughed, shifting uncomfortably in the chair. "No. You, Ethan, and Ignacio have fallen, but me—no. Maxwell and I will be bachelors for a very long time."

"Maxwell, maybe. You? Sounds like your days are numbered."

"No." He shook his head vehemently. "Love and marriage are not in my five-year plan."

"No one ever plans for love and marriage. They club you on the head and drag you away whether you want to go or not."

"How romantic. I see why Marissa fell in love with you."

Bruno laughed. "I'm serious."

"So am I."

"Okay, Mr. Confirmed Bachelor, do you want to end up like Father? Alone in your sixties, regretting you lost the woman of your dreams?"

"I won't be alone, and you know as well as I do why Father is. He didn't like being told what to do and revolted, just as he did with Mother."

"Mother was a different situation. They were toxic together. His marriage to Mama Rosa lasted a long time, but now he's alone, wishing he had made a different choice. All because she wanted to spend more time with him."

Thiago couldn't argue there. Their father had miscalculated, putting work and business before his marriage.

"Have you heard from Mother?" Thiago asked.

"The last time I spoke to her, she was still in California but said she would fly in as soon as the baby is born. Marissa is nervous about meeting her."

"I don't blame her. I understand Mother's desire to see her grandchild, but the whole idea of the visit feels off. She never came for the wedding, and all of a sudden, she's excited about being a grandmother. She was barely maternal."

Bruno's face turned thoughtful. "People change," he said.

"Maybe," Thiago said with a healthy dose of skepticism. "She didn't bring what's-his-face, did she?"

Their mother had been in a committed relationship with a man thirty years her junior for over three years. None of them liked him and viewed him as an opportunist, but Valentina wouldn't hear a negative word about him. After a while, they gave up trying to talk sense into her.

"She left him behind," Bruno replied.

"Good."

The sound of movement at the kitchen door caught Bruno and Thiago's attention. Bruno lifted his gaze, and Thiago turned around to see Marissa in the doorway, one hand supporting her large belly.

She flinched. "It's time," she said.

Bruno hopped off the stool and rushed to her side. "The baby?"

She nodded vigorously.

His brother turned to look at him. "Thiago, I—"

"Go! I'll lock up before I leave. Get out of here."

Marissa shot a grateful smile at him, the fingers of one hand gripping his brother's forearm.

Thiago followed them into the entryway and watched as Bruno removed a travel bag from the top of the closet and threw it over his shoulder. Then he helped his wife out the door, leaving Thiago behind.

He stood in the doorway until the car pulled off the property and then returned to the kitchen. He scraped what was left of their meals into the trash and placed the plates and other dishes in the dishwasher. When he was done, he stood in the silent kitchen, reflecting on what he had witnessed a few minutes before. His brother was about to become a father for the first time.

Did he want what Bruno and Ethan had? A wife and a baby?

He had never thought much about those things before. A family could derail his plans. Children needed care and attention. So did a wife, for that matter. For years, Thiago had only been concerned with reaching the upper echelon of his father's company and making more money. No woman had ever made him consider giving up his freedom.

Until India.

If he did pursue the life his brothers had, there was only one person he could imagine being with. Which meant Bruno was right, and he'd been living in denial and could no longer hide from the truth.

He was definitely, unequivocally, in love with India Monroe.

Chapter Twenty-Eight

"Whose car is that?" Rose asked, eyeing the dark sedan parked in Bruno's driveway, hoping her suspicions were wrong.

Balancing two foil-covered pans on one arm and a bag filled with items for the baby in the other, Benicio replied, "If I had to guess, I would say Valentina's. Bruno warned me she might be here."

"Warned" was the right word, and Rose's stomach tightened with dread. She had looked forward to spending time with her daughter-in-law, son, and their new baby boy, but Valentina had already arrived. She was Benicio's first wife and the mother of his three boys—now men—Bruno, Thiago, and Ignacio—whom Rose had come to love as her own when she married their father. Despite the wonderful relationship she had with her stepsons, the few times she'd met Valentina over the years, the other woman never hid how much she disliked Rose.

"Are you going to be all right?" Benicio asked, watching her closely.

"I'll be fine. I'd walk through fire to see my grandchild."

They had originally seen their grandson when he was first born at the hospital. That had been a short visit, and she looked forward to spending more time with him tonight.

She balanced a basket of fresh vegetables against her hip and led the way into the house.

As soon as they entered, she heard voices in the kitchen and went in that direction, immediately encountering Bruno and his mother. Mother and son stopped talking as soon as they entered.

"Good evening," Rose said in a bright voice.

"What is all this?" Bruno asked. He approached and took the basket from Rose.

"A little something to get you through the next couple of days. Fresh vegetables from the garden. I also cooked a few meals so you wouldn't have to worry about that while you're getting settled with the baby."

"I told her you don't need this food, but did she listen to me? No." Benicio placed the containers on the island.

"And I told him that even chefs need a break, especially when they have a newborn," Rose said.

Bruno pulled her into a warm hug. "Thank you, I appreciate you going to so much trouble. *We* appreciate it."

"You're welcome, my dear." Rose patted his back.

"How quaint of you to bring food," Valentina said, a thin smile curving her lips. "I suppose if I had nothing to do all day, I could do the same—cook for a man who is a Michelin-starred chef."

Tension heightened in the room.

Rose clasped her hands in front of her. "Hello, Valentina."

"Rose."

A glass of white wine pinched between her manicured fingers, Valentina looked like she had just stepped out of a salon. The former actress's glossy black hair tumbled past her shoulders and was held out of her face with sunglasses perched on her head. She wore cream slacks, a silk blouse, and a light cashmere sweater tied over her shoulders. Elegant and posh, she made Rose feel severely underdressed in her comfortable jeans and simple gray shirt, and decidedly frumpy with all the gray streaking through her hair.

Bruno shot his mother a look and picked up the food. "Are you ready to see the baby?" he asked, placing the container inside his stainless steel refrigerator.

"That's why we're here," Benicio said, stepping closer to Rose and placing a comforting hand at the base of her spine, which she appreciated.

She knew better than to let Valentina get under her skin, but somehow she always managed to do so.

"Follow me," Bruno said.

They moved into the living room, where Marissa was sitting on the sofa holding her son in her arms. Her russet-brown skin was makeup-free, and her hair pulled back into a neat bun. Though she appeared put together, Rose saw the lines of strain around her mouth.

"Oh my goodness, look at his little face and those full cheeks." She sat next to her daughter-in-law and rubbed her back. "How are you?"

"Tired. Happy. Excited. A lot of emotions at once."

Marissa was not close with her parents, so Rose had been as involved as possible without overstepping her bounds. This was Marissa's second child, but she had wanted her daughter-in-law to know she was available for support if needed.

She laughed. "It doesn't get any easier, does it?"

"No, but I can't wait to see the personality my new little guy has," Marissa said, gazing down at her son.

"Before you arrived, Bruno was about to explain the name

they have chosen—Liam Manuel Santana." Valentina sat in an armchair and crossed her legs.

Bruno remained standing. "Marissa has always liked the name Liam, and we added Manuel for my father's father."

"He would be honored if he were alive," Benicio said with a wistful smile.

"I was surprised by the choice. Liam. It is a very anglophone name, no?" Valentina's eyes landed on each person in the room.

Marissa glanced at Bruno, shifting uncomfortably on the chair as she rocked the baby.

"There is nothing wrong with my son's name," Bruno said stiffly.

Valentina lazily swirled her wine. "Sí, but a nice strong name can make the difference in a person's destiny. I gave all my boys strong names. And look, you are all very successful."

Rose couldn't believe Valentina was being so rude as to complain about Liam's name. "I like the name Liam," she said.

Valentina shot her a scathing look. "You would."

"That is enough, Valentina," Benicio snapped.

Her head whipped in his direction. "Of course you defend her. This woman has inserted herself into our family—"

"Inserted?" Bruno interjected, his face turning thunderously dark with fury. "She raised us."

Valentina looked as if she'd been slapped, red brightening the crests of her cheeks. "I knew it was a mistake to come here. I simply wanted to be supportive and see my first grandchild, but of course, I have to put up with the insulting comparisons between me and this... this woman!"

Benicio's jaw tightened. "This woman was my wife, and she helped me raise our sons."

Her gaze fixed on Rose, like a hawk sizing up a rabbit. "Ah

yes, she was perfect. Some of us worked hard for our wealth, others married into it."

Marissa gasped quietly.

"Enough, Valentina. Rosa is a good woman, and if you took the time to get to know her—"

"Rosa this, Rosa that. You are pathetic. That is not even her name. Her name is Rose, for God's sake!"

"Mother, stop this now!"

"I will not stop!" Valentina's voice rose louder with a cutting edge. "Why is she here? I am your mother! She knew I would be here. Why can't I have a few moments alone with my grandchild before she inserts herself into our family business? Why does everyone act as if she is so perfect? The perfect wife. The perfect mother."

"Because she is!" Benicio thundered, surging to his feet. "You sent the boys to live with me, and I met Rosa, and we built a life together. She raised them. When she discovered Bruno's love of cooking, she encouraged his interest and made sure he spent time in the kitchen with her. She taught him how to grow his own vegetables."

"Yet your perfect little wife divorced you, didn't she?" Valentina said with spiteful malice.

"Mother—"

"Don't you dare take her side against me!" Valentina yelled. "I am your mother. You will not treat me like I am the devil, and she is a saint!"

Liam let out a startled cry, and Marissa cradled him closer, rocking him back and forth.

The argument became incomprehensible as Bruno, Benicio, and Valentina lapsed into Spanish. The baby continued to cry, and Marissa's hands shook as she tried soothing him. Liam's face turned red and scrunched as he wailed his unhappiness, completely ignoring Marissa as she tried her best to calm him with whispered words.

Rose shot to her feet. "Enough!"

Everyone turned to look at her as the baby's cries continued to pierce the air.

"Oh good, she's leaving," Valentina said.

Rose spoke in a firm voice and elevated her normally soft tone to be heard above the baby's cries. "No, Valentina, I'm not leaving. You are."

The room went utterly still. Liam quieted to soft hiccupping sobs, as if he understood a monumental shift was taking place.

Valentina blinked, a stunned expression on her face. "Excuse me?" she said, her voice filled with incredulity.

Resting her hands on her hips, Rose met her gaze calmly. "All that talk, but you have a hotel room in downtown Atlanta because, let's be honest, you're not here to help Marissa and Bruno. I don't know why you're here, but I do know they don't need your drama. Marissa has a new baby and needs rest and peace. Bruno is a new father and needs guidance and help so he can support his wife. Liam needs a happy, comfortable home."

Valentina's hand balled into a fist. "Are you saying they can't have those things if I am here?"

Rose drew in a steady breath, keeping her voice quiet and suppressing the anger threatening to spill from inside her. She had never wanted to put her hands around a person's neck more than she did right then.

"That's exactly what I'm saying."

Valentina's mouth fell open, and she clutched her chest in a dramatic display of disbelief. "Who do you think you are?"

"Rose Santana. Mama Rosa. And I don't care if you like me, Valentina, but what you won't do—what I *will not* allow you to do—is upset my son and my daughter-in-law during what should be one of the happiest times of their lives."

Rose took a step closer, her gaze unwavering. "No more insults. No more drama. If you can't adhere to those rules, you should leave. Right now."

Suffocating silence followed.

Valentina looked around the room. No one spoke up for her. No one defended her.

Her chin lifted. "I see," she said coldly, carefully placing her glass of wine on a nearby table. "I know when I'm not wanted." She snatched up her purse and stormed out.

After a moment's hesitation, Bruno went after her.

Rose exhaled a slow breath and reclaimed her seat beside Marissa.

Her daughter-in-law blinked back tears. "Thank you. She's... a lot."

Rose patted her knee. "I know, but don't worry. We've got you."

She felt Benicio's gaze on her and looked up to see him watching her with an expression she couldn't read. Pride, perhaps—or something much deeper.

When Bruno returned a few minutes later, Rose was cradling Liam in her arms.

"She's gone," he said, sounding weary.

"It's for the best," Benicio said.

Bruno nodded. "I'm sorry any of this happened. Are you okay, *querida?*" He dropped into a crouch beside his wife and lifted her hand to his lips.

"I'm fine. Though when you said your mother was dramatic, I didn't know you meant *dramatic.*"

They both laughed, and Marissa leaned in, placing a soft kiss on Bruno's lips, as if to reiterate that she was okay.

"You should take a nap. Sleep while the baby is sleeping,

remember? And Theo is coming home tomorrow, which means we'll be busier."

Marissa looked at Rose, uncertain.

"He's right. Take advantage while we're here to get a few hours of sleep. I don't mind."

Marissa's shoulders slumped in relief. "Thank you. I'll take two hours, max."

"Go," Rose said, shooing her with one hand.

Bruno helped Marissa to her feet. "I'll be right back," he said.

"Don't rush. Take a nap too, if you like," Rose said.

When they were gone, Benicio came to sit beside Rose. He glanced over his shoulder to make sure they were alone, and then he kissed her cheek.

"What was that for?" she asked.

"You were magnificent."

Rose's lips curved up at the corners, and she shifted her gaze to look at the baby in her arms. "I wasn't trying to be. I was just protecting my family."

Chapter Twenty-Nine

The drive to the house passed in silence. One of the benefits of knowing someone for as long as Rose and Benicio had known each other—over two decades— was that words were not always necessary. They could sit in comfortable silence together.

Rose watched the city go by, fingers loosely locked together in her lap. Every now and again, she caught Benicio looking at her from the corner of her eye.

The confrontation with Valentina had happened hours ago, and she was still analyzing it in her mind, surprised by her own actions. She had always been a little intimidated by Valentina, with her big personality and biting words. Tonight, she had stood up to her and wished she had done so sooner.

Benicio was spending the night at the house with her. Monica was overseas, having been invited to promote a new resort along with other influencers. They would have the place all to themselves, except for the staff.

Once inside the master bedroom, Rose sat on the edge of the bed. "I looked up the meaning of the name Liam," she said.

"Did you?"

"I was curious after Valentina made such a big deal about his name and how very important it was to have a strong name because it determined a child's destiny."

"Is that a Spanish accent I hear?" Benicio asked with amusement.

"I might be mocking her a tiny bit," Rose admitted.

He outright chuckled this time. "What did you learn about his name?"

"Not that it matters, but Liam is the short form of the Irish name Uilliam, which is the equivalent of William. When you combine all the elements of his name, Liam means 'strong-willed warrior' or 'resolute protector.'"

"So he does have a strong name after all."

"Not that it matters, but he does," Rose confirmed.

A faint smile remained on Benicio's face. He leaned back against the wall, stuffing his hands into the pockets of his chinos. "You were incredible tonight with Valentina," he said, his voice soft and rough with emotion.

"You like me as a bully?"

"You were not a bully, *mi amor*. You commanded the room without raising your voice. I liked the way you handled her."

"I wasn't trying to handle her. I wanted to protect Bruno and Marissa. And the baby," Rose said.

"Which you did." He stepped closer, a fierce expression on his face. "Like a warrior."

Rose shook her head, folding her arms loosely. "You're exaggerating."

"No," he said in a sharp tone. "You were calm and steady as you stood up to her, and instead of agreeing to behave herself, she ran away. Your strength put her weakness on display. You have always been strong, Rosa, and the center of this family. My center. My home."

Emotion gripped her chest at his words.

Taking a slow breath as though steadying himself, Benicio carefully lowered onto one knee.

Rose's eyes widened, and she hopped up from the bed. "Ben, what are you doing?" Her voice came out breathless.

"What I should have done a long time ago to fix the mistake I made," he said simply.

"Get up. Stop."

She reached for his arm, but he caught her hands, gently but firmly holding her still.

"No," he said, shaking his head, his voice deep and unwavering. "I have lived with regret every single day since I let you go. I don't want to live without you anymore, Rosa."

"Ben..." Her voice trembled, and her heart ached as she looked down into his gray eyes.

"*Mi amor.*" He searched her face, his thumb gently stroking the back of her hand. "I love you, but I squandered my time with you, and I let my pride destroy the best thing that ever happened to me."

Her lips parted, a soft, shaky breath escaping. "Ben..."

"I see clearer now. I see you, my home, my heart, my everlasting love. You are the best part of my life, the reason I wake up every morning. Give me another chance. Let us try again. Marry me. *Por favor.*"

Rose's heart swelled almost to bursting. She cupped his jaw, her thumb gently caressing his bearded cheek. "I love you so much. I'm happiest when I'm with you. Yes. Let's get married again."

Relief flooded his face. Despite his words, he hadn't been confident she would say yes. She kissed his cheeks, his eyelids, and then his lips.

"My love," she whispered.

Benicio pulled her flush against his body, wrapping his

arms around her waist and resting his cheek against her bosom. He held her tight, as if he'd never let her go again.

Finally, they broke apart, and she helped Benicio to his feet. He grunted as he stood, and she laughed softly.

"I am not as young as I used to be."

"Neither am I, but that's okay. We'll grow old together the way we planned from the beginning."

"With all our aches and pains."

"And wrinkles," Rose added.

Benicio sobered. "And laughter. Good times and bad times, and everything in between."

They held hands and gazed into each other's eyes.

"Does this mean I'm officially off the market now that we're engaged?" Rose asked.

"Absolutely."

"When do you want to tell the kids?"

Benicio was quiet for a moment. "After Monica and Andre are married."

Rose nodded her agreement. "Good idea."

"*Mi bella esposa*," Benicio whispered reverently.

Rose raised onto her toes and kissed his lips. "Not yet."

His mouth curved in a slow, dangerous smile of promise. "Soon," he said, his voice husky. "Very soon."

Chapter Thirty

Someone was pounding on the bedroom door, disturbing Thiago from a fitful night of rest.

"Who is that?" India asked, her voice thick with sleep.

"I don't know," he grumbled, rolling away from her soft body to squint at the door in the darkness. "Yes?"

His housekeeper's muffled voice came from the hall. "Mr. Santana, your mother is downstairs in the foyer."

"Your mother?" Hugging the linens against her chest, India pushed onto one elbow.

"Remember I told you she was coming to see Bruno's baby and help Marissa? She flew in a few days ago, but I don't know why she is here at this time of night."

When Bruno had told him their mother was on the way, Thiago had wished him good luck and said he'd say a prayer for him and his wife's sanity. Marissa delivered a healthy baby boy in the wee hours of Sunday morning. Thiago had already seen photos of his nephew, fast asleep against his brother's chest, with a shockingly full head of hair. He planned to see his nephew in person in a few days but wanted Bruno and Marissa to get settled first before he went to the house.

Picking up his phone from the bedside table, he saw the time was ten after one in the morning. Groaning inwardly, he fell back against the pillows and stared up at the ceiling. His mother's presence at this hour could not be good.

"Take her to the den and tell her I will be right there," he called out to his housekeeper.

"Yes, sir."

Reluctantly, Thiago rolled out of bed, and India sat up to watch him get dressed in the dark.

"Something must be very wrong for her to be here at this time of night," she guessed.

"My mother is dramatic, and trouble follows her wherever she goes. The question is, did she cause the problem, or did someone else? One can never tell with her," he added dryly.

He went into the closet and pulled a robe over his pajama bottoms. "Go back to sleep. I will deal with my mother."

India lay back against the pillows, but he could feel her eyes on him as he walked to the door.

He went downstairs and entered the den to find his mother pacing the floor. He was mildly annoyed to have her show up so unexpectedly, but when she turned to face him, the irritation drained from his body. Her eyes were bloodshot red. She had clearly been crying.

"Hello, Thiago. I'm sorry to disturb you so late." The quiver in her voice confirmed her emotional state.

He walked over and placed a concerned hand on her arm. "What's wrong? You look like you've been crying."

"I have." She took a shaky breath.

Though he was concerned, Thiago knew very well that his mother was a talented actress. She didn't get as many job offers as she used to when she was younger, but he remembered how well she portrayed every role she accepted. For Valentina Arango, the world was a stage, and as a child, he had seen her histrionics contribute to the death of her marriage to his father.

Valentina sat down, dabbing her eyes with a crumpled tissue.

"Can I get you something to drink?" Thiago asked.

She shook her head, crossing one leg over the other and resting her folded hands on her knee.

"I've had a terrible night. I went to see Bruno to help him and Larissa with the baby."

"Marissa," Thiago corrected.

"Yes, right, Marissa. Rose and Benicio showed up. Rose kicked me out, and Bruno and Benicio let her."

Thiago sat down across from his mother, confident he had only heard part of the story. "What really happened?"

"You think I'm lying?"

"Mother, it's after one o'clock in the morning, and you came here for a reason. What's going on?"

He saw a flicker of vulnerability, a signal all was not well beyond what had happened at Bruno's house.

Valentina dropped her gaze. "I'm broke." She spoke in such a low voice, he barely heard her.

Thiago straightened in the chair, the unexpected confession taking him aback. "What do you mean?"

"Broke. As in, I have no money—hardly any money left. Because of Marco."

Marco Reyes was Valentina's lover, a man thirty years younger.

"How did you lose all your money because of Marco?"

Tears welled in her eyes. "It started small, with trips and expensive gifts. Then he asked me for money to invest in various businesses. We were a couple, so how could I refuse him?" Her voice wavered, and she wiped a tear from the corner of her eye. "Your father gave me a lump sum payment after we divorced, which I invested in legitimate businesses. I had done very well for myself, if I do say so. Coupled with the occasional acting part, I was comfortable. At my age, directors are not calling like they used to, so I was careful with my expenditures —until Marco. He took the money I gave him for those so-called businesses and spent it on himself and his friends. He made a fool out of me. He made me feel young and alive and pretty again. I know it's ridiculous, but it's the truth. I'm an old fool, Thiago."

Her vanity had been her downfall. He had never seen his mother so raw and honest. "You are beautiful," he insisted.

She waved a hand at him dismissively. "You're only saying that because you're my son."

"I'm saying it because it's the truth. You're also smart because you managed to maintain a comfortable lifestyle all these years despite no longer having regular work. You should be proud. That's impressive, Mother. Marco is a charlatan, and he took advantage of you."

He and his brothers had been worried about this very situation. They had never trusted her lover, but she'd been dismissive of their concerns, expressing anger when they suggested he had ulterior motives.

Thiago took a good look at his mother. Really looked at her and truly saw her. She looked frail and helpless, and his heart went out to her.

"Where is Marco now?" he asked.

"In the house I'm about to lose. He and his friends have taken it over. I couldn't stay there. I've been staying with family because he refuses to leave."

Thiago's temper flared. "Why don't you get the law involved?"

She shook her head. "It's embarrassing. I'm hoping he'll leave on his own."

"People like him don't leave on their own. He'll be there until the bank comes and tosses them out. I wish you had told me or Bruno or Ignacio before the situation got to this point."

"How could I tell you?" she wailed. "I had lost everything, and after you boys had warned me about Marco. I was humiliated and couldn't face you, knowing you had been right all along."

"Is that why you came to Atlanta?"

"I came to see Bruno and the baby. I wanted to meet my daughter-in-law."

"*Mother*..."

Valentina's shoulders slumped. "I also hoped your father might..."

Thiago sighed. "You and Father have been divorced since I was a child."

She shrugged. "He used to have a soft spot for me, once upon a time, but when I tried to arrange a meeting with him, he made up excuses for why he couldn't meet me. Then he showed up at Bruno's with Rose! Are they back together?"

Thiago wasn't sure how to answer the question. He and his siblings had their suspicions, but their parents had not stated they had reconciled. "They've maintained a good relationship since the divorce."

"Unlike me and your father," Valentina said glumly.

Thiago held his tongue about who he believed was at fault. "What happened at Bruno's? What really happened?"

Valentina hesitated at first, then told him everything, including how she'd left the hotel where she had been staying because her credit cards were maxed out. At the end, she stared down at her hands and said, "I had hoped to stay with Bruno and Larissa. My bags are in the rental car outside."

"Mother..."

She lifted her gaze, eyes shimmering with tears. The same penetrating, dark eyes everyone said he had inherited. "Don't be mad at me too," she whispered.

Thiago pushed up from the chair and sat beside her. Looping an arm around her shoulders, he pulled her into his side and took on the role of comforter. "You're certain that Marco is at the house now?"

She nodded, sniffing. "He was when I left."

"All right, you're going to stay here for the night. I can't have my mother sleeping in her rental car. Then tomorrow, we're going to the bank, and I'm going to transfer some money into an account—a separate account Marco does not have access to."

Valentina pulled away. "No, I don't want any of my sons to—"

"Would you prefer to ask Father for the money?"

Her lips turned downward into a frown.

"The option of my help isn't open for debate. I won't allow you to go without. *We* won't allow you to go without. I'm going to tell Ignacio and Bruno everything."

She nodded, shamefaced.

"Stay here tomorrow. Relax. I'll go into work and wrap up a few things, then I'm going to cancel all my appointments for the rest of the week because you and I are going to Colombia. I will make sure Marco moves out."

"You're a busy man with so much to do here with the company..." She seemed genuinely distressed.

"The company will be fine," Thiago assured her. "I want you to be okay, and we need to get this man out of your house and out of your life, once and for all."

Her lower lip trembled. "Thank you." She paused. "I've never liked Rose, and I didn't know why. She was always polite to me, and she took good care of you boys. But when she walked in tonight with Benicio, I understood why I never cared for her. She reminded me of everything I had lost. I was watching someone else have my life. She was the mother to my children, and she was living the life I should've been living with your father."

"She is a good woman. She has been a good second mother to us and loves us like her own."

"I love you too. You know that, don't you?" Valentina placed a hand against his cheek.

"Yes, I know." *In your own way*, he added silently. Not everyone was meant to be a mother. Valentina had done the best she could.

Thiago decided to call his brothers in the morning and give them an update about their mother. In the meantime, he had his housekeeper prepare a guest room for her for the night while he brought in her bags.

Once she was settled in the room, he returned to the master bedroom. As soon as he entered, India turned over to face him.

"What's going on? Is she okay?" she asked.

He placed his robe on the chair and climbed into bed. Pulling India into his arms, he answered, "No, but she will be."

Because of their newfound intimacy and the trust between them, he told her about the situation with his mother and what he planned to do.

"How long will you be gone?" she asked.

"As long as it takes to get rid of that piece of shit," he said grimly.

Chapter Thirty-One

"I should be back before midnight," Thiago said, talking to India via Bluetooth as he flew back to the States.

He had spent the last couple of days in Colombia with his mother. He could have waited one more day but didn't want to be apart from India for longer than necessary.

"It's Friday night. You timed your return perfectly," she purred.

He chuckled, relaxing into the seat. She was the first person he thought to call. She was the first person he thought of every morning when he woke up. If she wasn't in his bed, he looked forward to catching a glimpse of her at work.

No doubt, he was definitely in love with her. But how did she feel?

"Thank you," he murmured, accepting the bottled water the flight attendant handed him.

"So everything is all set for your mother?" India asked.

"For now. We're going to keep a close eye on her, checking in more regularly to make sure she doesn't fall for any of Marco's sweet talking again."

"Do you really think she would after what he put her through?"

"I'm not willing to take the chance. I believe she really cared about him, and she might be tempted to give in. If he or anyone else tries to take advantage of her, Bruno, Ignacio, and I will handle the situation."

He and his brothers had pooled their resources, and every month they were going to deposit an allowance into the account he set up for Valentina. They had also paid off her mortgage, so she never had to worry about having a place to live.

"How did you get Marco to leave?" India asked.

"I asked nicely."

"How did you really get him to go?" she asked with a laugh. "Your hands are lethal. You didn't hit him, did you?"

"His friends were easier to get rid of. Money and threats worked fine, but Marco was insistent he loved my mother and didn't want to leave. I convinced him to go with a simple arm bar move, nothing fancy. It's a taekwondo hold. I caught his wrist and turned it just enough to lock the joint, then pressed down on his elbow. He whined like a baby, and I was able to shove him through the door. We had the locks changed the same day."

"I'm sure your mom was happy."

"I'm glad I was able to help her," Thiago said, but he wanted to say more.

India hadn't had a chance to meet Valentina. His mother had slept late, and both he and India were gone to work before she woke up. At some point, he wanted India to meet her and the rest of his family.

When he landed, they needed to talk. Maybe not tonight because he'd be too tired, but tomorrow for sure.

The phone beeped in his ear, and when he looked at his phone, he saw the name Spencer Boyden on the screen.

"I have another call coming in. Business. I'll see you later?" Thiago said.

"Yes, sir."

He groaned. "Promise me you'll say that when you're under me."

"I promise. Take your call, and hurry up and get here," India whispered in a seductive voice.

There was a slight pause, and the words almost slipped from his lips—*I love you.* They seemed like the natural way to end the conversation.

"I'll see you soon," he said instead. He answered the other line. "Hello?"

"Hello, Thiago, how are you?"

The male voice belonged to Richmond Gallagher, a headhunter with Spencer Boyden, an executive recruiting firm out of New York.

Thiago couldn't remember when exactly he had met Richmond. Probably at a networking event. Over the years, he had learned that connections flourished when sweetened with generous incentives, so to get first dibs on top candidates, he gave Richmond perks, such as the occasional free vacation at one of his homes around the world and a regular supply of $500 bottles of Don Bene tequila.

Thiago ran his fingers through his hair and stifled a yawn. After dealing with his mother's problems, for the first time in a long time, he was running on fumes. He didn't think he had gotten more than four hours of sleep while in Colombia.

"I'm good. And you?"

"Fine and dandy. Happy summer's almost here."

"Do you have big plans?"

"My wife and I are taking the kids to Hawaii this year.

She's always wanted to go. You don't happen to have a place there, do you?"

"No, I don't. Why did you call?" Thiago sipped his water.

"Two reasons. Let me get the first one out of the way. I heard a rumor that you guys are going public. Is that true?"

Thiago bit back a sharp retort. Why couldn't people keep their mouths shut? The fact that Richmond, all the way up in New York, had heard rumors of them planning to issue an IPO meant the information had been leaked. Many more people likely knew about their plans. None of the other executives had mentioned staff asking about the IPO, and no one on the staff had approached him yet, but it was probably only a matter of time.

"I don't know what you're talking about," he said.

Richmond laughed. "I understand, you have to keep your moves quiet until you're farther along. Good luck with every-thing. Now for the second reason I called. Are you looking to fill any positions at the company?"

"Not at the moment, but if you have a good candidate, send over their CV like you always do, and I'll hold on to their infor-mation for when there is an opening."

"Really? You might have a vacancy soon enough, and I could help."

Thiago frowned. What was he talking about? "If there's someone you want me to look at, send their information."

"It just so happens a great candidate came across my desk recently. Fantastic candidate with stellar credentials. I thought of you immediately, though she caught the eye of one of our other clients looking for a vice president of marketing," Rich-mond said with meaning.

Thiago, who had barely been paying attention, froze.

He was giving Thiago a hint about India, but he had to be wrong. Why would she be looking for work outside of Santana

International? She loved her job, and besides, he was at the company. They were lovers. Leaving the company meant leaving him, which would be a bitter, unexpected betrayal.

After a low chuckle, Richmond continued. "Between us, this candidate already has an offer on the table from a firm in Miami. Happened a week ago."

Thiago's ab muscles contracted. "When exactly did this amazing candidate submit her resume to your company in search of work?"

Richmond rustled some papers. "Back in... looks like March eighteenth," he answered.

More than two months ago, and she never said a word. Thiago was under the impression they had become closer and opened up to each other. He'd shown her his watch collection, which many people might consider excessive, but he treasured it because of the history behind each piece. He had shared his past and explained his family dynamics. He'd opened his home to her.

She had also opened up to him, telling him about the estrangement with her father and her struggles with lupus. How could she not tell him she was looking for work? More importantly, how could she not tell him she had been offered a job? They spoke regularly and had spoken only moments before. Did she intend to keep this a secret until the last minute?

She had also kept the continued contact from Simon a secret, a little voice whispered.

"Thank you, Richmond. This has been an enlightening conversation. I always appreciate you letting me know about the incredible pool of talented executives in your database."

"I love my job bridging the gap between employers and employees. If what I hear about this candidate is true, I figured her current employer wouldn't want to lose her. They might want to counter any offer she receives."

"Yes, they might. I appreciate the call. I'll send you a bottle of Don Bene on Monday."

"Perfect. My in-laws are visiting next week, and a bottle of Don Bene will impress the hell out of my father-in-law. Appreciate it, *hombre*. Talk to you later."

Thiago disconnected the call. Remaining very still, he kept going over the conversation in his mind and circling back to one glaring fact.

India was good at keeping secrets.

Chapter Thirty-Two

India paced the living room with the phone to her ear. She had been restless all night, unable to sit still or concentrate. She had big plans and needed to talk to Kiara about her decision.

"Hey, girl," Kiara chirped when she answered.

One of her boys was crying in the background.

"You sound busy," India said.

"I'm not. Josiah is throwing a tantrum because I wouldn't let him eat a dead fly."

India laughed. "The life and hard times of a one-year-old."

"Tell me about it. What's up?" The sound of the crying toddler faded as her friend moved away from him.

"I want to have The Conversation with Thiago about our feelings and our future. What do you think? Am I crazy?" She had taken a shower a few moments before in anticipation of Thiago's arrival and continued pacing the living room in her lavender kimono.

"Crazy in love," Kiara quipped.

"I'm serious! You would tell me if I'm being an idiot, wouldn't you?"

"Of course, and you're not being an idiot. You're the smartest person I know."

"How smart was I to fall in love with my boss?"

Having a good friend like Kiara meant being able to bare her soul, and when she'd told Kiara she was in love with Thiago, her friend hadn't judged. Instead, she'd asked her what she loved about him, and India had paused, heat filling her cheeks as she expounded.

"I respect him. I respect his toughness and his drive. And there are moments—glimpses of genuine human kindness that peek through the tough guy act every now and then. He has a wicked sense of humor. He always smells good. His laugh is... addictive. His smile is gorgeous. He's gorgeous. It's obvious he cares a lot about his family. They're close, and any man who loves his family like that, who shows such respect and deference to his stepmother, can't be all bad."

"He's definitely easy on the eyes," Kiara said.

"I already said he was gorgeous, Kiara."

"I'm just agreeing," her friend said, laughing mischievously.

"Stop being so hard on yourself," Kiara scolded.

India sighed. "I don't plan to embarrass myself and profess my love for him, but I at least want to know where we stand, to know if we're on the same page, you know what I mean?"

She didn't need bold promises or a grand declaration of love right now. She simply wanted clarity, enough to know if the man who had become the center of her universe saw her as more than a sexual indulgence.

"I do. Basically, is this relationship going somewhere? Leading to marriage, maybe?"

"Exactly. You understand what I mean." She stopped and stared out the window. "Of course, there's the other issue."

"The job offer."

"Yes."

"Well, you wanted to know you had options, and now you know you do."

When Thiago had threatened her job during their argument about Simon, she contacted the headhunter to test the waters and see if she could find a job elsewhere, to confirm she wasn't stuck under Thiago's thumb.

"Yes, except Bridge Tech is persistent, though I've told them I'm not ready to leave my current employer. They think it's a negotiation tactic and offered more money. They're basically holding the job for me, and I didn't tell you everything. The job is in Miami, Kiara."

"Oh." She heard full disappointment in her friend's voice. "That sucks."

"Yeah. So if I accepted and left Santana International, I'd have to move out of state."

"Well, you've moved for a job before. You moved back here to work for Santana International, and I was happy to have my best friend back in town."

India had been working for a South Carolina firm when she applied for the job as director of marketing, which eventually led to her role as vice president of marketing.

"If I move, I won't see you and Josh anymore. I won't see my babies Jayden and Josiah or my new baby on the way."

"You won't see your Mexican baby, either," Kiara said pointedly.

"Him too," India admitted in a quiet voice. "I only contacted the recruiting firm because Thiago's asshole comment scared me and made me feel as if my position could be in jeopardy."

"Sleeping with your boss does have drawbacks."

India turned away from the window and started pacing

again. "Our relationship is different now. We're closer, and I've seen sides of him I never believed were possible. He created a wellness program, the Renew Initiative, at the company, which the staff appreciates. I'm fairly certain he created it because of me. He incorporated several of the methods I told him I use to keep my symptoms under control."

"Josiah, put that down! This damn boy. Hang on, India." Kiara put the phone on mute for a bit. "Okay, I'm back. Has Thiago told you he made those changes for you?"

"No, but I can't think of any other reason why he would add those specific benefits."

"So what are you saying?" Kiara asked.

"I'm saying, I'm going to talk to him and find out where his head is concerning us, and if he says what I want to hear—what I need to hear—then I'll give Bridge Tech a final no and tell them in no uncertain terms to move on."

If he didn't say the right words, she couldn't stay and face him every week. She'd had her health scare, and coupled with her mother's death and her own precarious health, she had truly come to appreciate that tomorrow is not promised. She wanted to live life to the fullest, and for her, at this stage in her life, that meant getting married and possibly having at least one child, if she could get her lupus under control.

"Come on, Thiago, give the right answer. I need my girl to stay in Atlanta," Kiara said.

India smiled and walked toward her bedroom. "Let me finish getting ready. I don't know what time Thiago will be here. He said he'd arrive before midnight, and I want to be ready whenever he comes."

"Call me tomorrow and let me know how your conversation went," Kiara said.

"I will, and kiss my godsons for me," India told her.

She hung up and tried to psych herself up. She had nothing

to be afraid of. She and Thiago were adults and could talk candidly about their feelings and the direction of their relationship. She finished getting dressed, pulling on a pair of bottom-hugging jeans and a form-fitting blouse. She brushed her hair and added small hoop earrings before spritzing perfume on her wrists and neck.

By the time Thiago rang the doorbell, she was torn between excitement at seeing him and anxiety for the conversation they needed to have.

India opened the door wide. "You made it before midnight. You get a treat." She flung her arms around his neck and kissed him.

He seemed stiff and didn't kiss or hug her. When she pulled back, he barely looked at her and wasn't smiling.

Her smile faltered.

Thiago didn't respond to her effusive greeting, not even with his customary grunt. He stepped into the apartment with his usual elegance, but this time it was wrapped in a chill that made the room suddenly feel colder.

India quietly shut the door and watched him from the entryway for a few seconds, her chest tight and heavy.

Had something happened since they talked on the phone?

Thiago's gaze swept over her in a detached, impersonal way. She couldn't understand the expression on his face. The coldness.

And why no kiss? Why no warm smile? That's not how they greeted each other.

"Everything okay?" India asked carefully. "Your mother? Your family...?"

"My family is fine. Everyone is in good health," he answered in a clipped tone.

"Wonderful." India hesitated as she watched him. "Can I fix you a drink?"

"No." The short, blunt answer was another indication something was amiss.

She cleared her throat. "You seem off. You were in a much better mood on the phone earlier."

"I must be tired," he replied.

He didn't look tired, but his eyes were unreadable. He wasn't simply watching her, he was studying her. Beneath the cotton shirt molded over his muscular chest, his body appeared coiled tight, as if he was preparing to spring into action.

India clasped her hands together, undeterred from the conversation she intended to have. "Let's sit in the living room. I'd like to talk to you about something."

"Talk." He said the word in a mocking way, and his mouth curved into an expression that wasn't quite a smile. "Yes, we should definitely talk."

His tone alarmed her. He was upset, at her, perhaps? But what did she do? They hadn't spoken since he took the business call.

India followed him into the living room. Instead of sitting, Thiago remained standing, so she followed suit.

She laughed nervously. "Is something wrong? Are you sure you're just tired? You seem upset."

"What did you want to talk about?" Thiago asked.

She inhaled deeply and released the breath. Clearly, he had no intention of answering her questions. Swallowing hard, she pushed past the pounding of her heart and started. "I've been thinking about our relationship. I know we didn't start out in the conventional way, but over the past few months, we've become closer and developed a deeper connection."

"Become closer? Developed a deeper connection?" He repeated the words with silken sarcasm. "Interesting choice of words, considering..."

Confused, India stared at him. "Considering what?"

"Considering you cannot be trusted. Considering you keep secrets."

"What the hell are you talking about? Get to the point," India said irritably.

He smirked. "I had a very interesting chat after you and I ended our conversation earlier. I heard from a reliable source that you had a job offer. In Miami." Cold accusation gleamed in his eyes.

Shiiiiit. India's stomach plummeted. "Who told you?"

"So it's true." His voice was steel.

"I was going to tell you."

Thiago looked at India in a dispassionate way. "When, exactly? Wait, don't tell me—tonight, right? Or were you going to wait until you signed the employment contract? No, no, probably better to wait until your bags were packed."

"*Stop.* I didn't mention the offer because I wasn't sure if I'd accept. Our conversation tonight was going to help me decide. I wanted to know where we stood before—"

"Before you left me?" Thiago finished, his voice flat.

"You're twisting everything," she accused.

He chuckled, but the sound was empty, mirthless. The laughter stopped as suddenly as it began.

"I thought I knew you," Thiago said.

"You do know me."

"No, I do not. You are a stranger to me, someone who hid a major decision, allowing me to believe we had something special. Something real."

India gulped back the pain. How had the conversation become so twisted? She hadn't expected their talk to be easy, but this—this was devastatingly difficult and not going the way she had hoped at all.

"I don't want to leave. I would prefer to stay in Atlanta and continue working for Santana International."

"So then why did you send a recruitment firm your CV? Your response does not make sense, *mi amor*. Clearly, you were ready to leave the company—leave me behind."

"Did someone at Spencer Boyden leak my job search to you? Because that would be extremely unethical."

"Answer the question."

India wanted to scream and pound his chest. "You don't understand," she said, shaking her head.

"Oh, I understand very well." Cold fury glittered in his dark eyes. "You didn't tell me about your lupus until you had no choice. You didn't tell me Simon was still contacting you until I forced the issue. I suppose I should question if you truly ended your relationship with him at all. And now this, a new job, a new city. Secrets, secrets, and more fucking secrets. Why should I trust anything you say?"

His words stung. "You're being unfair."

He laughed derisively. "I am being honest. Something you know nothing about."

The fingers of both her hands bunched into fists. "Do you want to know why I sent my resume to a headhunter? Because you threatened to fire me if I didn't stop seeing Simon. What did you expect me to do? I needed a backup plan in case you followed through on your threat."

His expression froze, muscles tightening until his face looked like it had been carved from granite. "You thought I was going to fire you?"

"You said you would."

"And because I said—"

"Yes!" India snapped.

"Is that what you think of me? That I am a blackhearted monster?" Thiago asked.

"I only know what I see."

His jaw hardened, his spine going ramrod straight.

The silence between them stretched to an uncomfortable length, vibrating with all the words they had said and those they hadn't.

"Are you taking the job?" he asked quietly, tension woven through every syllable.

"I don't know. I—"

"Are you taking the job or not?" he demanded.

"Yes! I'm going to take it!" India snapped. She hadn't meant to give that answer, but he'd forced her hand. "It's a good opportunity for me, with a pay increase and the possibility of a promotion in a few years. You're smart and ambitious. Tell me I wouldn't be a fool to pass on it."

"Good for you." He spoke slowly, dragging each word like an anchor across stone.

Her heart shattered into tiny pieces. "I'll give my official notice on Monday." She kept her voice cool and crisp to hide the emotions threatening to overtake her. She needed to hold it together and not embarrass herself in front of him.

"Don't bother," Thiago said, his voice colder than ice. "Your position is terminated effective immediately."

Her breath caught. Staring at him, she searched for a flicker of softness or regret. Anything to indicate he was the man she had fallen head over heels in love with. But there was nothing. Only his impenetrable mask of icy control.

"Thiago—"

He brushed past her without another word, his dismissal like shards of glass piercing her skin. She hurt everywhere.

She turned to watch him leave. Tall, broad-shouldered, uncaring that she was dying inside.

Shaking, she followed, hoping he'd have a change of heart. Hoping he'd say he had overreacted. Neither happened.

Thiago walked out, and she stumbled to the security monitor near the door.

In the past, he always looked up at the camera or turned back, offering one last glimpse of his magnificent features. Tonight, he did neither.

He strode down the hallway and out of her life.

Her throat ached, and she gulped back the pain, blinking furiously against the tears burning her eyes.

India tried. She really, really tried to hold it together, but her strength deserted her. She crumpled to the floor, and the dam broke, deep sobs rocking her body as she pressed her palms to her eyes and cried.

It was over.

Chapter Thirty-Three

Thiago drove his fists into the heavy bag, the sound of flesh hitting leather echoing in the empty gym.

He had come in early, not bothering with gloves this time. He wanted to feel each blow—the sting of his knuckles splitting, the pain of bone striking against the resistant outer shell of the bag.

He'd lost track of how long he'd been in there. His breathing was hard and ragged, sweat crawling down his forehead and into his eyes as he pivoted and struck with lethal force, again and again.

The pain should keep him from drowning in memories he couldn't escape, but no matter how many times his fists landed, he couldn't beat back the images of India. He couldn't stifle the scent of honeycomb soap and guava hair conditioner that clung to the walls of his bathroom and lingered in his lungs, torturing him, though she hadn't stepped foot inside his home in what seemed like an eternity.

Each day this week, he had walked into Santana

International without a glimpse of her in the hall or the sight of her captivating walk as she strutted into his office in one of her monochrome designer suits. She was gone for good. He would never see her at the company again.

Thiago growled low in his throat and landed a series of rapid blows, each one harder than the last. Sweat rolled down his back, and his knuckles screamed in protest, but he kept punching, ignoring the pain. Welcoming it.

Finally, his strikes slowed, muscles burning and knuckles throbbing. He let his arms fall loosely to his side and rested his forehead against the bag. Squeezing his eyes shut, he took deep breaths into his lungs.

God, he missed her.

Thiago stumbled back and collapsed against the wall. Lifting his hands, he examined the torn and bruised skin, mesmerized by the blood smeared across the back of his hands. The pain finally registered, but it was nothing compared to the tightness that wouldn't leave his chest.

He had felt this before, when he had thought he was losing her, only this time the sensation was worse because he *had* lost her. His chest cavity felt too small to accommodate his grieving heart.

He pushed away from the wall and shuffled toward the showers. Employees would start arriving soon. He couldn't allow them to see their CEO in such bad shape.

* * *

"Your father is here to see you," Amir said.

His father? He hadn't seen him in the office in weeks. Before Thiago could reply, Benicio strolled into the office and closed the door.

Thiago put down his pen to give his father his undivided attention. "Hello, Father. What are you doing here?"

"I came in to work today and thought I'd stop by and say hi. You still haven't put any guest chairs in front of your desk, I see."

"And I don't plan to. Do you need something?" Thiago asked.

"Let's sit over here, shall we?" Benicio directed him to the sitting area between his desk and the conference table. Benicio sat down and stretched his arm across the back of the sofa. "Have you talked to your mother lately?"

Thiago sat opposite his father. "Two nights ago."

"How is she?"

"Better."

"Bruno told me what you and your brothers did. I had no idea Valentina was in serious financial trouble."

"None of us did, and she wouldn't have been if she'd listened to our warnings about Marco. Of course, he turned out to be much worse than we had anticipated."

"Some people have to learn the hard way, but at least she's better now," Benicio said. "I went by India Monroe's office, but I was told she no longer works here."

"She found a job in Miami. Company named Bridge Tech." He had done some digging and learned the name of the firm that had stolen her away from him.

Benicio's eyebrows jumped higher. "I'm surprised. I always believed she enjoyed her job here. Have you started looking for her replacement yet?"

She's irreplaceable, Thiago thought. "Not yet. I'll give Spencer Boyden a call soon to see if they can find someone for us. In the meantime, her staff has been picking up the slack."

Benicio nodded slowly. "What happened to your hands?"

Thiago dropped his gaze to his bruised and red knuckles. "I went to the gym this morning, and I forgot my gloves."

"You've been boxing since you were a boy. You've never forgotten your gloves."

"I did today," Thiago lied.

A beat passed.

"What happened between you and India?" Benicio asked, and that's when Thiago realized his father knew everything.

"Bruno told you?"

Benicio nodded.

"You're upset."

"Disappointed. You know better than to sleep with a subordinate."

"It just happened."

"A sneeze just happens. Sex—for months—does not just happen."

Thiago rubbed the back of his neck. "Fair enough. I can confirm our relationship was consensual, but I may have said something... I messed up."

"What did you do?" Benicio asked.

Thiago blew out a breath and told his father everything—minus the graphic sexual details—from the time he and India slept together, her dating other men, his ultimatum, which he swore he didn't mean, their trip to Brazil, and their painful breakup. When he finished, he sat and waited for judgment.

"Well, you've been busy."

Thiago laughed, and his father chuckled in response.

"Do you know why I never had serious relationships with women? Because I saw what happened with you and Mother and then you and Mama Rosa—how they always wanted more of your time. I love to work. I love a challenge. To me, nothing is better or more satisfying than to have a goal and smash it. I didn't want a woman coming between me and what I loved."

Looking off to the side, Benicio didn't speak at first. After a few moments, he met Thiago's gaze. "What are your fondest memories growing up?"

Thiago was confused by the question. "What do you mean?"

"Do you remember with fondness all the times I stayed away because of work, or the times I flew down to see you and your brothers in Colombia—if only for a few days? What about when I came to your kickboxing matches, or the time I arrived late to see you win the spelling bee in ninth grade? Do you remember those times?"

"I do."

Thiago remembered all those events and the joy he'd experienced when his father was present. The day of the spelling bee was particularly vivid because Benicio had been working on a lucrative contract with a company in another time zone. He had told Thiago he wouldn't be able to come, and he'd been disappointed but hopeful a miracle would allow his father to wrap up his business early and attend.

He had been sad during the first thirty minutes when he looked out into the audience and didn't see his father, despite other family members being there. Then he experienced excitement when he saw his father striding down the aisle, still dressed in his suit, take the empty seat next to Mama Rosa.

"I understand the importance of spending time with family, but work is important too."

"Of course, but there has to be balance. How many more women like India will you lose because you can't loosen the reins a little?"

Thiago swallowed. He didn't want anyone else. He wanted India. He wanted the woman who wasn't afraid to glare at him when he pissed her off or smile at him with those sexy lips and warm brown eyes and make him believe that walking through life alone was a mistake. He wanted the woman who had made him understand that the reason he had prioritized work and hadn't settled with anyone else was because he'd been waiting for her.

"How do you feel now that you've lost her?" his father asked.

Thiago buried his head in his hands. "I can't breathe. My chest hurts. I miss her so much. I feel as if... as if..."

"As if you're missing a limb?" Benicio supplied.

Thiago lifted his head. "*Yes*. Tell me it gets easier."

Benicio shrugged. "It gets easier, but the emptiness never goes away. Some days will be worse than others, but you'll always feel as if you're missing a limb."

"I wish you had lied to me."

Benicio smiled and leaned forward, resting his elbows on his knees. "Do you love her?" he asked gently.

"Love is too tame a word," Thiago admitted huskily.

His obsessive need to hold onto her and keep her for himself had been love all along. He'd simply been too blind to see.

"Then go get her."

"I doubt she'll want me."

In the past week, he'd picked up the phone no fewer than a dozen times to call India. Each time, he had placed it back on the table. He had never considered himself a coward, but deep down, fear of rejection kept him from dialing her number.

"That's a chance you'll have to take, isn't it, son? For once, you'll have to humble yourself. Pride caused me to lose your stepmother. Pride made Valentina almost lose everything instead of facing the truth about Marco. Pride, son, is a terrible crutch to lean on, and do you know what it leaves behind? Regret. Let me tell you, regret is the heaviest load a man can carry. It doesn't just crush you. It gnaws at you, following you into every room and whispering in your ear at night when you're lying in bed, *alone*. It's impossible to live comfortably with regret."

Long after his father was gone, his warning echoed in Thiago's head and inspired him to act. He was a fighter, and he was not going to lose India for good—not to pride, not to fear... not to anything.

Chapter Thirty-Four

Her heart was racing.

India sat in her car, parked across the street from a little red brick house. She double-checked the address on her phone to make sure she was in the right place, though her GPS had brought her there.

8255 Treetop Lane. The home of Karl Monroe.

She probably wouldn't have ever come here if she were still working, but she had a lot of time on her hands nowadays, so she'd looked into finding her father instead of crying. She'd never been one to cry much and had spent the past week making up for it. The first few days after the argument with Thiago had been bad, but when her personal effects from work showed up in a box, another bout of sobbing had commenced. At this point, she had cried enough to last ten lifetimes.

She stepped out of her car and smoothed a hand down her dark slacks and straightened the bow at the neckline of her blouse. She had dressed up a little, wanting to impress her father, but did her appearance matter if he didn't want anything to do with her?

"You're here. If it doesn't work out, at least you can say you tried," India said, giving herself a pep talk.

She looked both ways and then walked across the residential street. She climbed the stairs to the front porch and rang the doorbell.

She nervously waited until the door creaked open. A heavyset woman wearing a floral print muumuu peered at her through the storm door.

"Yes?"

India licked her suddenly dry lips.

"Is Karl here?"

"No, he's not, baby. He's at the store..." The woman's voice trailed off as a frown took over her face. "Can I help you?"

She didn't know who this woman was to her father and wasn't sure how to respond. She glanced down the street, hoping he would appear so she wouldn't have to have an awkward conversation with a complete stranger and explain she was Karl's daughter—a daughter she probably knew nothing about.

"My name is India—"

"Indy Monroe! I knew that was you! My name is Verna. I'm your daddy's wife. We got married a few years back." She pushed open the storm door and extended a hand.

India shook it, surprised. "Nice to meet you."

"You got his whole face. Same cheekbones and everything. Would you like to come inside and wait?"

India had never felt so out of sorts and unsure of herself as she did in that moment. Should she go inside and wait or come back another time?

"He won't be long," Verna added, as if sensing her dilemma.

"Sure, I'd love to come inside."

India entered the dim living room—dim because the

curtains were drawn, shielding the interior from the brightness of the sun. Dark furniture, mostly brown and worn, filled the space. The pieces had obviously been there for years, the sweet scent of cigar smoke clinging to the fabric of the chairs.

India's gaze swept the room. Except for a magazine askew on the leather recliner, the place was neat and tidy. But there was no mistaking the pared-down life her father and his wife were living, and sadness filled her. It was far removed from the life she lived but reminded her of growing up in her grandmother's home.

"He talks about you all the time, you know."

Verna's voice pulled India from her thoughts, the words shocking her. "He does?"

His wife nodded. "Since we've known each other. He got a bunch of pictures of you. Let me show you."

Her father had pictures of her?

Verna spun toward a built-in bookcase. As she searched the shelves, India's gaze landed on a couple of drawings hanging on the wall.

"Did he draw those?" she asked, pointing.

"Mhmm. He always drawing something, chile. He has a bunch of paintings too, but he mostly draws now. He's real talented, ain't he? Do you do any artwork?"

"I draw a little. Charcoal, like those."

While she was pleased to see her father hadn't given up on his passion, she wondered how great he could have become if he'd been given the same opportunities as other artists.

Verna removed a photo album from one of the shelves. Moving to the sofa, she sat down and patted the spot beside her. India joined her, leaning closer to look at the first page.

"This was when you was first born," Verna said, tapping a picture. "He said his momma wrapped you in that blanket."

They spent the next fifteen minutes going through the

photos, and there were plenty of them, many India had never seen before. All from when she was a little girl.

"Look at all that hair," Verna said with a laugh.

In the photo, India was sitting between her mother's legs while her mother braided her hair.

She smiled wryly. "I used to hate getting my hair braided." She smoothed a hand over her short hair.

"You took care of that, didn't you?" Verna said, eyeing her short cut.

"Yeah, I did," India replied.

The front door opened, and Karl walked in. "Verna!"

India immediately stood, watching as he closed the door. He looked older than his fifty-one years. His dark skin was lined with wrinkles, and though he was a tall man, his stooped shoulders made him appear shorter.

"Well, hello," he said when he saw her, wiping his feet on the mat inside the door. He rested a paper sack on the table near the door. "Didn't know we had company. Howdy."

India had a sudden, sinking feeling. He had referred to her as "company." She was standing in his house, and he still didn't recognize her. She swallowed back the pain and humiliation.

"Hello." This had been a mistake.

"Karl, put on your damn glasses," Verna said, setting the album down and standing.

"What do I need my glasses for?" Karl groused.

"To see!" Verna shot back. "I can't believe you got behind the wheel of that truck without your glasses on. He only wants to wear them when he's watching TV or doing his art." She shot India a look, as if to say, *See what I have to deal with?*

"I didn't go far, and I know the way. Where are my glasses, anyway?" Karl asked.

"Over there on the table next to your chair. Hurry up and put them on so you can greet our guest."

Karl let out a loud sigh, as if putting on his glasses was an unreasonable demand. He muttered something to himself as he shuffled over to the chair.

Verna rested one hand on her hip. "Hurry up," she said.

"I'm hurrying. Damn, woman." Karl settled the bifocals on his face. "Satisfied?"

He faced India. Then he blinked. He took a step closer and eyed her like a scientist discovering a new species of bug under a microscope.

"Indy?" he whispered in disbelief.

Relief, gratitude, and joy flooded through India. Was that why he hadn't recognized her two years ago? Because he hadn't been wearing the glasses he clearly desperately needed?

"Yeah, it's me," she whispered.

Karl's mouth fell open. He looked at Verna as if needing confirmation. She gave a slight nod, and a smile overtook his face.

"Look at you. If I'da seen you in the street, I woulda walked right by you," Karl said.

You did, India almost said.

"I don't know how. She look just like you. Got your whole face," Verna remarked.

Karl smiled, showing off his pearly white teeth. "Sure does. A prettier version. How you been?"

"Okay."

"Why you here?"

"I wanted to see you. I thought maybe we could..." Emotion clogged her throat.

Her father nodded, clearly understanding the unfinished sentence.

"I would like that," he said quietly. He cleared his throat. "Would you like some iced tea? Verna makes good iced tea."

"I sure do. Everybody loves my tea."

"I would love some," India said.

"Be right back."

Verna hurried out of the room, leaving them alone.

"Would you like to sit down? That couch ain't pretty, but it's comfortable. No, you know what, you can have my chair," Karl said, moving to the recliner and removing the magazine. "Bought it brand new a couple of years ago. Christmas gift to myself. Here you go. You can sit right there." He stood back, presenting the chair to her with an extended hand, like a model during a game show.

India didn't move, though. She couldn't take her eyes off her father. She was in the same room with him for the first time in forever. She didn't feel any of the anger and disappointment she had expected to experience. Instead, overwhelming happiness filled every cell.

"Can I hug you?" Her voice quivered.

His face softened into a smile. "You can hug me for as long as you want."

India moved immediately into his warm embrace and lay her head on his shoulder. He rubbed her back as he held her, and tears welled in her eyes.

Verna came out of the kitchen with three glasses of tea on a tray. A smile of approval touched her lips as she watched father and daughter cling to each other.

Considering her recent breakup with Thiago, India was relieved to experience a moment of true happiness.

She didn't have to report to her job in Miami for another month, and she would spend every moment she could with her father, getting to know him and letting him get to know her.

This new relationship would soften the blow of losing Thiago, and in time—hopefully—thoughts of him would no longer make her heart ache.

Chapter Thirty-Five

"Are we ready?" Thiago asked Amir.

Amir had set up the audiovisual equipment. Nodding, he sat down with the rest of the employees crowded into the conference room. Thiago took his place behind the microphone and placed his hands on the podium.

Normally, he liked to have prepared notes to refer to, but he had decided to speak off the cuff to the thousands of employees around the world via videoconference. The screen in front of him showed images of staff in various locations, waiting for the big announcement.

"Good morning, good afternoon, and good evening to all of you."

He paused for a moment to collect his thoughts and then looked directly into the camera, speaking to each and every employee.

"In the past year since I took over as CEO, Santana International has grown into an extraordinary company. Not solely because of me or any one person or office, but because of each and every one of you watching right now—in North America, South America, and other parts of the world. Each of you has given your time and effort to make this company successful. Thanks to you, we have reached a major milestone. The preliminary numbers will be confirmed in a few weeks at the end of the quarter, but I am pleased to announce we have achieved our revenue goals. Santana International is officially a billion-dollar corporation!"

Applause and cheers filled the room and filtered in from the overseas locations via the screens. They had seized twenty-three percent of Santiago Migos's market share while the company continued to struggle with the fallout of the tequila scandal, surpassing Santana International's goals for the quarter.

Thiago waited until the commotion quieted down. "Despite the good news, that's not why I requested this company-wide meeting, the first of its kind. For months, you have probably heard whispers about what's next for our company. You may have heard we were planning to take Santana International public, and yes, I considered that route. In the end, I realized something important: we do not need Wall Street to define our worth. We already know our value."

There were a few gasps and whispers from some staff, including members of the executive team, who appeared bewildered as they looked around the room and came to the realization that his goals had changed.

"I do not wish to reduce our company to numbers on a quarterly report. We are much more than that. Our strength was, is, and will always be in the talent and dedication of the people who show up each day, solve problems, build relationships with our vendors, and simply make us one of the best companies to work for and work with.

"So today, I am announcing a new chapter at Santana

International. One that I know the previous CEO, my father, Benicio Santana, would be very proud of. In honor of his vision of a company that stands for more than profits, instead of selling shares to strangers, we are going to invest in each other. We are going to invest in you. Starting at the beginning of the fourth quarter, we will launch a profit-sharing program delineated by region. Bonuses will no longer be limited to the top executives. All permanent employees will share in the profits of their individual region—from the mailroom to the boardroom."

More gasps and big smiles as the admins and other support staff processed the information.

"This is not a gift," Thiago continued. "This is recognition. You are the heart of our organization, and when you put in the work, you should share in its success. Details will be forthcoming from your managers and supervisors, but I wanted to thank you myself for your efforts. You have earned this. The future of Santana International belongs to all of us, and together, we will continue to win and succeed. Thank you."

Half the room shot to their feet and started clapping. More cheers could be heard on the screens as the international locations also celebrated.

Standing at the podium, Thiago experienced a great sense of accomplishment.

He only wished India could have been there to share the moment, which simply didn't feel complete without her presence.

* * *

Late in the afternoon, Thiago cruised along the highway in his red Ferrari Roma. This morning's announcement had gone well. He'd felt a moment of self-satisfaction when staff heard the news, instead of what they had expected, which was the *we're going public* speech. Seeing their reactions, he had no doubt he had made the right decision, and his father had been ecstatic when Thiago called and told him of the change.

Now he was on his way to India's apartment. On the seat beside him were peace offerings: *arepas con queso* from Bruno and chocolate chip cookies with macadamia nuts from Mama Rosa. He hoped they were enough to get him in the door.

Traffic was tight as he pulled onto India's street and crawled to a stop at the traffic light a couple blocks away. The light turned green, and he slowly accelerated, when he saw India up ahead on the sidewalk.

Then he registered the man with her. He grabbed her arm as she tried to walk past him.

Simon.

With a surge of anger, Thiago hit the brakes without thinking. The car jerked to a stop in the middle of the street. As he hopped out of the vehicle and slammed the door, horns blared behind him.

"Hey, what are you doing?" someone yelled.

"This ain't no damn parking lot!" another person yelled.

He ignored the commotion and took long strides toward India and Simon, his eyes zeroed in on where the doctor gripped her arm so she couldn't get away.

"I said, let go of me!" India yelled, pushing at Simon and simultaneously trying to yank her arm out of his grasp.

"Hey!" Thiago yelled.

Both India and Simon swung their heads in his direction.

"Thiago!" she said with relief.

Simon's face twisted with annoyance.

"Let her go," Thiago said.

"What is your problem? You're just her boss."

"I said, let her go." Thiago stopped just a few feet away

from them, his body tense as he barely restrained the urge to hit the guy.

"Get the hell out of here. She doesn't need you!" Simon shoved Thiago in the middle of the chest.

Thiago snapped.

His fist whipped out and connected with Simon's jaw. A clean, sharp jab that knocked the doctor to the pavement with a thud. He lay sprawled on the ground, his body unmoving.

India gasped, pressing both hands to her mouth. She dropped to a crouch. "Oh my goodness, what did you do? You didn't kill him, did you?" Tentatively, she shook Simon by the shoulder.

Thiago knelt beside Simon's still body and pressed two fingers to his neck, checking his pulse with a practiced touch.

"He's not dead. If I wanted to kill him, I would have hit him in the temple."

As a martial artist, he knew a temple strike was a particularly dangerous move. The skull bone is thinner in that area, with an artery running underneath. A blow to that part of the head could cause a skull fracture, brain bleed, or even death.

India stared at him. "You said that way too casually. What do we do? We can't leave him here."

Thiago's attention was drawn to the curious onlookers, several of whom had taken out their phones and were recording from a safe distance. "I'll move him inside. Call an ambulance."

Holding Simon under the arms, he dragged him the short distance to India's apartment building, and the doorman followed them inside.

"What happened to him?" he asked.

Thiago propped the unconscious doctor against the wall. "His face collided with my fist."

India hung up the phone. "An ambulance is on the way."

"When he wakes up, tell him if he touches her again, next

time I won't stop at one punch." Thiago handed the doorman a C-note and then ushered India out the door.

"Where are we going?" she asked.

"I need to move my car." He nodded in the direction of his vehicle.

"You left a two hundred and fifty thousand dollar car in the middle of the street?" she asked, winding through traffic alongside him.

He shrugged as he opened the passenger side door. "I had something important to take care of," he said, looking directly into her eyes.

Her lips turned up a little at the corners as she slid onto the car seat. A good sign if he ever needed one.

When he settled behind the wheel, she asked, "What's this?" She held the paper sack with the two containers inside on her lap.

"Something for you. I'll explain when we get upstairs, if that's okay?" He paused, their gazes meeting.

"Upstairs?"

"If you don't mind."

A beat passed.

"No, I don't mind," India confirmed.

Relieved, Thiago parked in the garage below street level, and they took the elevator up to her apartment. Inside, he felt immediately as if he had come home after a long, arduous journey.

The familiar floors, the dining area where they had eaten their meals, the sunken living room where they relaxed afterward, all brought back a flood of memories.

He followed India into the kitchen.

"So, what are you doing here, Thiago?" she asked.

"I came to talk."

"About...?"

"Us. Before we get started, I said I brought you something." He removed the glass containers from the bag. "Bruno made arepas. They're best when eaten right after they're cooked but still good if we heat them up. My stepmother sent you a batch of chocolate chip cookies with macadamia nuts. Tonight marks the end of the reign of oatmeal raisin." His lip curled up in mock disgust.

"I'll be the judge of that, thank you very much. Are you going to join me?"

"Yes, I will," Thiago said.

"I'll get the plates." Her eyes softened and another smile, broader this time, touched her lips before she turned away.

For the first time in a long time, hope stirred in his chest.

Maybe he wasn't too late.

Chapter Thirty-Six

I ndia placed the last piece of cookie in her mouth, cognizant of Thiago's laser-focused gaze across the table. She finished chewing and swallowed.

"Well?" he asked.

She purposely took time to answer, as if she had to think long and hard. "The arepas were delicious. I could definitely eat those again."

"And the cookies?"

"The cookies..."

Seconds ticked by.

"India!" he exclaimed impatiently.

She giggled. "All right, they were delicious! Oatmeal raisin has been dethroned."

"Thank you!" Thiago threw up his hands with exaggerated finality.

After some additional laughter, they both fell silent.

"I heard you established a profit-sharing policy."

"I only announced the plan this morning. How did you find out?"

"I still have contacts at Santana International," India replied. "It's a great idea."

He nodded. "Profit-sharing is good for the company. It boosts morale and lowers turnover."

"That's not why you did it," India said.

A statement, not a question. She had come to realize Thiago enjoyed the role of gruff overlord, but his complex personality included a softer edge beneath the steel, which most people never saw. He often spoke about numbers and efficiency, and though he could be harsh at times, he was also quietly generous, exhibiting pragmatic compassion when it was least expected.

"No, that is not why I did it," he admitted quietly.

India cleared her throat and stood. She picked up her dishes and came around the table to collect his.

"Thank you," he said.

"You're welcome."

She took the plates and glasses into the kitchen, using the time to shore up her defenses for the conversation ahead. Having Thiago there felt good but was extremely difficult. She had missed him and wanted to touch him—anywhere. She longed to run her fingers through his soft hair or stroke his beard as he held her in his arms.

Taking a fortifying breath, she pushed away from the sink and left the kitchen.

Thiago was standing at her desk in the living room. "You're drawing again," he said, holding up two sheets of paper. One contained a raven on a tree branch, and the other was a halfway completed image of a hummingbird.

"Yes. I took your advice and went to see my father."

He carefully returned the pictures to the desk and gave her his undivided attention. "What happened?"

"We got along. Turns out, he didn't forget about me. As I

grew older, he became embarrassed about his financial situation. He believed I was better off without him since he hadn't contributed much to my life—his words—but he was always proud of me. He just didn't see where he fit into my world. Of course, I made sure he understood I love him, he's my father, and he will *always* fit into my world. Oh, and the reason he didn't recognize me at the gas station is because he can barely see." She laughed, shaking her head. "He wears bifocals and didn't recognize me without his glasses."

"I'm glad you found out because I was angry at the man for no reason. Has he seen your work?"

"Yes, and he acted like a proud papa. He sketches, like I do, and he also paints. I told him I would work on a marketing plan for him to see if we can generate publicity and get him some sales."

"If anyone can help him, it's you," Thiago said.

"Thanks." India smiled faintly. "You said you wanted to talk?"

"Yes." He paused. "I don't know where to begin."

"Try the beginning."

"The beginning..." Thiago rubbed his hand across his jawline. "Okay. Did you accept the job in Miami?"

"Yes."

His Adam's apple bobbed up and down. "I don't want you to leave, India. I want you to stay here and continue working for Santana International. Stay here with me."

"We're past that point, don't you think?"

"I will match whatever they offer you in salary, benefits, and bonuses."

India laughed, but it was a hollow, empty sound. "You weren't saying this two weeks ago."

"Because I was a fool. I was angry you were trying to leave me, and when I found out you had a job offer, I felt betrayed."

"Can you understand why I called the headhunter? You threatened my career. My livelihood."

His face filled with shame. "I know. It was a shitty thing to do, and I'm sorry. I hurt you and scared you, and I hate myself for it. I used my power in a way I shouldn't have, and it was unforgivable. I know that." His voice roughened. "But despite what I said, I never intended to follow through on my threat. Your job was never in danger. I swear to you."

"There was no way for me to know, Thiago."

"I understand, but can you understand how I felt when I found out about your job offer? I thought we were closer, and it seemed you were keeping yet another secret. You hold so much back. I still don't understand why you took so long to tell me you had lupus."

India shrugged. "I was afraid."

"Of what?"

"Maybe you wouldn't... want me anymore." During their time apart, she had analyzed her actions and come to this sobering conclusion.

"How could you think such a thing?"

"I have an incurable disease, Thiago."

"I don't care. I love you."

She blinked. His words shocked her.

"Yes, I love you. I want you in my life, and I don't care that you have an illness."

"You should care since one day my situation could become so bad I'll have to be taken care of. What then?"

"I'll still love you."

Her chest tightened with emotion. "This isn't a fairy tale."

"No, it is real life. Do you think you're the only person with health problems? My father has a bad back. My brother Ethan is deathly allergic to shellfish. Someone once told me I was mean and an asshole."

"I wonder who that was," India said. "By the way, that's not a health problem. It's a personality flaw."

"The point is, we all have issues. I know those examples are not the same, but when you love someone, you love all of them. I love you, India. I want to marry you one day."

He said the words she wanted to hear, but he didn't fully understand the gravity of her illness.

"Thiago, I may never be able to have children. I would like to have at least one baby, but a child might not be in the cards for me."

He shrugged in a *so what?* way.

"Think about it. What if I can't have kids? What will you say when people ask?"

"I'll tell them to mind their damn business, and so should you. Did you hear what I said? I love you. I want *you*. If we never have children, my life will still be complete because I'll have you in it. Besides, you have your godchildren, and I have six siblings who I'm almost certain will all have children. There will be plenty of kids running around for us to love. We could be the rich aunt and uncle everyone wants to hang out with."

He was easily knocking down every one of her arguments.

"How do you feel about me?" Thiago asked, his shoulders taut.

For the first time ever, she saw uncertainty in his eyes as he waited for her answer.

"I love you. So much," India admitted.

His chest deflated as he released a long breath. "Then don't leave me." Thiago took her hand in his and lifted her knuckles to his lips. "And lean on me. You do not have to struggle on your own with the symptoms and the treatments."

India stared at their hands together—his tanned, hers chocolate-brown. She lifted her gaze. "I need to tell you something. One more secret, in the interest of full disclosure."

He visibly tensed. "Okay."

"I don't know how to cook," she said.

Thiago visibly relaxed. "I know."

"What do you mean you know?" India asked.

"I know," he said again, adding a shrug.

"How?" India demanded.

"I guessed a few months ago when we had lasagna for dinner. I saw the restaurant bag you had stuffed in the trash."

Her mouth fell open. "You didn't say a word!"

"What does it matter?"

"It matters because—because I *lied*. I lied for months!"

"Do you really think I give a damn that you cannot cook? I'm rich! I have a personal chef and a housekeeper who prepare most of my meals. When I don't want to eat at home, I go to a restaurant. I thought it was cute you were trying to impress me."

"I wasn't trying to impress you." India slapped his hand. "I was trying to feed you because I knew you left work and came straight to my apartment. I was surprised you didn't pass out in the middle of sex."

His sculpted lips slowly expanded into a smile. "You were concerned about me."

"Yes, I suppose." India rolled her eyes but smiled at the same time. "For the record, I didn't set out to deceive you. I had ordered food, put it on nice plates, and you assumed I had cooked. You made such a big deal about how thoughtful it was and how much trouble I'd gone to, I didn't have the heart to tell you I hadn't done much except take the food out of the containers."

"But that's the point, don't you see? You made the effort. You once said it's not the grand gestures but the small acts of kindness that make the difference. I don't care if the food you serve me is home-cooked. All I care about is how you made sure

I had something to eat and drink. That's very thoughtful. Do you know how rare that is for people to do something like that, especially for a man like me? A man who has everything. What could I possibly need? You saw a need and filled it, which is all that really matters."

Perhaps sensing her pending acquiescence, Thiago stepped closer, forcing her to tip her head back to look into his eyes.

"We are perfect for each other. We were made for one another. I don't want to live without you. I would be utterly miserable. My life would be incomplete. It would be so much sweeter, so much happier, so much more enjoyable with you in it."

"I agree." India slid her hands up his chest and locked them around his neck, pleased she could touch him again. "You love me?"

"If I could find a stronger word to express my feelings, I would use it. Love will have to do. I love you, with every fiber of my being." His hands tightened on her waist. "Do you forgive me for what I said, India? I know I don't deserve it, but I'm begging for your forgiveness anyway."

India touched his cheek. "Yes, I forgive you."

Holding her close, he buried his face in her neck. "Thank you. I never again want to know what it's like to not have you in my life. The past two weeks have been torture."

India stroked his hair. "I agree. Thank you for coming to get me."

They moved at the same time, their lips meeting and searing together in a kiss of love and the promise of a shared future.

Chapter Thirty-Seven

The ballroom shimmered under the glow of crystal chandeliers, every detail designed to dazzle as family and friends awaited the arrival of the wedding party at Monica and Andre's reception.

Flowers wound around the handrail of the staircase leading to the second-floor balcony. Linen-draped tables held towering arrangements of ivory flowers in slender gold vases, surrounded by sparkling plates and silver cutlery.

The gold and silver decor with blush accents was the perfect palette for Thiago's glamorous social media influencer sister. Monica's own videographers and photographers moved discreetly through the room, capturing every moment for the millions of fans who would later devour the content she shared on her Instagram feed.

"I can't believe our little sister is a married woman," Thiago said, speaking to his brothers in Spanish.

Ignacio stood beside him, his hair in a man bun, and Maxwell stood on the other side of Ignacio, looking less harried than at the engagement party when he had been ducking his two dates.

"Never thought I'd see the day she gave in. She was so adamant she wasn't getting married," Ignacio added, taking a drag from his beer.

"You're next," Maxwell said, with a pointed look at Ignacio.

"Don't expect wedding plans any time soon. Delta's tour only wrapped up last month, and we start production on *Wrong* in July," Ignacio informed them, referring to his passion project, an indie film loosely based on the true story of one of their family members who had been wrongly accused of murder.

"When are you going back down to your normal weight?" Maxwell asked, gripping one of Ignacio's large biceps under his suit.

He had packed on muscle for his last role as a soldier in an action-thriller.

"No time soon since Delta likes my new body," he answered with a smirk.

Maxwell chuckled. "The hard workouts are worth the reward?"

"Every minute," Ignacio confirmed.

As his brothers talked, Thiago's gaze swept the venue, filled with the bride and groom's many family and friends. He spotted India chatting with Connor-Santana wives Skye and Marissa.

She was radiant in Chanel, wearing a powder blue sheath dress adorned with imitation pearls on the sleeves. Her hair was styled higher than usual in soft curls, but as always, she wore very little jewelry—only simple pearl earrings and one statement piece, the gold and diamond bangle that had become an almost permanent fixture on her wrist of late.

He was pleased she wore it often because he'd picked the

bracelet himself, agonizing over various options before settling on the one he believed perfectly encapsulated who she was: a classy, elegant, and strong-as-a-diamond woman. He was now on the hunt for a new gift to commemorate their one-year anniversary in July.

"How is the situation with Simon?" Ignacio asked Thiago.

Simon had threatened to press charges against Thiago for hitting him.

"Handled. My private investigator found a bystander who captured the moments leading up to Simon's knockout. The video showed him manhandling India and shoving me. He showed Simon the evidence and told him we'd share it with law enforcement if he didn't leave me and India alone. The weasel backed down, so I don't expect to hear from him again."

Aunt Florence shuffled over, a gleam in her eye as she said, "I see you took my advice." She didn't stop, a self-satisfied upward tilt to her lips as she continued on her way.

Maxwell's eyes followed her jaunty steps. "What is she talking about?"

"Nothing but the usual," Thiago said with amusement, taking a sip of champagne.

Minutes later, the soft music the band was playing changed to an upbeat tempo, the doors to the ballroom opened, and the wedding party filed in. Audra led the way in a gold dress, hair piled on top of her head, with her escort, Andre's cousin Phineas, on her arm. Cheers, whistles, and laughter spilled over as the bridesmaids and groomsmen danced in to the music.

Then the doors closed, and the lights dimmed. The room went still and quiet in anticipation. Delta's beautiful voice broke through the silence as she started singing "At Last." The R&B singer was dressed in a sequined gold dress. She wore her hair parted in the middle with extensions cascading down to her butt, crooning the emotional words in her angelic voice.

Everyone looked at the front doors, waiting for the arrival of the newlywed couple. But a spotlight landed on the stairs and illuminated Monica and Andre at the top. The guests started clapping and cheering. Anyone sitting stood. Then, arm in arm, the couple slowly began their descent to the beautiful, romantic song.

Monica wore a strapless, blush-colored, floor-length gown. Thiago had learned from Audra that Monica had wanted to wear the nontraditional dress to the wedding ceremony but changed her mind at the last minute and opted for a traditional white gown. This entrance and this color befitted her big personality. The dress complemented her narrow frame, and the oversized flower-inspired prints on the full skirt added additional details of grandeur.

A brilliant smile suffused Monica's face. The smile on Andre's rough-hewn face was equally wide—the kind a man wore when he'd won the ultimate prize. Thiago enthusiastically joined in the applause and cheering, his chest overflowing with joy for his younger sister.

Dinner and speeches filled the next hour. With India seated beside him, the time passed in a blur of laughter and conversation with his brothers and their wives.

Much later, as the night was winding down, Thiago stood with the single men as Andre tossed the garter into the crowd. When their cousin Joe caught the piece of lace, some of the men wiped their foreheads in relief while others teased him with good-natured ribbing.

Then it was time to toss the bouquet. Monica stood on the staircase with the single women gathered around, jockeying for position. But instead of throwing the flowers behind her, Monica turned around and walked down the stairs.

The laughter stopped as everyone stared in confusion. She

walked directly to her mother, Rose, and placed the bouquet in her hands.

The room went completely silent.

Benicio appeared at Rose's side and slipped an arm around her shoulders. Speaking into the cordless microphone in his hand, he said in a strong, proud voice, "We have an announcement to make. Rosa and I are engaged. We are getting married again."

Gasps and laughter rippled through the gathering.

"Did you know about this?" India asked beside Thiago.

"No," he replied.

Monica grabbed the mic. "Congratulations, Mommy and Papa Ben!"

The room erupted into loud cheers, and Thiago made eye contact with Bruno across the room, silently asking if he'd had any idea of this development. His older brother shrugged, shaking his head, then joined in the clapping.

Thiago watched as his father dipped his stepmother over his arm, kissing her as if he had waited a lifetime for such a moment. The thunderous applause increased and filled every corner of the ballroom.

When they straightened, Rose gently hit his chest, mortified but leaning closer to Benicio, her eyes filled with happiness as she took in the excited reaction of the crowd.

Thiago's gaze slipped to India, who was clapping as loudly as anyone. He knew how much she respected his father, and her joy was genuine.

After the excitement died down and some of the guests left, those remaining hit the dance floor, including Thiago and India. Fortunately, she liked to dance as much as he did. Much later, with her head resting on his shoulder and her hand in his, Thiago led as they slow-danced to an old R&B tune.

"You have a great family. They're very welcoming," India said.

He had introduced her to them earlier, making their relationship public and official. Come next week, the employees of Santana International would also be made aware of their relationship.

"I get the feeling Mr. Santana knew about us already," she continued.

"He might have helped get us back together. He adores you," Thiago said.

She briefly lifted her head and looked into his eyes. "Good to know. I'll go to him when you act up."

He laughed softly as she placed her head on his shoulder again.

Across the room, Audra and her husband Damon were one of the couples on the floor. They stood in one spot, arms wrapped around each other as they swayed to the music. Thiago hadn't always been a fan of the former baseball player, and when the couple was on the brink of divorce, he had been staunchly on his sister's side. But after counseling, they reconciled, and he had no doubt their marriage was now unshakeable and would last.

His father and stepmother were also among the last couples dancing, whispering and laughing as they moved around the floor. Something fierce stirred inside him as he watched them. He wanted what they had. An enduring love.

He kissed India's forehead, certainty settling deep in his chest. One day he would have the honor of marrying her and spending his life with her.

No five-year plan. No carefully chosen night.

Just the two of them. Together. Treasuring each moment.

Always.

Bonus Content

If you enjoyed this story, join my mailing list to read a steamy bonus scene of the night Thiago and India saw each other in the sports bar.

Use the QR code or enter the link below in your browser.

geni.us/DDBonusContent

Also by Delaney Diamond

More from the Family Ties series!

Audra - The Prequel (Family Ties #0)

Thanks to an unexpected pregnancy, they both realize that some risks are worth taking—especially when love is at stake.

Ethan (Family Ties #1)

After seven years together, one night, Skye broaches the subject of marriage and learns the devastating truth. Ethan has no intention of marrying her.

Monica (Family Ties #2)

Andre is engaged to marry the daughter of the man who gave him a chance when no one else would, but seeing Monica causes old feelings to resurface and calls his plans into question.

Audra (Family Ties #3)

When Audra asks for a divorce, she and Damon are forced to face the truth about their marriage. Can they rekindle the fire in the relationship... before it's too late?

Bruno (Family Ties #4)

When Bruno hires a matchmaking service to find him a wife, sparks fly between him and the matchmaker, blurring the lines between love and professionalism.

Ignacio (Family Ties #5)

A fake romance could catapult the careers of actor Ignacio Santana and R&B singer Delta James to higher levels—or reignite heartbreak they never recover from.

Thiago (Family Ties #6)

A no-strings workplace affair spirals into a tug-of-war of emotions. Every glance holds a question. If neither surrenders, they might lose the one thing they never meant to risk at all: each other.

***

More family series are available!

Visit my Books page at delaneydiamond.com to learn about all my books and the

Johnson Family

Brooks Family

Hawthorne Family

***

Audiobook samples and free short stories available at www.delaneydiamond.com.

About the Author

Delaney Diamond is the USA Today Bestselling Author of sensual, passionate romance novels. Originally from the U.S. Virgin Islands, she now lives in Atlanta, Georgia. She reads romance novels, mysteries, thrillers, and a fair amount of nonfiction. When she's not busy reading or writing, she's in the kitchen trying out new recipes, dining at one of her favorite restaurants, or traveling to an interesting locale.

Enjoy free reads on her website. Join her mailing list to get sneak peeks, notices of sale prices, and find out about new releases.

Join her mailing list
www.delaneydiamond.com

instagram.com/delaneydiamondbooks
x.com/DelaneyDiamond
pinterest.com/delaneydiamond

www.ingramcontent.com/pod-product-compliance
Lightning Source LLC
Chambersburg PA
CBHW070850250626
47159CB00003B/1015